Warning Signs

By

Sheila Englehart

Abyss Books
Published by Indigo Sea Press
Winston-Salem

Abyss Books
Indigo Sea Press
302 Ricks Drive
Winston-Salem, NC 27103

First Abyss Books edition published
February, 2016
Abyss Books, Moon Sailor and all production design are trademarks of Indigo Sea Press, used under license.

For information regarding bulk purchases of this book, digital purchase and special discounts, please contact the publisher at
indigoseapress.com

Cover design by Tracy Beltran

Manufactured in the United States of America
ISBN 978-1-63066-392-6

Praise For

WARNING SIGNS

"Warning Signs will grab your interest from the beginning and keep you turning pages as you can't wait to know what happens next. Ms. Englehart has a gift not just for writing, but for fleshing her characters and scenes out and interweaving different parts of the story in a way that makes the events real and whets your appetite for more. This novel will introduce you to some metaphysical and spiritual concepts in an authentic and non-Hollywood, stereotypical way, in keeping what authentic metaphysical practitioners experience. *Warning Signs* is a great read that you won't want to pass up. When you read the last word, you'll find yourself wishing that it would go on and wondering what happens next with the characters."

> *Diane Brandon,* Radio Host, Author of *Invisible Blueprints: Intuitive Insights for Fulfillment in Life,* & Integrative Intuitive Counselor

"This suspenseful story both entertains and educates by offering a broad range of opinions about the survival of consciousness after death and what may lie on other side. Scientists, spiritualists, shamans, and skeptics all have their say during the dramatic events that unfold after the "spirit virgin" protagonist's first séance. The frustrated would-be writer reluctantly embarks on a quest to understand and fulfill a spiritual mission. Surprising synchronicities lead her to the target of her search and a confrontation with the dark force that has her in its own crosshairs. *Warning Signs* is a well told cautionary tale packed with the kinds of experiences that parapsychologists love to investigate."

> *Dave Roberts,* Managing Editor, *The Journal of Parapsychology*

"Sheila Englehart has a flair for creating quirky characters that are utterly believable whether they're dead or alive."

"This is a terrific, sometimes funny, sometimes terrifying book, and I recommend it to any fan of urban fantasy, supernatural, or just plain good writing out there."

From Indigo Sea Press
By Sheila Englehart

Warning Signs

indigoseapress.com

Acknowledgements

I applaud my first readers Pat Barber, Mary Ann Peden-Coviello, Tony R. Lindsay, Mary Kay McAllister, Carol Roan, Rachel Schneider, Debra Slack, Dr. Michael Stephan, and Susan Williamson for their critiques and support. Special thanks to Michael for being the game-changer.

I honor Sandra Ingool for sharing the journey and helping cut the path to the real story. Without your expertise, this wouldn't have seen the light.

I celebrate Mike Simpson and everyone at Indigo Sea Press for rolling the dice and making the process a pleasure.

And most importantly, I adore my husband Bob for indulging my eclectic nature and making my writing life possible.

Chapter 1

She would have sold her soul for a story. Chalk on the blank slate in her mind made agonizing noises as her level of anxiety grew. Kellan took a couple deep breaths and rubbed her hands together to generate an imaginary spark. "Day one, do or die." She had convinced herself that the next thirty days would decide if she had what it took to live her fantasy writer's life, or if she needed to let go of her childhood dream.

Her thumbs tapped the space bar in anticipation.

Any minute now.

After ten minutes, she typed: *This sucks. Why did I think I could do this? I haven't written more than a grocery list in three years.*

She knew her day was about to go off the rails when the phone rang. The time on the computer read 4:22 AM and she didn't need Caller ID to know who was calling.

"You need to come with me tonight." Jade never bothered with preliminary greetings.

"Not with a gun to my head." The last time Kellan let Jade talk her into going out, it was Ladies-Drink-Free night at a men's strip club. Women pushing forty didn't belong in strip clubs.

"Don't tempt me." Jade's southern lilt was slanted with sarcasm.

"What are you doing up this early?" Then Kellan remembered the Danish boyfriend was in town. His band had just begun to get airtime stateside. She could also hear Jade smoking. "Putting a few clicks on the rock star?"

"Not writing in the middle of the night, that's for damn sure."

Kellan stared at her twenty one words. "Makes two of us."

"See there? You have to come. Get your juices flowing."

"I'd rather stick needles in my eyes."

"Oh, come on. This is something you only get to do when opportunity knocks, and it's pounding the door off the hinges."

Kellan's stomach fluttered as she fingered the peeling edges of her mouse pad. Her writer's block had been reinforced with steel, and she felt like a convict trying to dig her way through a cell with a pencil nub. But she conceded, knowing full well she'd live to regret

1

it. "No drag strips, no sex toy parties, no men's clubs, biker bars, two-for-one tattoos, and no checking out a new band in the basement of somebody's grandma's house."

"God, you're worse than my mother," Jade said. "I'll have you know that this happens to be a very classy soiree at the Crestletter Mansion. Seven thirty."

"Seriously?" Kellan perked up. What she wouldn't give to see inside of those gates. "What are you doing, a private class?"

"It's a surprise."

"Jade."

"You already agreed, so don't wimp out."

"I clean these people's houses. Well, not that house, but you know what I mean. I can't sit at the same table with them."

"Trust me," Jade huffed out another puff into the receiver, "tonight you can."

The words 'trust me' never went down without a strong chaser. The needle on Kellan's suspicion meter swung to its highest level and she had prickling up her spine that warned her not to go. Seeing inside of the Crestletter Mansion would be worth any humiliation Jade might spring on her, right? Facing a long night staring at a blank screen was option two. Option three was nonexistent, since her boyfriend was busy dealing with a family matter.

"I swear on Opal's life, if you don't come home with a story idea, I will. . ." There was a long pause as Jade thought it over. "Well, you know I'm good for something."

Kellan closed her eyes. Jade's daughter was usually not in her good graces. "If some stripper shakes sweat on me or some old fart tries to cop a feel--"

"There won't be any men there."

"Well, women either."

"No one will sweat, slobber, or paw on you."

"Wait," Kellan sucked in a breath, and her eyes flew open. "What would I have to wear?"

* * *

Regret set in seconds after she hung up. Kellan tried to regain focus on her word count. After typing another sixty seven, she decided a snack might help. Guilt would surely follow at this hour, but maybe just a little pick-me-up.

Four steps and she was in the kitchen unwrapping a Little Debbie Snack Cake. She was about to bite in when she got a harebrained idea. Couldn't hurt, right? Kellan rummaged through the junk drawer by the refrigerator, found a white, briefly used birthday candle, poked it in the middle of her cake, and lit it with the long barbeque flame-thrower. She closed her eyes imagining words flowing from her fingers to the screen without effort, scrutiny, or planning.

"Help me find a story, a good story, that will speak to someone. A story bigger than my boring little life. For this, I will be grateful."

And she blew the candle out.

* * *

Kellan didn't perspire, she sweated and her clothes were now sticking in the wrong places. She adjusted the vent on the dash to blow right on her chest. "This is a bad idea. One of my clients could be here."

"Relax," Jade stopped her red Porsche Carrera at the intercom box. "It's going to be great."

"You don't understand. You're a professional," Kellan said, trying not to focus on Jade's spiked hair, layers of black eye make-up, and Japanese letters tattooed up her arms. Not to mention the red and black she could pull off anytime, anywhere. "I'm The Help. I can't sit at the same table with these people. Small town like this?"

"So you'll shake things up a little. We're here now, so just roll with it."

And before Kellan could argue, a man's voice came through the intercom. "Name please."

"Jade Hayes and guest for the party."

Kellan eyed her. "Party?"

"Go left, park in front of the tennis court."

The gate parted in the middle granting them access to a cobblestone drive. Real cobblestone long enough to warrant beverage service for the ride.

"Okay, it's not so much a party as it is a séance."

"Are you kidding me?" Kellan brightened. "Wait. Oh, God."

"What now?"

"Candace Litchfield. Was she invited?"

Jade barely avoided scraping a hedge for staring at Kellan.

3

"Maybe. I don't know."

Mrs. Litchfield was Kellan's bread and butter and part of a group of women who felt if they only dipped their toes in the water and tithed to their church on Sunday all would be forgiven. They liked to put on a conservative show, but behind closed doors they dabbled with things they found naughty: strip tease parties, psychic readings, and high stakes poker passed off as bridge. They may have even had a pot party or two. Kellan had heard Mrs. Litchfield talk about Mary Crestletter yesterday on the phone as if they were bosom buddies. Why hadn't she picked up on that sooner?

"I have always wanted to go to a séance."

"I know. Surprise!"

Kellan frowned. "But Candace Litchfield? She's the reason I can pay my bills. She'll want me dead on sight."

"Please," Jade grinned. "I could tell you some things about her that'd have her licking the bottom of your boots to keep quiet."

Kellan's eyes cut to Jade. "Great. A séance and blackmail in one convenient stop." They were quiet for a moment. "Does it always work? I mean, do you always get somebody?"

"Not always. So this will either be a total bust or," Jade glanced at her, "some really cool material."

"Isn't this a little Scooby Doo for you? You're not worried this kind of thing might tarnish your spiritual integrity?"

Jade tossed her cigarette butt out the window.

Kellan smacked her arm. "You don't throw your butts out the window in a place like this. The world is not your private ashtray."

Jade waved her off like a gnat. "Okay, so I'm a little out of my element. But if someone like me doesn't supervise, you know what can happen? A couple martini's, they break out a Ouija board and flat out ask for trouble. I'd rather do it right than have to clean up the mess."

Kellan eyed her with suspicion.

"I'm acting in service of my spiritual integrity."

Kellan winced. "How many of these have you actually done?"

"Plenty, okay?" Jade met Kellan's eyes. "Come on, I want you to have some fun tonight, alright?"

Kellan studied her in silence.

"You gave me your list of no's and this was not on it."

A flash of something dark caught Kellan's breath in her throat. A red-tailed hawk dove down at the hood of the little car. Jade jammed on the brakes and they both lurched forward as the large raptor ascended up to the tree tops that now blocked their view of the house.

"Holy. . ." Kellan braced herself against the tiny dash. "I've never seen one dive down on a car before."

Jade wore a mystified grin. "Messenger."

"What?"

"Hawks are messengers. The Egyptians and Native Americans believe that when a hawk crosses your path you are about to receive an important message."

The bird bobbed on a swaying tree branch. Kellan's skin prickled and a strange uneasiness crept into her. "Like 'go home, stupid, before they see you here.'"

"Oh, please." Jade grimaced. "You watch. Somebody is going to get a very big message tonight." Jade patted Kellan's arm. "And you'll have a front row seat."

* * *

The tennis court's white lines and tape along the net tape were bleached bright. Even the paint of the parking bumpers was void of dirt. Kellan made sure Jade stopped the car before touching one, lest some poor groundskeeper be assigned the task of removing the mark.

They examined the carriage house from the passenger window. Double doors looked wide enough for an actual carriage and a second story above could have been for tack or hay storage, maybe a tiny room for groomsmen. White brick and oak framed by gas lanterns gave it old world charm. Matching iron hooks held the upper shutters open to window boxes overflowing with peonies.

"It's going to be fine." Jade took her hand. "I will make it fine."

Kellan climbed out of the car to greet a short older lady who was not as slender and toned as Mrs. Litchfield and her friends. Mary Crestletter's hand fingered a long doubled strand of pearls against a smart lilac pantsuit. Short strawberry blonde hair, dyed to the color of her youth, no doubt, feathered as if she'd just come from riding in a convertible. What struck Kellan most were the pink bedroom slippers.

Jade was out of the car and halfway across the drive before Kellan could offer her hand.

"And who have we here?" Mrs. Crestletter didn't smile as her

5

eyes took Kellan in.

"I'm sorry. If I shouldn't be here. . ." Kellan hoped for an easy out before the rest of the group arrived.

Jade linked arms with the lady as if they'd known each other for years. "This is my friend Kellan Brooks. I thought we might kill two birds with one stone, if that's all right? Kellan has never attended a séance."

Mrs. Crestletter grinned like a child with a secret. "Then welcome, my dear."

"Thank you, but if you feel your other guests might be uncomfortable. . ."

A gray haired man in forest green coveralls opened the side door and pushed the double doors open. Inside was indeed a carriage; one with more than a several hundred horses beneath the hood. The very old, carefully pampered Rolls Royce Silver Cloud reminded her of the car in the movie *Arthur* with lanterns on each fender behind the rear doors. Kellan felt her mouth open then clamped it shut, hoping Mrs. Crestletter hadn't noticed.

"Grady, would you kindly set another chair upstairs for us?"

He nodded without a word and disappeared.

"I daresay I needn't implore you to exercise discretion."

"Of course not." Kellan shot a laser glance at Jade.

"Shall we?"

And she followed the pair up the staircase with a growing sense of dread.

* * *

Lace filled the windows beneath moss and mustard draperies. Seat cushions in various textures served to compliment the sunflower table setting with a simple white ring of carnations and a white pillar candle. Several other white, yellow, and green candles stood on lace swathed stands in front of the windows. The floor of beautiful resin-polished tongue and groove glistened beneath her shoes. A six by eight section near the seating area draped in a heavier olive fabric invited lounging on large throw pillows.

Kellan strolled around. She could not reconcile her presence in such a place. *Leave, right now. Just leave. They really won't want you here. Demand Jade's keys and pick her up when they're finished. Do it, now!*

But the window of opportunity closed when the rest of the ladies came up the stairs in a group. They milled away from her as expected. Kellan thought she'd choke when she saw Candace Litchfield come through the door wearing a look of uncertainty behind a practiced smile. The minutes dragged like hours before they settled into cushioned seats around a circular table. Grady hit the light switch by the door, leaving them in the golden glow of candlelight.

"Ms. Hayes has brought a guest. A spirit virgin, which might help raise the energy."

What did that mean? Was she some sort of bait? An array of looks passed between the ladies. Kellan had to work hard not to meet anyone's eyes directly.

"Shall we begin?" Mrs. Crestletter gestured for Kellan to sit next to her. Great, now her clients would think she was privy to private information about them. Kellan's face now matched the rest of the group as she sat rigid as a grave marker, trying to think of a way out. There would be uncomfortable days ahead once this was over she was certain.

Jade offered some preliminaries and answered a couple questions before instructing them to join hands. A painfully thin Bella Truss hesitated at taking Kellan's hand. Why did they have to hold hands anyway? She tried not to think about it. Bella took Kellan's hand as delicately as a soiled tissue. Self-consciousness helped her swallow a snicker. To her right, Mrs. Crestletter, who before closing her eyes gave Kellan a wink as if they shared some secret.

Kellan couldn't resist opening one eye again to see Mrs. Litchfield's face had drained and her accusing gaze bore into Kellan. Elise Barton, recent widow, sat opposite Mrs. Crestletter, dressed appropriately in mourning black. Kay Van Kesler sat next to her several layers of gypsy rags. No one had bothered to introduce the dark woman with long black hair that shone blue in the candle light. Dark eyeliner, shadow, and lip color brought out her inner Morticia Addams. In simple shimmering silver, she exuded the elegance of a slinking panther. Kellan had trouble not staring at her, just as Candace Litchfield couldn't take her eyes from Kellan.

"If you'll take three deep, cleansing breaths," Jade instructed. "Imagine the silvery umbilical cord of your core going through your seat, down through the floor, into the ground and deep into layers of the earth. Feel yourself anchored by this cord."

Kellan felt this happen instantly, while feeling eyes still on her. She wondered for a moment if she was the only one with her eyes closed. Stop thinking about it, she commanded herself. Just let well enough alone, and try not to laugh. The moment she had the thought not to laugh, that's all she wanted to do. The situation was quite ridiculous by anyone's standards. The longer she fought to suppress it, the more she wanted to crack up. She forced a couple deep breaths and the feeling subsided while seriousness settled her. In minutes, the mood in the room felt smothered in wool.

Okay, when this was over, she would torture Jade. For now, go with it and be open-minded in the name of research. This could be construed as research, right?

Jade took command. "We fill this space with light and love, asking the powers that be to protect us from harm. Ladies, let us imagine a column of healing light coming from above, surrounding and protecting us. We ask Archangel Michael to protect us from anything negative. In this space, no harm will come to us. Only beings of like mind and highest intention are allowed in this sacred space."

Kellan cracked an eye open to see the ladies in various stages of effort.

"We ask for our loved ones who have crossed over to come forward to this safe, loving space and deliver any messages they deem appropriate. If there is anyone present who needs help, you are invited to step forward as well."

Silence. Nothing moved. This group might not generate enough spiritual electricity to disturb a candle flame.

"We call the man specifically known as Frederick Barton. Frederick Barton, if you are present, please come and be heard."

"Freddie. It's me, Elise."

Here we go. Kellan bit her lips together to keep from laughing.

"If you are with us, give us a sign, please," Mrs. Crestletter added in a raised voice as if Jade hadn't been loud enough. Kellan imagined a hand with a sign dropping from the ceiling reading, Here! Then she struggled to contain the urge to laugh again. Where was this coming from? She had gone from nervous to giddy in a few short breaths.

Someone whispered, "Nothing's happening."

"Patience," Jade said. "It's not exact, and he may not be ready to come back yet." A pause before she said again. "If there is a

Frederick Barton here, please make your presence known."

Behind Kellan's closed eyes, a shadow moved to her left. Was it from a flickering candle casting a shadow beneath her eyelids? She forced herself not to open her eyes.

"I feel a presence," Jade said.

"Male."

Kellan assumed this was the voice of the panther woman because she didn't recognize it. Next to her, Bella caught her breath as if she had been holding it the entire time. In her mind's eye, all Kellan saw were orange and brown swirls.

Jade tried again. "If there is a loved one connected to anyone at this table who would like to relay a message, we are open to hearing from you now."

Kellan saw a bright golden bubble of woven light around her. A heavy drapery of deep purple fell around the bubble, as if a magician might make her disappear.

Blackness.

Kellan listened. Nothing. She strained to find something in a void. Jet black. No shadow, no light, no form, no movement. Silence. When she remembered to breathe, she could hear herself as loud as from inside a closed space.

The scent of freshly broken earth, moist and musty found her. She could taste it on her tongue. Kellan no longer felt in the presence of the other ladies. Where was this?

A light flash. A dark shape. Stillness. Another flash: a strobe lasting only a half beat revealed a curved shape. Kellan steeled herself not knowing what it was or if it had seen her at the same time. Another strobe showed the edge of the largest bird wing she'd ever seen; larger than the garage door on the firehouse.

Darkness.

Her ears pricked to a soft rustling. Fabric moving? Parting of curtains? Where were the others? Feathers. It sounded like of a bird stretching a wing.

Another strobe showed a silhouette of a tall figure. Not a bird, more like a man with gigantic wings. He was three times the size of any normal man. How strange to feel on such high alert while unafraid, almost safe.

Darkness.

What are you?

Az-ra-el came a deep whisper, forced out as if from a last breath.

Kellan's mind searched. What was Azrael?

An-gel of Death.

You have *got* to be kidding. Until that moment Kellan had been sure there were no such things as angels. People thought their deceased relatives went on to become angels, but she knew, that if angels were real, they were not human, and they were not sweet and loveable. According to religious texts, there were only two humans to ever become angels, and she had never heard of an angel having black wings.

Rustling grew louder behind her. The flashes came faster, revealing more. Great black wings reached to encircle her, and climbed high over her head.

Stillness. The sound of her own breathing was unsettling. Was this thing really death in disguise?

The blast of a train horn made her jump. She could still feel the chair beneath her. The horn came again, two more short blasts, then the rumble of the fully charged engine pushing closer, as though a track were right in front of her.

Her mind raced. There was a track she crossed at least twice a week that had not been used in many years. She could only think of one active railway that ran through the area, but it was miles east of the city. In the nearly three years she'd lived there, she had never heard a train.

Hushing her haggard breathing, she could feel another presence.

The flash of a middle-aged man standing at an iron gate confused her. He wore a white shirt, sleeves rolled to his elbows. He looked familiar, but her eyes failed to distinguish clear facial features.

"Please, you need to open the gate," he said. "I beg you."

Then he was gone. She searched in futility but saw only darkness and a gate, ancient and rusted in spots, suspended in the darkness. Rails of iron woven together without having been straightened. There was no lock or handle anywhere she could see.

If that guy needed it open so badly, where did he go? Kellan searched for a way to open it. No hinges, no framework, nothing held it in place. It just hung by itself in the blackness. How could she open it? Was she even supposed to? This was nuts. Looking around she decided there was nowhere else to go. Behind her was nothing but solid black, and no one else present.

Kellan reached a hand to the gate trying to think of something to say. No words were required as the iron bars rose silently into the darkness above. Hindsight was a killer and it now occurred to her that something scary might come out.

Blackness. The scent of copper found her nose.

Emotion swirled around her in a fury of confusion that jolted her body. Did a creature await her? Was it large? Hungry? Kellan steadied her breathing and felt she was not alone.

Another flash revealed a profile in silhouette of someone sitting on the ground. The image came so quickly she couldn't be sure of if it was a male or female.

"You see me?"

This was not the deep whisper of the dark angel or the voice of the man in the white shirt. It was lighter, younger, and nearly panicked.

"Who are you?" Kellan strained to see what was moving to her right. Black, then charcoal, then black again.

The strong scent of cedar, balsam, talc and sweat came. Kellan could not see his face clearly through the dark.

"I'm so tired. I can't. . . I didn't mean to do it. I'm so sorry. I'm so tired."

"What are you tired of?"

The flesh on her back rose like a dog's hackles.

Another flash showed an enormous dark shifting thing with no definitive shape. A charcoal swatch of fabric in the breeze shifted thick, gray, and alive. When the shape moved toward her, she felt the blood in her veins firing and a blast of cold. Whatever it was, it felt angry.

There was a little more light giving the space a negative hue. A young man knelt, his head bent to his knees, short bangs feathered over his left eye, hands bracing the floor like a runner propped on blocks. Sheer terror ran through her, followed by fury. The dark shapeless shadow rose to tower over them both. Kellan thought she could make out bottomless black eyes but it wouldn't stay still long enough to discern. Her mouth went dry and sucked at the prickling cold as her skin turned icy.

"It lied to me. It made me do it. It just stepped in, and I couldn't fight it anymore."

Kellan felt weak, her inner core siphoned and her energy evaporated. This is what It did, she knew. She could feel it. And It held no remorse for leeching energy from its prey.

11

Bright pictures followed. A montage of people she didn't know rushed around her: a young boy; a man in a casket; a sallow woman; a child with striking eyes; flashes of light; crowds of people swirling around; blue sky; red kite; and a hawk in flight.

Shadow returned to pitch black. Despair and exile built walls around her. Tears, pain, silence.

Light came. A brown-haired boy peeked through door cracks. Hopeful seawater eyes bore into hers.

Then came a pretty girl, strawberry blonde, pale skin, crying. Kellan could feel her fear, anguish, and sadness. The girl backed away shaking her head in confusion, disconnection, and fright.

Cold—freezing cold—made Kellan's body shake.

Darkness.

A razor sharp voice screamed in her head. *Let go. You're a burden to them.*

Do it!

She felt heat beneath her fingers that dug into hot stone. Scalding and hard, it ripped at her skin.

You spineless, gutless, pathetic excuse. You belong to me now.

Kellan's breath was sucked from her, as she was pulled from the stone, then falling, falling, her hair whipping behind her, her body turning, speeding, then . . .

Cold. Freezing cold.

Blackness.

Where am I?

She felt herself strain for sound. No sound came.

The void again.

Warmth ran down her right arm into her fingers. In her hand, she gripped a long pair of gold scissors fitted perfectly to her hand, almost part of her.

Where had they come from?

"No, don't!" The young man called to her. "I'm not worth it."

Why would he want to stay tied to this thing?

Through the dark came a shift of grey. Barely enough light to see the looming shadow and the thin umbilical cord that connected It to the young man. The thing launched at him. Without thinking, in one swift turn, she thrust her arm out and snipped the cord that connected them. The dark thing recoiled and Its rage straightened her spine. It would come at her now.

Before she could think or It could strike, she thrust her left hand open in a stop gesture. Golden light shot from her palm like netting, trapping the thing, shrinking It into a bundle. It stretched, squirmed, and strained in Its fury, pushing with all its might to breach the light and free itself.

No time to wonder how she had done that because the young man was in her arms. His body shook and convulsed in a sort of seizure. Kellan wrapped her arms and legs around him trying to force warmth to his icy limbs, but she had none to offer. His muscles fought against her as she failed to still his shivering. Her conscious mind questioned, how could this be? He's dead, right? In death, there is no body. How could she feel him in her arms having a physical response?

Kellan felt him as any live person pulled from a frozen lake. Straining, convulsing, every muscle, every tendon tight, and utter despair traveled through her interior. Every organ seemed to freeze and fight, yet her blood pumped as slowly as cooling lava. Robbed of her breath, tears came. She fought to control her panic as her lungs strained for air.

It's not mine, Kellan told herself. It's not mine. It's not mine. It hurts. It hurts. Please, somebody, take it out. Take it out. Take it out!

Fear burned inside.

"Don't be frightened."

Kellan didn't know how she how felt the young man was safe. She just knew.

"He belongs to you now," Azrael said, before vanishing.

What?

The young man's fear did not ease. His every breath, every sensation, but most of all his panic crawled into her skin as if he were trying her on like a suit.

What now? Where was the guy who wanted the gate open? Kellan called out, "Hello? Is there someone here for this kid? If he belongs to you, please come and take him."

Light beams pierced the edges of the darkness forming a tent-like flap above until a star burst forth to reveal a stone staircase. A shadowy silhouette of a man appeared in the doorway and descended the stairs. Kellan fought for breath and tried to stop shaking while he gathered the young man from her lap. She stopped breathing. This was the man who asked her to open the gate. The kid collapsed, unable to speak, yet she felt his relief. She took a breath watching them inspect each other.

They could not break eye contact as the man practically carried the kid up the stairs. Once inside the doorway they were absorbed by light. Relieved of wrenching emotion but still shivering, Kellan watched the flap fall over the light and cast her into blackness once more.

Chapter 2

Kellan opened her eyes to find the ladies' faces crowded around her. Jade had a hand on the pulse in her neck. She was freezing and could feel her lower lip still quivering. An afghan covered her.

"Kellan?" Jade asked. "Can you hear me?"

"What?" Her voice shook from cold.

"You dropped like a ton of bricks," Jade whispered. "Don't try to get up."

Kellan's eyes saw the rest of the ladies peering at her.

"You were out there, a million miles away," Bella offered.

"All the blood drained from your face," Elise said. "Then you shouted, 'Take it out!'"

Rolling to one side, Kellan tried to sit up. "I don't. . . I'm just. . . Let's. . ."

The ladies looked at each other. She couldn't see Candace Litchfield past the rest of them. The dark Morticia rose from her chair. "Now that she's alive, I need to run. It's after nine."

Jade turned to the women. "Can someone get her a glass of water, please?"

Elise delivered the water. "You just fell out of your chair right at the end. I thought you were dead."

She took the glass offered and drank it dry in one go. Why was she so thirsty?

"Can you tell us what you saw? Who were you talking to?"

Kellan saw the expectant stares. She couldn't tell them. They were here to contact loved ones. Besides, she didn't have names, well, except for the Angel of Death. Yeah, that'd be pleasant, and would provoke questions she couldn't answer.

"I don't know. It was. . .dark," she struggled. "Did you not see anything?"

Jade's eyes met hers, but there was no connection.

"You came out of it too fast," Kay offered. "Like when you're dreaming, the alarm goes off and you sit right up? You forget the dream by the time you get your robe on. Look at you, you're still shaking."

Elise leaned over her. Her face was plump and shiny from too much moisturizer. "It wasn't Freddie, was it? Because there were a few times I wanted to yell at him to take it out."

"Elise!"

"Oh, let's just be out with it." Elise scowled. "He was a pervert. Probably had women all over town. I'm willing to bet one of you knows some of them."

Mrs. Crestletter poured Kellan more water, and cut Elise away from her. "If we did, we would have exercised the proper discretion. Dear, if you thought he was cheating, why on earth would you want to contact him in the hereafter?"

Kellan wondered the same thing.

Elise searched the faces around her as if she couldn't believe what they were asking. "Well, obviously to ask him why he stayed with me? If we had gotten divorced when I wanted to, when Sam went to college, I might have had time. . .but he wouldn't hear of it. Now, I'm. . .I'm. . ."

"Past your freshness date?" Kay said.

Someone spat a horn sound and burst into fits of laughter.

Kellan took that opportunity to toss back the throw, dive for her bag, and flee out the door. On the staircase her head swam and she gripped the handrail for dear life. An ache crept from her left eye, over the top of her head, and down the back of her neck. All she wanted to do was run as far away as possible, release the rigidity from her neck muscles that felt like they'd had a railroad spike hammered into them. The July night wasn't warm enough. But before she could get to the bottom of the stairs, she realized she had not driven herself.

Jade was right behind her.

Kellan spun to face her. "Give me your keys."

"You can't drive like this, Kellan. You need to let your body readjust."

Kellan's lip quivered. "I need to get out of here. Just give me your keys."

Mrs. Crestletter appeared in the doorway. Their eyes met. Kellan's stomach dropped, and she turned and ran down the rest of the stairs.

"Kellan, wait."

She ran for all she was worth down the long cobblestone drive.

Those women would want to pump her for information and she could not yet process what had just happened. As she approached the security gate, her anger inflated. Again with a gate. Well, this gate would not prevent her from leaving this place. Kellan moved to the stone wall, pulled her bag over her head, and hauled herself up and over. Just as she hit the sidewalk on all fours, she heard the gate click open and the purr of Jade's Porsche pulled around to her.

"Get in before they call 9-1-1."

* * *

She didn't hear a word Jade said all the way home. Before the car was in park, Kellan bolted up the stairs to her apartment and pulled the comforter from the bed. She couldn't get warm and she didn't feel safe. Wrapped in a cocoon, she climbed into the tub and made a tent over herself holding her knees to her chest. Her cattle dog, Riley, moved to the bathmat on guard. She snaked a hand out of the wrap, over the side of the tub to stroke his back. He usually preferred doorways to camping right next to her, but he sensed her fear.

Afraid to close her eyes, she stared. The images rushed back: black feathers, black curtain-like shape, that poor kid. Who was he? And why was she the only person at that table to experience all that?

God, what would those ladies think of her? She'd surely lose some of her clients once Candace Litchfield got on the phone. She could hear the gossip now.

"She'll be jumpy. More apt to break things."

"Dabbling in the dark side? We can't be associated with anyone like that."

"Necromancer. No witch will come inside our home."

Jade must not have done something right. What was that thing? Was it a demon? In Kellan's mind, demons were only in people's minds. They were manifestations of anger, depression, illness, and substance abuse. There was no such thing as a demon or an entity, was there? This thing was as real as that kid was, as real as anyone. The fire in her blood, the rage in her heart, she'd felt all that. Its need to launch at her, to overtake whatever power she had to wield against it was real. That thing was not human. Where had she gone, all pitch dark and freezing cold?

Riley didn't bother to get up when Jade came in the bedroom.

Kellan didn't want to see her right now.

"You going to talk to me yet?" Jade set her bag down outside the door. "Kellan, tell me what happened."

"You tell me," Kellan was angry and needed to vent. "What did you do?"

"I didn't do anything."

"How could you not see the kid or the thing chained to him, hovering around him like some ghoulish cloud?" Kellan's voice cracked and tears breached her lower lids.

"I heard your breathing, so I put up protection. But I thought you had angelic assistance." Jade kept her voice calm.

"Yeah? What kind of angelic assistance has black wings?" Kellan said knowing the answer.

Jade thought for a moment. "Archangel Azrael. He's the angel of. . ." she paused. They shared a look.

Kellan pulled a wad of toilet tissue from the roll to mop her face. "I knew I shouldn't have gone. You said you'd make it okay. Look at me? You call this okay?"

"I have never seen anything like this happen. How was I supposed to know?" Jade said. "You should cleanse in a salt bath."

"I don't want a salt bath," Kellan snapped.

Jade stood straighter folding her arms in front of her. Kellan could feel her trying to figure out what to do to make her feel better.

"At least let me smudge you." And she left the room a moment.

Kellan mumbled, "Go smudge yourself." She didn't want to entertain any unorthodox remedies or rituals. She just wanted to know what happened. What was with that gate? If that thing was actually a demon and Mr. Black Wings was actually an angel, then why didn't he do something?

Jade returned carrying a candle for light in lieu of snapping the bathroom lights on. She also had a bundle of sage leaves bilging smoke from an abalone shell, a vial of essential oil, and a small fluorite stone. Kellan was not in the mood for any of this. Riley sneezed twice before abandoning his post for the fresh air of the bedroom.

"What kind of god would let somebody have a thing like that attach to them?" Kellan asked.

"No one can interfere with free will," Jade said, prying Kellan's hand open to place the crystal in it. "Dark entities do what people let them. It had to be invited somehow. Like when drunks get draw a

18

pentagram on the floor and demand 'a sign of their presence.'" She dabbed oil on the crown of Kellan's head, forehead, and her heart. Recapping the vial, she waved the smoke from the abalone shell in circles around her.

"Why would anyone invite a demon to attach to them? That makes no sense. Don't demons come from people?"

"Ssh, breathe."

"You breathe. I want answers."

Jade's voice remained calm and neutral. "Self-created demons can come from people's anger, pain, frustrations, but there are also things that aren't human."

Kellan tossed her a wary look.

"And not all dark entities are demons. Wherever they come from they are very real. I know you and I don't share the same philosophy on some things, but I have seen lower energies before."

"This place was freezing cold, like Arctic Circle cold," Kellan said. "My whole body was turning into a block of ice from the inside out. I'm still freezing." She slapped the piece of fluorite on the tub wall and waved Jade's smoke away. "Stop this. Just get out of here with this. It's pissing me off."

"That's what it wants, Kellan. Wants you to get angry, lose control. That's what attracts them."

"Well, I wasn't pissed off before it showed up, so I'm entitled." She launched herself out of the tub to pull a heavy sweater from the chest in the corner. "Will you just go? I can't deal with this right now."

Jade stood in the doorway of the bathroom that was now filled with smoke. "You shouldn't be alone. Kellan, please tell me about what you saw."

"Not now," she paced. "Tomorrow."

"I'm booked till eight thirty tomorrow."

Kellan threw a hand. "Well, Tuesday then."

Jade gathered her things and made her way to the bedroom door before stopping. "Everything happens for a reason."

"I didn't ask for this," Kellan said. "I didn't belong there. I wasn't supposed to be there."

"But, you were, and you know there are no accidents."

Kellan sat at the edge of the bed, hands locked behind her neck. "I never asked for this," she whispered.

"You asked for a story." Jade slung her bag over her shoulder.

19

"Looks like you got one."

* * *

Connor Clarke walked the wood floors in his bare feet. Cool and clean, everything smelled of lemon oil. More importantly, there was light and color everywhere; beautiful white and earth tones. He was in an apartment he didn't recognize and looked around as amazed as a blind man seeing for the first time. Where was this?

"Hello?" he called.

Rustling came from another room and the strangely welcome thump of a refrigerator door closing followed. Connor waited. Looking around, the place was modern, comfortable, and simple. Buckskin leather couches faced each other with no coffee table to divide them, high-backed chairs on one end of each, dark side tables with lamps on the other. A large stone fireplace sat empty as it was too blissfully warm for a fire. Loaded white bookshelves lined two walls.

A painting on an adjacent wall caught his eye. He'd seen it before, but where?

A sand colored canyon with a wide river flowing past a hiker that walked the edge of the blue water. Yes, his mother had painted that. The pop and crack of a screw top cap opening turned his attention to the doorway. He nearly dropped to his knees on the sight of him.

"Tony?"

Connor's brother wandered in examining a small black device that looked like it came from a movie. In the other hand, he carried a bottle of Coke. He wore pajama bottoms and a T-shirt and walked right past him. Connor couldn't believe how different he looked and trailed him like a dog out onto a small balcony. *So grown.* Gone was the stringy kid with the unruly bangs; they were now hints of silver. He was filled out, chiseled, a spooky duplicate of this father.

Panic fluttered in him. "Tony, look at me."

Connor stood across from where Tony sat in one of two white webbed chairs at a glass table focused on the small contraption in his hand. Staring at it, he placed the bottle on the table and pulled *The New York Times* from under his arm to lay it by its side. He had no idea Connor was even there. How could he not see him right there? Why couldn't he hear him? Connor crouched to eye level three feet from his brother who went about his business. Tony's eyes focused only on the little screen while he tapped the little buttons with his thumbs. When he was finished he set the device on the table and opened the paper.

Connor didn't know what to think. He was back now, wasn't he? What had happened? He was in the dark. It turned light. There was a woman. He couldn't remember much after that. Now he was here, looking at a man where he last saw a boy. How come he can't see me? How long had he been gone?

"Twenty years," a voice found him.

Connor saw black wings towering over his brother who remained oblivious to anyone. He knew this dark angel on sight and watched him shrink his size to accommodate the small space behind his brother. He placed a hand on the back of Tony's head. Connor waited as if he were going to get some kind of test result.

"Pain lives."

"What pain? What's wrong with him?"

When their eyes met Connor saw two frames merge into one screen like a television. He saw his own body in a casket in his best suit. His face was different and his hair was combed wrong. It frightened him. He wanted to close his eyes, make the vision go away, but couldn't or didn't dare. Images came at him. His mother dressed in black, pale faced, eyes pleading as she shook hands with a long line of people.

His brother, too slight for his suit, droned a solemn monotone. "Thank you for coming."

Connor looked at Tony, sucked in a breath and felt his sadness. "I did this."

The angel moved one hand over Tony's heart. Tony worked at pressing the buttons on the little black device. Connor could feel an emptiness, isolation, exhaustion, and loneliness. A strange knowing settled into him that his brother functioned in the world, body still breathing, moving constantly, thinking, always thinking, and surrounded by people, yet he was alone. Fiercely independent, he'd structured his life to need no one: no roommate, no spouse, no children, and no one. Friends saw him little and moved on with their own families. A precious few persisted in getting him out now and then.

The angel's face was void of expression. "He works."

Tony's fear and frustration, pain and anger swirled around him,

21

gently followed by a strange peace. The angel closed his dark eyes breaking contact.

"What do I do?" Connor said, his gaze glued at Tony.

"Must you do anything?" The angel's face showed no sign of emotion.

"He's my brother and what I did changed him."

"And what would you have him be?"

"Not alone." Connor reached out and grabbed Tony's arm. It didn't move and he didn't notice.

"You no longer possess the abilities of the physical."

"That lady felt me. She held me in her arms, talked to me. She saw me. How come he can't?"

Dark eyes pieced him yet his face didn't move. "His door to spirit is sealed."

"What does that mean?"

The angel put a hand on Tony's forehead then pulled it slowly away a few inches. A blue light stretched between his hand and a spot between his brother's eyes. "You are no longer in his world."

"Then why am I back?" Connor asked. "Right here, in front of him?"

"Desire."

The device on the table buzzed. Tony picked it up to look at the little screen, and then set it down and went back to the paper.

Connor moved closer to examine the device. "What is that thing?"

"How he communicates with his world."

"Could I use it?"

The angel turned toward him tilted slightly as if the notion was one he had never heard. "Not today."

* * *

Kellan's cell phone chimed with an incoming message that snapped her awake. The clock on the nightstand read 6:40. Kellan weighed the options: shower and coffee or her dreaded messages? Making her way to the bathroom, she checked what she had in the cabinet; nothing stronger than ibuprophen. She dumped four in her hand and bent down to drink straight from the faucet, and drank, and drank.

After several minutes of trying to remember what she couldn't, she grabbed Riley's leash and took her phone along to check the messages. Might as well see what awaited her before trying to wash it away. She grabbed her sunglasses and a ball cap, and let the dog drag her from shrub to tree while hearing that she had nine unheard messages. She took a deep breath before thumbing the number one to get the first.

"Kellan, Dee Meyers. Listen, the week has just gotten away from me, so I just can't have anyone here today. Let me give you a call next week and see what we have then. Just don't come this week, kay? Thanks."

Apparently, last night was not a dream. Dee Meyers was a secretary at her boyfriend's family church. Having heard of her episode, Kellan had no doubt that Dee would never call again. She punched the button to delete the message and listened to the next.

"Kellan, its Misses. . .Elise. Just wanted to see if you were all right. And I want you to know that no matter what the talk, I know you're not really a witch and I will tell anyone who dares call you one. I mean, who knows what's out there really, and it could've been any one of us last night. Please let me know you're okay."

Her thumb hit the delete message. Perfect. Elise Barton, rumored tequila lush, would explain to everyone *Kellan's really not a witch*.

If she'd been smart, she would have just hung up and not listened to anymore, but the next one came before she could finish the thought. Mrs. Crestletter.

"Kellan, we need to discuss what happened last night. Avoiding it will not solve anything. You be here at one o'clock and we'll have a nice lunch by the pool."

A summons from the Queen herself. Life just keeps getting better.

The next message was from her friend Stefan who ran the floral shop of choice in Landon. "If you are in hiding, I can't say I blame you, but I'm dying here. I need the real dope. Whatever really happened, know that someone else will take over as headliner tomorrow. Think Brangelina after Beniffer."

Nice.

Kellan snapped the phone shut not wanting to hear any more. Meyers was her only booking of the day, so there would be nothing to get her out of lunch with Mrs. I-own-you-because-I-own-all-your-clients.

This ranked right up there with Tom Cruise doing a dance on

Oprah's couch. Her sanity would be questioned, speculation would abound, and people would stop talking in her presence, shield their children and stare open-mouthed. And Gayle's mother. . .she couldn't even think about it. Her clients would go to Merry Maids and she would gain thirty pounds washing down brownies with white Russians. In this town, she was officially the couch-jumper.

Just because Mrs. Crestletter left her a message didn't mean she had to return to the castle and kiss her ring, right?

She showered and then surfed the net for articles on séances and channeling to try and understand her experience. They ranged from parochial to ridiculous, and were of no help. Much as she lived by the law of simplicity, in this case, it was most dissatisfying.

Someone drop-kicked her into the middle of a place so foreign, she couldn't speak the language or comprehend what she saw. Who let that kid through with that thing tethered to him like a goblin? If there was a god, where was he in this? And why did this happen to her? Was it someone's choice or a mental misfire?

No answers dropped out of the blue. If she sat in her apartment ignoring the phone all day she'd lose her mind, if she still had one to lose. She grabbed her keys, shooed Riley from the door and headed out. The door pulled shut, she turned right into her boyfriend who looked like she felt: rigid and confused.

"Just what in the hell happened last night?" Gayle Lee Schick ran the family's hardware store and had been a volunteer fireman since he could drive. Outside he was bricks and steel, but inside he was cashmere and silk.

Kellan reopened the door, backed inside, and flung her bag on the couch. He stepped in and closed the door quickly. "I'm having my eggs when Sarah Timms starts in with a million questions. Did you really go to a *séance* last night?"

She bit her lip. He waited, not sitting down, both hands on his hips.

"It was at the Crestletter carriage house."

"You know that woman is nuttier than peanut brittle."

"Well, I didn't know it was going to be a séance until we got there."

"And you stayed anyway?"

She could only look guilty. "I was curious and they didn't kick me out."

"Kellan, those people can afford to do whatever they want. They

24

don't sit in the back of the church on Sundays, they don't count their money in public, and they don't invite people beneath their station to anything they do. How in the hell--"

"Mrs. Crestletter seemed happy that I was there. I considered leaving, but. . ." There was no point. What was done was done. And she was not about to blame anything on Jade. Gayle was leery enough about her with her mood-changing hair and tattooed sleeves. She was mad at her, sure, but Jade was her soul sister on many levels. No boyfriend would get away with throwing stones at her. "It seemed innocent, silly even. I mean, I was trying not to laugh for the first five minutes—thought I was going to pop a vessel in my forehead."

"Sarah said you blacked out then lit out of there like a branded calf."

She squinted. "Was Sarah there?" She had not blacked out as much as traveled somewhere else. "I didn't black out. I just had a strange experience. But it's over so. . ."

"What kind of strange experience?"

She moved around him so she wouldn't have to look him in the eye. The kitchen counter always needed wiping so she headed there. "It was nothing."

"Nothing, that scared you enough to tear on out of there."

"They were all staring like I'd landed from Mars and I didn't want to add to the rumors I knew would circulate, so I got out of there as fast as I could."

"Get back to the strange experience," he said. "What made you hit the floor?"

She had to think fast. She couldn't tell him what she really saw. He'd flip, not that it was any of his business. "I'm not sure. It was all dark and something moved. Looked kind of like a big crow's wing."

"That's it?"

"Well, there was a kid too."

"A kid?"

"Well, maybe not a kid, kid. An older kid. It was dark. I couldn't tell, but he looked kind of young."

He looked like he was having difficulty hearing. "What do you mean? You saw a dead kid?"

"I don't know. I guess."

"Well, what'd he look like?"

"A kid, Gayle! God, what do you want from me here?"

"You saw a dead kid during a *séance,* now you're trying to act like its nothing?"

"Well, what am I supposed to do with it?"

"Ho-ly shit, Kellan."

This startled her. Gayle rarely swore, at least not when she was in earshot.

He dragged a hand over his freshly shaved face. "How do you know it wasn't the devil himself?"

Her mouth dropped open. She knew it wasn't. But how did she know?

While he paced, she wiped, grateful to have the bar counter between them. "It was not the devil. Come on. Have you ever seen the devil to know what he looks like? I'm not even sure I believe in such a thing."

"That's exactly what he wants you to think."

Kellan ignored the comment, knowing how he was raised and that his mother still taught Bible school.

"You don't know what kind of Pandora's box those crazy women opened up." He moved closer. "And how come they didn't see this kid? I heard you were the only one to see anything."

"Now, just how am I supposed to know that?" She said hand on her hip, mirroring Gayle. "But hey, I'm fine, really. Thanks for asking."

This got his attention. "I'm sorry, Baby. I just. . .are you really fine?"

She felt stupid pandering for attention like a child. "If we can just move on, I will be."

His eyes did the talking and she could see this bone was not yet buried. "Well, we have Uncle Mick's viewing tonight."

"God, I forgot," she sighed.

Gayle's Uncle Mick had suffered congestive heart failure while sitting at a black jack table in Vegas. His body had arrived yesterday and they had wasted no time trussing him up for display.

"Maybe it would be a bad idea for me to go. If Sarah Timms is already spreading the word, I don't want people asking me at the funeral home about it."

"Momma would snuff that out in a hurry," he leaned over and kissed her on the forehead. "She'll be worse if you don't come. I'll never hear the end of it."

She met his gaze that looked weary, like he wasn't sure what to do with this information.

"Seven o'clock?" he said.

All she could do was nod while dreading having to see his mother, who went out her way to find her flaws in the hopes of saving her only son from being led astray by the 'wrong kind.'

Chapter 3

The parking lot at Taft's Funeral Home was overflowing. Kellan eyed the strip plaza across the street where a tax accountant and home health care company resided. She did a glance for security cameras and pulled the El Camino into a space on the far side of the building. As accustomed as she was to changing her clothes in her car, she didn't care to be the morning show for any security people. Peeling off her polo shirt, she dried her armpits and regretted not running home to shower. The Matthews had not yet gotten wind of the previous evening and called for an emergency cleaning to accommodate their new furniture. The job turned into a rearranging extravaganza that made her sticky, but paid for three extra hours. She made a note to replenish the baby wipes in her kit.

The viewing started at seven and she was forty minutes late. Add that to her growing list of flaws. Kellan hoped her tardiness would not cause more drama. It didn't take much to disturb Betty Ann Schick and she certainly needed no encouragement to share her thoughts openly.

Funeral parlors had all the comfort of dimly lit parking garages with attendants dressed like they had crawled out of caskets themselves. After last night, she was not looking forward to this.

She tugged a simple black velvet dress over her head, pulled the elastic tie from her ponytail and shook her long mousy hair out as best she could. The windblown look would have to work. She used her finger to apply some flaking gray eye shadow and scraped an old lipstick on a McDonald's napkin to get it going. Probably she should replace it, but as little as she wore makeup, it seemed a waste. She reached for the box of business cards on the floor, then cursed herself for the inappropriateness of leaving a stack on a coffee table next to a box of tissue, especially since she didn't know what the tide of gossip might do.

A change of shoes and one last check in the rearview to insure her teeth were free of mauve smears and she hurried across the street. The heavy door was opened by a somber-suited zombie whose pelican neck spilled over the knot of his tie. The receiving line still stretched into the foyer and was hard to shrug past. Gayle's immediate family could fill a theater. Peeking into the Twilight Room, she spotted a few of them clustered between the maple casket and the photo laden easel. Betty Ann saw her first, made a disappointed face, pulled the paisley silk scarf from her neck, gestured toward Kellan while handing it to one of her six daughters. Kellan sucked in a deep breath.

Gayle looked handsome yet uncomfortable in his only navy suit. He had bought it for his youngest sister's wedding, worn it to his nephew's graduation, and on their first date. He did have a new tie though, at least one she had not seen. It made her smile, the thought of him having only one suit. Like she only had one dress. Simple, long-sleeved and machine washable, it lived in the kit in the back of her El Camino.

Kellan smiled her sweetest at an older gentleman inching past her on a cane. She waited for him to get completely by before starting the approach that was halted abruptly when Gayle's oldest sister grabbed her arm.

"There you are," Carrie Ann roped her with the scarf and made quick work of arranging it around her shoulder. "Duck's been antsy. Tried your cell." It had taken Kellan weeks to get used to everyone in town calling her boyfriend Duck, but Carrie Ann's Southern accent hit it with a thud. "You have to come meet everyone." She sang as if it they were at a birthday party instead of a funeral viewing.

"Everyone?" Kellan hoped this wasn't an inquisition committee ready to interrogate the snot out of her. Sniffing the red and gold scarf that smelled of orange blossom hand cream, she let herself to be pulled through the crowd. Carrie Ann stopped her at a gaggle of ladies in hats robbed from a model of the solar system. Carrie Ann appeared to be the youngest of the group, and had opted for a pantsuit and loafers over pantyhose and sling-backs. Kellan still felt plain next to her.

"Here she is. This is Duck's fiancée, Kellan Brooks."

Kellan's head snapped around and her eyes flew as open as the O her mouth made. Her voice vanished but her mind screeched *fiancée?*

"Proprietress of K.B. Cleaning." Carrie Ann smiled megawatts, as if that would impress a Southern woman's social club. If Kellan weren't so shocked she would have made careful note of their names to send them brochures and business cards.

The shortest, roundest woman in skin tight turquoise and shiny black hair grabbed her left hand in search of a ring. Finding none, her face shifted from where-is-the-ring to you-poor-thing. After an eye flutter she recovered quickly. "It's so wonderful Duck has finally wiped the mud from his eyes to settle down."

All Kellan could do was raise an eyebrow and try not to back away when the woman felt it necessary to pinch color into her cheeks for her.

"Have you set a date, sweet pea?"

"Date?" Kellan said.

"Oh," the woman stepped back and waved it off. "Well, you know, you just need to go out and get the dress. Once you have the dress, he'll have to get off his butt and set a date."

They all laughed, except Kellan.

A woman in black sparkles seized her arm away from Little Miss Turquoise. "Date or not, congratulations, Kellan. You must come by the emporium and pick out your pattern."

Kellan frowned as if she were listening to a foreign language.

"Your china is your calling card, as my Mama always said."

"That's your parties, darling." To Kellan it sounded like paw-tees.

A red-head in an enormous straw wide-brim intervened. "Don't listen to any of these witches." They responded with mocking cackles. "I'll accept Duck's marrying a Yankee, long as she knows where to get her cake." This drew an 'Amen' from somewhere. "My daughter is Mrs. Sugar Plum Confections. Does those real fancy decorator cakes, not all slathered in butter cream."

"Nothing wrong with butter cream. That's the best part," said another.

"Congratulations, Sugar. You must *really* be something to snare the last good bachelor in town." This was followed by a wink that sent chills up Kellan's back. The ladies drifted by, smiling cruelly, their eyes criticizing her lack of fashion sense. She found herself searching for an exit sign. Maybe this was how Southerners mourned.

Once they were away, Kellan latched onto Carrie Ann. "Why did you tell them I was his fiancée?"

She waved a hand. "Oh, they already knew."

Kellan was stunned. "How?"

But Carrie Ann was abducted by another guest. Kellan turned to find Gayle, who greeted her with a bear hug.

"Thank God. I was about to send the dogs after you. Daddy's all hinky. Believe he's hit the shine early."

She didn't care about his turkey-hunting, moonshine-swilling father. "Are you aware your sister is introducing me to people as your fiancée?"

He sighed. "Aunt Adele put it in the paper yesterday."

She shook her head. "What? Why?"

"Surviving family?"

Her head rolled back. "A little heads up would have been nice."

"Momma latched onto it and went out of her way to spread the word this morning." He met her horrified gaze with apologetic eyes.

Kellan could hardly believe her ears. "This is her idea of damage control?"

He wilted. "Not the worst thing in the world, being engaged to me, now is it?" Then he forced a sheepish grin in attempt to lighten things up.

"What is she hoping to distract everyone with happy news? So when they find out we really aren't engaged, they will think you dumped me because of last night, making you, and therefore her, look good, smart, and sensible even."

Then someone pulled Gayle away and she was left to be congratulated by half the town. How appropriate. A man was lying dead down front and everyone was in the back planning her wedding. Her eyes found Betty Ann who forced a scary smile when she spotted her glaring. A satisfactory nod answered the scream in her head of why. Kellan looked over at Uncle Mick resting peacefully amid the chaos and thought, *lucky you*, then immediately felt ill. She scanned the crowd for Gayle's father. Maybe he had some shine left.

Chapter 4

Kellan needed a voice of reason, and at this hour she hoped Jade was still at the shop.

Opal was tidying up the front desk when Kellan walked in. "Wow. Look at you in a dress."

Kellan touched a hand to Betty Ann's scarf that she'd forgotten to return before leaving the funeral home. She smiled at Opal. Ah, to be that young and thin again. Opal was nineteen; all eighty six gothic pounds of her. She could easily fit inside a duffle bag. When she wasn't in school, she ran her mother's place when Jade needed an extra hand. The Peaceful Energies Healing Center had four small rooms for acupuncture, reflexology, massage therapy, and a variety of alternative modalities. A few shelves in the front displayed the herbal and aromatic products used by the practitioners.

"I'd ask if you had a hot date, but...," Opal said. The phone rang and she nodded down the hallway before answering. "Blue room."

The blue room was painted robin's egg and Jade was cleaning as if it had never been done before. Like her daughter, Jade was slight and favored dark colors to go with her short black hair. Kellan envied Jade's ability to eat anything she wanted without gaining an ounce. It wasn't fair. Her legs were the size of Kellan's arms and her waist. . . it really wasn't fair.

"Thought you had plebes for that," Kellan greeted her.

Jade was bent over picking crumbs or something microscopic from the carpeting. "They don't do as good a job."

"Yet you keep them."

"You didn't need an evening gig." Jade grabbed a chair to help herself up.

"You never asked," Kellan raised her voice.

"You don't belong in the cleaning business." Jade tossed the extractions into the trash with a big fake smile. "I don't want to encourage you." Her eyes took in Kellan's attire, but she chose not to comment. "How'd Uncle Mick look?"

Kellan took one chair and Jade followed her, drying her hands, and settled into the other. "Peaceful, which is more than I can say for the rest of that family."

"So you want to talk about what happened last night?"

"Not really."

Jade waited her out. She had the patience for that. The title on her business card read: Life Coach. And Jade had some rather affluent clients who flew her wherever they happened to be when they needed their hands held. She also had the intuitive ability to touch someone and tell them what was wrong, then shift energy so the body could employ its healing. She was mysterious and just seemed to have the right touch.

"I am so screwed," Kellan said.

"You didn't break something again, did you?"

"Not in three whole months."

Jade worked lotion into her hands with a suspicious grin. "Get proposed to?"

Kellan froze a moment, but recovered. "No, actually, I didn't."

Jade bit her lip. "Stefan called. Heard from Luisa."

"God, how did they get it this fast? I just heard two hours ago." Kellan closed her eyes. "I'm supposed to be doing this writing competition and now. . ." She threw a hand in the air.

"This is perfect timing," Jade said calmly. It took a lot to rile her up, but when you did it was like dodging a tornado.

"My life is in total chaos. I made this stupid wish on a stupid candle thinking that maybe it would land on some mystical force or a dead writer."

Jade cocked her head. "Thomas Wolfe is probably not doing anything."

"Nice." Kellan shot her a look of disdain. "Why did you want me to go with you last night?"

Jade lit a cigarette. "Duck doesn't take you anywhere and you needed story ideas."

Kellan closed her eyes. Jade was just trying to be a good friend and she might just be short of those by tomorrow morning. She yanked Betty Ann's scarf from her neck. "I could strangle this woman."

"Now that'd make a good story," Jade said. "How's the Duck taking the betrothal?"

"Like any good little Momma's boy," Kellan picked dog hair from the skirt of her dress.

"You'll have a good laugh over it sometime."

"Especially the part where I kick your butt for opening this can of worms."

"Your life needed a zap. And it'd take more than you to kick my butt."

"Me and that little cancer stick." Kellan pointed to her cigarette. "How do you keep the smell out of here anyway?"

Opal chimed in from the hallway. "White sage and eucalyptus."

Jade screwed up her face.

Kellan rocked on the back legs of her chair. "I can't believe I have to face all those people again tomorrow."

"Be sure to wear red to the cemetery," Opal said. "Duck's uncle made a pass at my friend Dana at the homecoming game last year. Total perv."

Jade smiled. "Marry into that family, you might just become interesting."

* * *

Kellan didn't take Opal's advice, but she didn't wear the black dress either. Instead she selected black Dockers, a white button down and black blazer. The sunglasses made her look like a federal agent, but that was just as fun as harlot. She was the last to arrive, as planned, and the pastor was deep into the reading. Part of her wanted to show Betty Ann some respect and not stand with the family, the other part just didn't want to endure more congratulations.

The cloudless sky had the temperature was rising faster than she'd hoped. She parked the El Camino and hiked over knolls lined with stones to stand discreetly behind the large gathering. Gayle spotted her and with a little head toss motioned her to join him. She shook her head and pointed up at the tree providing shade forty feet from the back of the green tent.

Kellan scanned the attendees. The women looked dolled up for a black and white pageant; splashes of color only graced hats and handbags, with the exception of the woman in turquoise from the viewing. She was in lavender today; a color that accentuated her size. Mrs. Humpty Dumpty. Kellan was about to laugh when Betty Ann's laser glare induced a fake cough.

Searching for a diversion, she spotted a man sitting at another grave about fifty feet to the left of where she stood. Her heart jumped and she held a hand over her eyes to block the sun and to get a clearer look. He sat on a stone bench, elbows propped on his knees watching her and he was wearing a white button down shirt, sleeves rolled up to his elbows. She caught her breath when he waved and held it while reaching a hand up to wave back. Self conscious about being watched, Kellan glanced back to the cluster of mourners to see if anyone had caught her. When she looked back toward the man, he was gone.

* * *

In her daily life, the woman was not brave. He'd been watching her for weeks and until last night, he had serious doubts she was the Gatekeeper. But with her ability to manifest a weapon and severe the cord that attached his son to The Leech, he held high hopes she could do more. From his observations, the dead did not bother her, but she was truly spooked by the living. He needed help and The Gatekeeper was all he had been given.

* * *

The service was wrapping up. The family tossed roses onto the casket and there was still no sign of Mr. White Shirt. Mourners formed clusters of chatter before drifting to their cars. Gayle hugged her from behind.

"You gonna be late to your own funeral?"

"If I have anything to say about it." Kellan smiled. "Your mom mad?"

"Probably," he said without care. "Wanna go to Fireside?"

"You want pizza when your mother has probably got a whole hog smoking at the house?"

Gayle took off his jacket and loosened his tie as they headed toward her El Camino. "Just not ready to go home to her right now." He rubbed her neck with one hand. "We could kill some time."

Kellan faked shock. "Your mind is on sex at your uncle's funeral?"

"My mind has been on sex since I took the tit. It's in my blood."

She squinted. "So I've heard."

"Unlock this thing so I can sit down. My back is killing me in these shoes."

"You're just getting old," she said, unlocking the car door.

"Yes, I am," he said. "Wanna do it with me?"

"You should be at the house." She settled into the driver's seat and Gayle climbed into the passenger side. "Don't want to give her any more ammo."

He fumbled around with his shoes and getting his butt situated. "I meant, do you want to grow old with me?"

Kellan's heart skipped a beat, then screeched to a stop when she saw what was in his hand.

The box was pearl colored with a silver ribbon around it tied in a perfect bow on top. He held it out and her stomach dropped. *Please let it be earrings.* But she knew better, what with the funeral-engagement party. This was the same feeling she got when a rollercoaster plummeted straight down. And today she couldn't see any water to break her fall.

Gayle was sweet-faced with lightning-struck eyes and a dimple in his chin. Everyone adored him and secretly pondered what freakish anomaly had occurred in his bachelor brain to attract him to her. She was nothing more than a no-account Yankee divorcee who cleaned houses.

He took her hand. "I felt bad about yesterday, Momma and everybody swooping in to congratulate you, and all."

"It wasn't appropriate at a funeral home. And now," her eyes scanned the acres of headstones, "we're in a cemetery."

"Thought you'd appreciate the irony," he grinned. "Good story, too."

Of course, what was she thinking? "You did not go get a ring because you thought I'd expect it."

"Baby, you know better than that."

Kellan had always hated men calling her Baby, but somehow didn't mind when Gayle did. It fit his vernacular. She stared at the offered box and forced a smile. Did it look forced? She couldn't stand when people forced smiles moments after being aggravated to their eyeballs. An honest, caring, and compassionate man was offering to marry her, and all her gut could say was: run.

"I know this is sudden, but I think you should open it anyway."

Kellan had to steady her hands as she fumbled with the bow, electing to slide it off and untwist the loops that held the package. Impatient, Gayle took it from her shaking fingers. Did he notice she was shaking? He lifted the lid, dumped out the felt box nested inside and placed it in her hand.

"You don't have to say anything right now."

"The whole town already thinks we're engaged."

"I knew it when I met you," he smiled. "I knew."

God, who was the girl here? He believed in the romantic notion of knowing the right one on sight, as if there were only one. She had learned long ago that buying into such fantasies worked only for people in movies.

Her neighbor's car had caught fire and she called 911. Gayle was one of the volunteer firemen to show up. Geography, not destiny, ruled. He'd spent more time watching her than actually putting the fire out, and his chief had yet to let him forget it.

If she said yes after seeing a beautiful ring, it would feel like a lie. If there was no ring, the no would come more easily. "We've only. . .it's only been a few months."

"I don't want you to feel pressured, but it takes a long time to plan a decent wedding. Janie says you have to reserve the hall and the photographer nearly a year in advance."

Ah, Janie, the sainted older sister who could raise five kids, cook gourmet meals, and volunteer for every church mission without ever seeing the need to raise her voice.

Wait, did he say church?

"So you want the full court press?"

He shrugged. "I thought you sounded disappointed about eloping the first time."

"I'm not religious, and your family. . ."

Gayle grinned. "Won't kill you." The first time she'd heard him say the word it sounded like part of a boat, keel.

She sputtered a silly laugh. "Suppose that means I'd have to wear a costume."

"It's called a dress," he said. "Preferably not that black one."

Kellan stared out the windshield. On the list of things she loathed, girl clothes landed just behind Brussels sprouts. It wasn't the dress so much as all the crap required for it to look right: make-up, hair adornments, foundation garments, and impossible-to-walk-in shoes. How come men didn't have to do all that?

"For pictures. One day out of your life, I think you'll live."

"Your sales pitch needs tweaking."

"You won't find this much fun in another man." Gayle leaned back in the seat and gave his belt a tug. "And wait till you see the fine little spread over in Yadkinville I got picked out. It's already got sixteen head o' hog. Once the young-ins are big enough, you won't have to haul the slop buckets anymore."

Panic overtook her before she noticed him laughing. "I can't start having babies at my age. I'd be sixty by the time they got out of high school."

He composed himself. "I got enough nieces and nephews for a little league team."

"I mean, look at me. Do I look like mother material?"

"Between Janie and Hilary. . ."

"You're the only boy. Aren't you expected to procreate?" Kellan could hear herself nearly shouting. "Isn't it your duty to carry on the family name?"

Gayle did a boyish giggle. "Damn, woman. You think this town needs more Schick's? Have you missed the last couple days?"

She saw a car pass with three women and two kids squeezed into the back seat. "I'm sorry. I'm ruining this."

Gayle leaned in and put his chin on her shoulder. "Marriage is supposed to be a joyful adventure, not a life sentence. You need to relax and let me show you what it's supposed to look like."

What planet was he from?

He took the box from her. The lid opened with a squeak to reveal a plastic bubble ring that looked like an eyeball straight out of a gumball machine.

She laughed. "Well, we won't have to worry about insurance."

Gayle watched her with a mischievous grin and said nothing.

"Is there gum inside?"

He cocked his head and swiped his chin with a finger. "Could be."

A little shake and she heard something clack against the dome. Her thumb found a tiny catch on the side that unsnapped with pressure. The casing popped open and a large Princess cut sapphire jumped into her lap. Her mouth fell open as she picked the stone carefully from a fold in her pants.

"I thought you'd want to pick out your own setting. Didn't know how fancy you'd go, working with your hands and all."

She stopped breathing, holding the stone as if it might melt to her touch.

"How?"

"You always get mad when that diamond commercial comes

38

on." He was a tad smug. "You do wear a lot of blue."

Kellan couldn't take her eyes off the stone. A big part of her had always hated being a girl, mainly because she had never learned to be any good at it. But this moment spoke to the small part that didn't. How could she dream of saying anything but yes?

Chapter 5

The Meadow was the florist of choice in Old Landon. Kellan gave Stefan a weak wave. A generic man somewhere in his forties who wore a corporate haircut, cargo pants, polo shirt, and reading glasses that hung from a black silk lanyard. She'd always assumed he was gay, but he never mentioned his personal life, and she didn't care enough to bother finding out. His Cairn terrier Tallulah usually greeted her just inside the door, but not today.

Stefan begged off his call and hustled over to her. "Get over here. You look awful. Tell me." He almost knocked her over with an attack hug.

"This is new," Kellan said into his shoulder as she tried to sound lighthearted.

He pushed her back, holding her shoulders. "My god, you're so pale. Out with it."

"I think Gayle and I just got engaged." She struggled to hold tears back. She didn't cry. Where was this coming from?

His mouth dropped open. "For real or cover?"

Kellan sagged. "You tell me. I thought it was just a ruse, but he actually gave me a sapphire to pick out a setting for." She slapped the box in his hand. "What have you heard?"

He moved the hands on the clock sign to say he'd be back by 2:00 and locked the door. It was only eleven. Business must be extra slow. He pried the lid open on the box and gasped seeing the eyeball.

"Oh, this is hysterical." He smiled then worked to get at the stone. "I didn't hear a thing about this, are you kidding?" Then he took the stone to a worktable, snapped on a lamp and examined the stone as if it came from an ancient civilization. "Yesterday's talk was all about the séance. I heard you were stoned, writhing on the floor, shouting at something nobody else could see."

He pulled a stool from beneath a workbench for her, and hopped up on one opposite. "You can tell me anything, you know that," he said, with a seriousness that unnerved her.

"Are they dropping me? I'm already getting crap messages."

He waved his hand. "They might pull back for a little while, but only the holy rollers will kick you to the curb. Tell me what really happened."

Kellan hung her head and closed her eyes, mustering the strength to tell him without mentioning the dead kid. "I'm not sure. One minute I'm trying not to laugh, and the next, it's two hours later and they're standing over me, telling me I was saying things."

"What kind of things?" He leaned toward her.

"I don't know. But I lost time, and saw things I can't really explain."

"Scary things?"

How could she answer that? "I don't really know what I saw," she said. It was an honest answer. At the time she didn't. She couldn't explain any of it.

Stefan cocked his head. "Okay, so you're not ready to share."

"It's not that. It's just. . ."

"Unbelievable? Crazy?"

She let her eyes do the talking.

"You saw someone," he said, searching her eyes. "A dead someone?"

She swallowed.

He grabbed up her hands. "Did you ever read any of John Edward's books? You know who I'm talking about, right?"

"I'm not a psychic."

"But you saw something. And his books talk about what he experienced when he first started out, full of doubt. I think you should read them. Come on."

Stefan hopped off his perch and handed her the sapphire box. He hit a couple buttons on the answering machine, grabbed the keys protruding from the side of the register, and motioned her to follow him out the back door.

"I didn't know you were into that stuff," she said, as he led her to his car. "Where are we going?"

"Why?"

"This is weird, but I'm hungry all of a sudden."

"We'll go to my house, get the books, and have some spinach dip and cheese cake. You can tell me how The Duck proposed, and I'll show you something unbelievable."

Stefan owned a restored two-story colonial just outside the city. Not as large as a plantation home, but far too big for one person. The decor was subtle and earthy, more rustic than she had imagined. An array of refinished antiques were strategically placed and elegantly adorned with vases and stones. Spacious, yet lived in, and very clean. Kellan didn't dare ask who cleaned for him. Probably did it himself. She half expected a couple Labradors to lope by when little Tallulah greeted them in a snit from the top of the stairs.

"You shush," he said to her. "She's mad 'cause I left her home today."

He gave her a tour of the house, dog at his heels, while he talked of turning it into a bed and breakfast. Afterward, he warmed some dip to serve with carrot sticks and celery. They sat before a television in a den on the south side of the ground floor. The room was cozy, upholstered in deep elegant plums and oranges. Plump pillows cried out to be snuggled with a good book by the picture window. With the wooden blinds drawn, the library converted to a home theater. Kellan smiled. She could live in this room. His video equipment was a little dated, but steps above anything she'd ever owned.

"First things first." He held both hands up. "Brace yourself."

She sat in the middle of the couch opposite the television while he put a VHS tape in. He took a seat close to the set and fumbled for the remote.

"Okay, so five years ago, I go up to Virginia to visit my mother's sister. She lives in Fredericksburg and you know there's not a divot in that area untouched by the past, right? They do reenactments up there, which, you ask me, just keeps restless spirits hanging around. I mean, if you died in the Civil War and every weekend people did battle around you? Well, how could anybody rest in peace like that?"

Kellan wasn't sure where this was going, but she had a feeling he had some sort of visual proof. She motioned for him to speed up.

He raised a hand in recognition. "So, we are out behind her house throwing the ball into the lake for Brando. He's gone now, but he loved to jump into the lake."

"Brando?"

"Sheep dog," he said, fast-forwarding the tape. "So we film him because he's a riot, and there's nothing else to do." He froze the frame. "I came across it weeks later. I'm about to pop the tape out of the VCR when I notice. . ."

He hit the play button. Kellan watched the dog haul down a small dock after a tennis ball and hit the water in a belly flop. Stefan leaned to the screen to point.

"See this bunch of trees? It's about three acres belonging to the neighbors. Keep your eye right here." He pointed to a cluster just short of the water's edge.

The dog emerged, shaking water all over everyone, as dogs do. There was a blip near the trees, a shadow of movement. Then a man dressed in a dusty blue Union uniform, complete with crinkled cap, and rifle in hand, stepped into view from behind a tree. Kellan leaned forward, mouth open. He was blurry, not nearly as clear as the dog, Stefan's aunt or even the trees.

"You're sure it wasn't the neighbor, or someone dressed for reenactment?"

Stefan glanced at her, then back at the screen. "Positive. They were in Nova Scotia for a month and both reenactments were rained out."

"Rained out?" Kellan grinned.

"I know, right? Like fighting actually stopped for rain." Stefan then turned back to the screen. "Keep your eyes on him now."

She watched. The man stood for a moment, then raised his rifle to rest the stock on his shoulder and let his arm slide down the length of the barrel. Then he turned to retreat back into the woods but, before he could take a full step, his image dissolved like a hologram from a sci-fi movie.

She sucked in a breath. "Rewind it, please."

They watched it five more times.

"This is amazing. Did you show this to anyone, like a ghost-hunting group, or a TV station?"

He shrugged. "Gave a copy to the local tourist company. They do ghost walks on Halloween, things like that. I did have a professional verify that the tape wasn't tampered with or double-exposed."

"You could send it to one of those investigation shows on cable."

"I only wanted you to see it, so if you saw something you couldn't explain, just know, it might not be your imagination." He gave her arm a squeeze.

She put her hand over his. "Thanks. The only thing I do know is my imagination doesn't go places like this."

Stefan waited.

"You'll be the third to know when I figure it out." She held up her right hand.

"I can't believe Jade didn't pick up more."

43

"Said she was busy running interference."

He raised an eyebrow. "So what can I tell the girls when they ask? Luisa's got a mouth so big she could blow out a homecoming bonfire. Thank God, or I'd be making things up to get through the summer."

"Let them stew for a while," she said. "I really don't know what to tell anyone."

She gave Stefan the details of Gayle's proposal while they enjoyed extra-large slices of cheesecake with strawberry sauce.

"So you're really marrying our hardware hero."

"I don't know," she said.

"What?"

"I can't help but think that he only proposed because his aunt put it in the obituary."

"You don't think that stone says more than that? He did not just pick that up yesterday at the mall."

"You think?"

He gave her his owl scowl. "You're mad at him about something."

She thought she was hiding it, but alas. "You know Sarah Timms?"

"Timms Tires?"

"She heard about last night. Blabbed to Gayle at breakfast."

"With all his fireman buddies there," he offered.

Kellan closed her eyes. "I didn't think of that." She climbed out of the sofa and took both plates back to the kitchen. "He shows up just as I'm headed out this morning, demanding to know if I actually attended a séance, without ever asking how I was or if I was okay. And then his mother goes and tells half the town we're engaged, in case they didn't notice it in the paper."

"And you think she was trying to divert their attention away from the evil doings of the previous evening."

"Exactly."

Stefan followed her to the kitchen with his plate. "They do fear the devil more than death, you know. The idea that you might have been dabbling in the dark side would scare the pecan stuffing out of them, which, you would think, would have them stonewalling you."

"I know." Kellan washed the two plates and forks they had used. "I don't trust that woman. She's always looking for things wrong with me. How can I tell if he's sincere and not just going along with her twisted little plot to get him to dump me and put him back on a pedestal?" She dropped a plate into the drainer. "I never said a word and the whole town was planning the wedding."

"You think that stone was a parting gift?" He cocked his head. "Kellan."

Okay, she knew it wasn't, but hated the circumstance that led to its offering.

Stefan smiled. "You want to know what I think?"

"Only if it can turn back time," Kellan sighed.

"Well, it won't do that, but my grandmother always said if the answer to the question isn't yes without a doubt, it's no." He leaned over to rub her shoulder. "If it is yes, you might be the star of the biggest event this town has seen since Gracie Northrop shot her heating oil tank with a .44 magnum, chasing Lester and that nasty Lane girl buck naked into their bean field. Blew a hole in her living room. . ."

"Big enough to drive a fire truck through," Kellan finished. "I heard."

They nodded in agreement before Stefan said, "Janie's probably already planning the theme for the fire hall, and you know that family takes their barbeque more serious than a heart attack."

She sobered, and looked at him with sad eyes. "What's wrong with me? I mean, besides what they all think? I know he's the best thing in three counties according to everyone. And he's been nothing but good to me, which is a first. Now, I'm starting to think--" she stopped.

"What?"

"I really am no good for him."

"Kellan."

"No, they all think that, and they might be right." Kellan sighed. "I mean, what does he see in me anyway? I'm nothing like his mother or his sisters."

"Aside from your utilitarian apparel and unmanageable hair, you are pretty attractive."

"I just flipped out at a séance where no one else saw anything. They used to burn people at the stake for that, you know."

Stefan shoved her away from the sink and turned the water off. "You're not a witch because you saw something that scared you. And just because you don't fit the mold of people's perceptions doesn't mean there's anything wrong with you. This is nothing that can't be fixed with a good raucous roll in the hay."

"With cheesecake like this, who needs sex?" She bit her lips together.

Stefan held his right hand over his heart.

Kellan dragged the sponge over the sink's edge. "He could bone up on a few skills in that department." Her eyes widened with immediate guilt, and a smirk snaked across her face. "You did not just hear me say that."

"Well," Stefan lifted his head. "Explains why our superhero's been flying solo for so long."

Kellan covered her mouth with the dish towel to conceal her laughter.

"He's trained to put the fire out."

* * *

Starbucks used to be a place where Yuppies in their top coats and loafers camped out with the latest bestseller or *The New Yorker*. Now it was where mothers met to remind themselves that being out of the work force was in their children's best interests and only temporary. Then there was always the single man on his cell phone, laptop open, lamenting over some painfully important problem that could only be solved his by shouting.

Kellan's Starbucks catered to the college study groups and stayed open until 1:00 AM, offering a free espresso shot with any specialty beverage ordered after midnight. It had limited seating, but that didn't stop the kids from camping on the floor, craning over books. Being summer, she wouldn't have to step over bodies. Even empty, it was a welcome sight. Kellan wondered if that was the feeling people with real families had when they went home for holidays. To her there was something safe about a Starbucks. The fact that the lousy economy was closing a lot of them was troublesome, but she found solace in knowing hers was near a college campus.

Anytime Riley was with her she parked in a far away spot close to grassy divides or perimeter hedges. Tonight, it meant the back corner near a new Italian bakery. Riley's needs were always the first to get attention. He hopped out, hiked his leg even though his tank had been emptied at the park, kicked up some grass and had a sniff near a utility box. Kellan ordered him back in the car, and headed inside.

The place was empty, save for an overdressed middle-aged man who wore the disappointed look of having been stood up. Kellan had to do a mental head-slap. She, too, was middle-aged, but never really thought of herself that way. She'd stopped caring how old she was after thirty and didn't concern herself with how other people saw her.

She felt out of place, removed in some way. As if this man would look into her and see that she was losing her mind, her clients, and possibly the most eligible bachelor in town. Being at Starbucks was normal, real, and rational.

She ordered a decaf and a peanut butter bar to share with Riley. Coffee and a cookie were good medicine. Her mind went over to the proposal. Gayle was great in so many ways, but, there were buts. They hit it off and she couldn't remember them ever having had a fight. But did he really want to marry her, or was this just a decoy to throw the town off the scent? Did she love him really? Enough to marry him, and his mother?

Stefan was right. If the answer wasn't an immediate "yes," then it was "no." Then again, her past and her concerns about his family could be ruining a perfectly good thing. She glanced at the man lost in thought and felt secure in the notion that her misery had company, even if they'd never met.

Riley drooled at the sight of her and the little flat bag. She let herself into the car, secured the coffee cup, and pushed his vacuum nose away so she could to break off a corner of cookie for him. He swallowed it without chewing.

"You didn't even taste that," she told him as a string of drool reached for the napkin she'd placed under him. She ate half and he got the rest. Her mind went from Gayle back to the séance, which had been the most bizarre experience of her life. The cold, the dark, the thing would always be there in her head, even if it was just placed on a shelf and ignored. No one could tell her anything now. It would only be speculation. Where was the evidence? The harder she tried not to think about it, the more questions came, the more frightening scenarios sprang up.

Her biggest fear was talking about it. People in this town were pretty much like Gayle's mother; "The Bible tells me so." If she were to be like the chick on TV, talking about it like it was normal, they would lock her up and commence with the deprogramming. Kellan used to have nightmares about imprisonment; her choices taken away. Those fears had no foundation so she had never known where they'd come from. Being locked in her room for punishment would be nothing compared to being institutionalized or imprisoned with other crazies.

She turned the key in the ignition. Click, click, click, then nothing. She closed her eyes. "Not now. Come on." She tried again. One click, then nothing. "Of course! What next?"

Calling Gayle for a jump was the last thing she wanted to do. He was probably at the firehouse. Bending down, her hand felt around for the long Maglight she kept beneath her seat. Its weight alone could crack a cranium. She pulled the lever to pop the hood open, and climbed out to take a look.

Under the hood she saw nothing unusual. The battery was connected and no visible corrosion oozed from the posts. A dead battery looked no different from a live one. Go figure. She shut the flashlight off to save its batteries and looked around. The place was dead. She could ask the sad-sack guy for a jump, but then she'd feel obligated to listen to his possibly depressing story. Jade was working, and she was still mad at her anyway. Stefan was a possibility, but after scrolling through the numbers on her cell phone, she only found the floral shop which had closed three hours ago, and she suspected his number home number was unlisted.

Riley startled her by barking from inside the car. She turned and saw a tall kid standing by the passenger door. Kellan hadn't heard a sound.

"I need to talk to you," he said.

"I'm sorry?" She clicked the flashlight back on to get a better look at him, but it flickered and died. "Do I know you?"

In the darkening light, he looked clean-cut in his white Izod and his Calvin Klein jeans. He could have been any kid out walking, having car trouble, bumming a cigarette, but her stomach took a dip, and her guard was up. There was something familiar about him, but she didn't know anybody his age in this area. *He's just a kid.*

"What are you, locked out of your car? Need money? I only have a couple bucks left since. . ."

He stepped closer and she instinctively took one step back. Riley barked. Kellan flinched and dropped the flashlight to the asphalt. She heard it clack, then roll underneath the car.

It was him; the kid from the séance.

Kellan took a couple steps backward, not taking her eyes from him. He was much clearer now as her eyes readjusted to the dark. Yes, definitely the same kid she'd found behind the gate, just as solid and alive as the guy in the coffee shop.

"You remember me," he said gently.

His head rose slightly and she wished the Force was real so she could retrieve the flashlight. The streetlight over the parking lot was at the opposite corner making it darker where she stood. Images flashed back to her: the black wings, the cord, the Thing. A deep shiver covered her back with goose bumps.

Kellan stepped carefully to the opposite side of her El Camino to get to an angle where the street light shone toward him. He was young, but grown; possibly drinking age. God, what she would give for a drink. Intoxication would be an excuse for what she was seeing. His eyes came into focus, but too shadowed to tell color. He was frightened, innocent. She could feel him, his confusion, and his loss all at once. He turned his head revealing one full side of his face.

"Who are you?" she said on an inhale.

He stared her down. "Who are *you*?"

She heard the name "Connor" whispered into her right ear as if someone stood directly behind her. Shooting a glance over her shoulder, she found no one, and then she started shaking.

"Connor," she whispered.

He seemed confused as he studied her. Her foot found that the flashlight had rolled back to her. Without taking her eyes from him, she crouched to retrieve it. He didn't move.

"You cut the cord. How did you do that?"

Her thumb tried the button on the flashlight again. It flickered and expired.

Kellan shook her head. "I don't know. What was that thing?"

He surveyed his surroundings. "The Leech? A liar."

Riley pawed at the window, nails clacking on the glass. Kellan hesitated, but her hand found the passenger door handle and opened the door for him to hop out. If the kid became threatening, Riley would remedy the situation. The dog hopped down with his tail wagging his whole body and trotted to greet him. Connor looked cautious but Riley seemed to offer him comfort. It was then she noticed he was barefoot.

Kellan lowered the useless flashlight that she had been holding like a club. "I don't understand. Are you real?"

Connor stroked the dog's head, and looked up at her. "You tell me."

Standing, he was a good six, seven inches taller than her, slender, with straight shoulders and unblemished face. He couldn't be any more than twenty, and he was here now, physically right before her.

"Twenty-three," he corrected.

She caught her breath. Mind reader? He took two steps toward her. She did not move away, but did flinch when he reached his hand out. Slowly, she mirrored him, her hand meeting his half way. He placed his over hers with a touch so gentle it might have been a feather. It sent goose bumps up her arm and down her neck. Expecting cold, she was surprised at the tingling energy she felt.

"Kellan," he said.

She couldn't move, forgot to breathe and lost her ability to form words. His touch felt so real. How was that possible? Tears welled, threatening to blur her vision, before one tumbled over the edge of her left lower lid. She couldn't put her finger on what she felt: part despair, part relief, part hope.

When her voice returned, she asked, "Why are you here?"

"You brought me," he said taking a step forward.

She took a step back. "No, that man came for you. You went with him."

"I need your help," he said, with absolute conviction. "Please, you have to keep the gate closed."

Kellan's heart dropped, and her breathing quickened. A drumming beat in her ears.

"I already. . .you went up the stairs and. . ." her voice shook. "Are you even supposed to be here?"

"You don't refuse people who ask for help," he said.

Guilt stung her in the chest. She and Jade had once made a pact that they wouldn't turn anyone who asked for help away. How did he know that? Of course, at the time they had meant live people. Now her instinct was to pull a Forrest Gump and run.

"I'm asking."

He could definitely hear her thoughts. Kellan looked away, then back. He was still there. "But I don't know how."

"You're the Gatekeeper," he said as if she already knew. "You opened it. You can keep it closed."

The image of the man in the white shirt asking her to open the gate flashed before her. How could she be something she knew

50

nothing about?

"Whatever you do, don't open that gate again," he said. "If It is still in there, that will buy me some time."

"Time for what?"

"I need to talk to my brother."

Kellan glanced around. "So, go talk to your brother."

"He can't see me like you can."

Of course not. Her head felt lighter and she fought to not wobble. "Your brother is here? Living?"

Connor nodded.

Kellan let out a sigh of distress. "So all I have to do is keep that gate closed?" How hard could that be? Just refuse to open it again, if it appeared. "Wait, how do you know that thing is still behind the gate? What if it got out while. . ."

"We would have known by now." The kid shoved his hands into his pockets. "But Tony needs to know."

She waited, holding her breath. The word no repeated itself in her head.

"Can you tell him for me?" Connor said.

Her stomach did a flip. She'd rather pick up a hooded cobra than talk to some dead kid's brother. Kellan swallowed so hard her voice dropped to a whisper. "Tell him what?"

"It wasn't me."

* * *

Kellan sat in the truck long enough for her coffee to go cold. Connor had been there one moment and when she glanced back, he was just gone. Riley had curled up, head on his paws, burrowed deep in doggie dreamland. She stared out the windshield remembering the one time she had tried to watch that TV show where a pretty medium woman delivered messages from dead people. It had made her nauseated. The show had a supporting cast that completely bought into the woman's 'gift,' as if it were normal.

This was no gift. This was more like a live grenade and she was not going to be the one to pull the pin.

"Yeah, remember when your brother committed suicide? Well, he wasn't screwed up in the head or on drugs. He was taken by an evil thing. Oh, and he wanted me to deliver this telepath-o-gram. Ready?" She could blow a kazoo and sing a song. *Not going to*

51

happen.

The mere idea of doing such a thing made her want to vomit. And if she talked to said brother, she was certain he would too. That is, if he didn't run her over with his car first. Kellan would lay money there would be no sappy, precious, feel-good ending in real life. She would keep the gate closed for Connor, nothing more.

With an audible click, the blue digits on the dashboard clock reappeared: 10:32. She straightened in her seat. The battery seemed to have awakened from its coma. Her bladder pulled her back to reality and she tried the key, not at all surprised when the engine turned over.

Chapter 6

At home, Kellan tossed four aspirin into her mouth and leaned over to drink from the faucet. When she caught her reflection, she was startled by how frightened she looked. It took a lot to shake her up. Maybe it came from having to rely solely on herself for so long. She did not have time for this. The new writing project was moving and couldn't leave it hanging now that she'd placed so much weight on its completion.

In the mirror, Jack Nicholson's face from *One Flew Over the Cuckoo's Nest* laughed at her. Was she losing her mind? Had what she just seen real or a figment of her imagination? Where did horror writers get their material anyway? If she was truly crazy, would she know it? How many perfectly sane people were locked up in institutions, having to endure other crazy people laughing, talking nonsense, babbling how they were aliens or Jesus Christ? With everyone telling them they are crazy, they would eventually start to believe it.

She climbed into the empty tub. "What do I do with this?"

The next morning, she woke with a neck ache, having fallen asleep in an unnatural position in the tub. The unforgiving surface had her tailbone throbbing and her left leg asleep. After forcibly regaining her circulation, Kellan stumbled from the tub and turned on the computer.

Day three of writing was starting late. Her mind was numb. Maybe she just dreamt up the dead kid. Yesterday had been a long day: Stefan had shown her his ghost video, and perhaps that got her mind going. The kid couldn't be real, right?

Coffee in hand, she sat before the computer and opened the file she had not looked at since Jade called: three whole paragraphs of nothing. She could plot Jade's murder. That might be fun. It occurred to Kellan that she had plenty to write about now: the séance, the funeral home, the cemetery proposal, and the dead kid at Starbucks; each more absurd than the last.

Kellan typed: What do I do with this?

Then she kept going. Without outline or thought, her fingers moved over the keys as if they were plugged into something the rest of her wasn't.

* * *

"You want to make movies, you go make movies," Naomi told her younger son. "I certainly won't stop you. Just be careful."

With a degree in political science, and four months in the Peace Corp, Anthony pulled a one-eighty and went to L.A., where he was greeted with steel-toed boots. He quickly learned that he had no specific skills, so he found a second hand video camera and shot anything that came his way. Street Theatre 101 yielded roadside sobriety tests, neighbors arguing in the street, dogs burying items stolen from the yards of careless children, dime-bag drug deals, and the dramas of homeless people. He'd even taken to following people randomly just to see what they did. This created problems, for some thought he was a casting agent and performed when they realized he was shooting them. Others confronted him, spouted right-to-privacy laws, lectured him on propriety, and threw whatever they had in their hands at him. He filmed every attack like a member of the paparazzi.

It was the short film he made of the kleptomaniac dog that got him noticed, purchased by a pet food company, and shortened for a commercial. A director saw it, liked his no-nonsense honesty, and offered him an internship, which meant working eighteen hour days to be fed a lousy lunch.

California had more beautiful people than cockroaches. All he needed to say was he was a cameraman or anything remotely related to the industry, and he could have any one of them. Who needed a date with an agenda? If they only wanted to sleep with him to get on set, gain access to an actor, or use his name to do the same, he couldn't be bothered. Diversions were nice, but usually cost far more than they were worth. That was how the game was played. He reminded himself that he was there to work, make a name, earn his independence and most importantly, not get screwed.

"You got a big voice in silence kid," Hal Martin, one of the giants of cinematography told him. "In meetings, get right to the point. Less is more. Smile when they immediately reject your ideas. Directors, it's what they do. Producers are even worse. Then watch them dance. Later, they come back, ask your opinion, stand by your first one. They swallow it down like baby birds.

"In a visual medium, your job is to make the picture look real. Picture looks bad, no one will buy it. Picture looks good, De Niro could scratch his ass for two hours, its box office. Actors and directors get all the awards, but it's what we do, makes it real. Everyone knows this."

Hal was right, and Anthony was smart enough to take his advice to heart.

"Watch, wait, and learn through the lens. Answers are like animals, kid. They sneak into the frame when they think they're alone."

From that moment on, Anthony had searched for answers to all his questions through his lens.

Now his heart raced from the cola he'd sipped to avoid meaningless conversation with people with whom he did not identify. With the last of his antacids gone, no drugstore within reach, his mind was preoccupied. He was unaccustomed to sitting in one place for long. Four hours seated in a theater clapping on cue felt like such a useless activity. There was so much that he could have been doing, and he got bored easily. He supported people being rewarded for their work, but having to endure a slow-moving ceremony made him wonder if the accolades were worth it. But major awards meant bankability, more opportunities, time extensions, and larger budgets. Never forget these things.

The woman seated next to him looked so perfect God might have sculpted her by hand. He had to force his eyes forward so she wouldn't think he was staring at her bejeweled chest. Most men would kill to be in his shoes, but Anthony was uncomfortable and her perfume did little to relax him. She'd already given him an odd aside for his incessant watch-checking and knee-bouncing. Anthony was no good with idle hands and averted his eyes to find the past had crept right up to the door of his present.

Anthony's greasy roommate flopped himself on the bed. "I'm telling you, you're gonna come crawling back with your tail between your legs and you're gonna be marked, like, like with a scarlet letter or something: a giant L for loser. You can't turn your back on your lord and master. Hollywood, this place, is like the Mafia."

Anthony packed his bags, ignoring Sid.

"The only real way out is death, cause once you're out there, making ten bucks an hour, editing college entrance videos, or shooting wedding receptions when the rest of us are doing real work, getting Oscar nominations, you'll want to be dead, my friend."

"Real work?" Anthony said. *"Hell on Prom Night, Dragon Warriors, Saw*, what is it eight now?" Anthony kicked an empty dresser drawer closed. "And when was your last Oscar nomination, Sid? What film? *Thirst for Blood? We Got No Game?* No, *Daughters of Doom.*"

"Hey, that was a good film." Sid rolled over to talk into the pillow. "We just didn't get distribution."

"Yeah, that was it," Anthony said, struggling to zip an overstuffed duffle.

"Hey, you worked on your share of crap too."

"I know, Sid. I'm tired of crap. You and Jerome and Phipps can keep making crap, taking scraps from the guys who actually had Oscar nominations, waiting for Spielberg to call. And all those bleached blondes who changed their names, and think a boob job and a visit to Hef's house will make them millions? They're all yours."

Sid rolled over on his side. His stringy hair was long and always in the way, which made his habit of combing it with his fingers extra annoying. "But you're the one who's worked with names. You're our in, Buddy. You've met Bruckheimer."

"Yeah, we almost did lunch once," Anthony said.

"New York is harder, you know?"

"Harder than waiting six hours for some spoiled teenage principal to calm down because the director reamed her for being too hung over to remember her lines?" Anthony felt himself heating up. He hated losing his composure over nonsensical happenings. He wanted to do something real, even if it meant washing dishes in a restaurant. At least he'd be home. "I'll be a doormat for a New Yorker any day over that."

"But cable documentary? You're going backwards, you know. Blockbuster to B-movie?" Sid tossed a sock ball in the air. "Do you know how cold it gets in New York? Probably never see a chick in a thong."

"I'm from there." Anthony tossed a script at him. "And indoors, they don't need thongs."

Sid sat up, the image in his head written all over his face. "Still, you'll want to come back."

"Only to work for one of you guys," Anthony said.

"And we won't be able to hire you. It's like, against nature to hire a defector."

"The mother country always wants her defectors back."

Sid was right. Here he was watching to see if his old friend would win his Oscar for comedy writing. The Academy rarely bestowed the honor to comedic work, but every year usually offered one surprise, and Anthony had agreed to be present in case that would be Sid's moment. As a nominee, his friend was seated near the aisle, just in case, and he shot him a nervous smile before the music cued up.

Anthony watched a woman in sequins mince to the podium in a dress so tight at the knees her steps weren't but a few inches apart. His hands responded with everyone else's. When the applause faded, she read her lines from the teleprompter announcing the category of best documentary.

"Film can inspire, enlighten, and educate. Only a handful of filmmakers seek the far reaches to bring to light the darker places. Documentary filmmakers are a breed of their own, often risking their own safety in pursuit of their story. They venture into uncharted territory to capture the story as it unfolds before their camera lens."

Anthony had been nominated once before, but he'd been beaten by a guy he highly respected. This year, he hadn't looked to see who was nominated since he had not been. Sid's category would be a while yet. He could sneak out later, check messages; drift in late to an after-party for an hour of necessary networking. As his eyes watched the screen showing clips from each nominee, his mind was on the exit door, and how he could breeze past the people milling near the entrance.

"And the Oscar for Best Documentary goes to. . ."

Anthony imagined how he might respond if his name was called one day. He'd probably step on the Jimmy Choo's of the woman next to him, and stumble into the aisle with all the grace of a one-legged stork, while the camera caught his flushed face and his worried brow. Thank God he wasn't nominated.

His hands clapped in response as he recognized the name of a guy he didn't much care for. Tiny Miss Tight Dress leaned in to touch her cheek to his with an air kiss, handed the guy his statuette. Anthony didn't hear a word he said, wishing he had not told Sid he'd be there for his big moment. Blood might be thicker than water, but friends help clean up any blood spilled.

* * *

Where is this coming from? She didn't know any filmmakers. Kellan read the words on her screen as if they'd been written by someone else. Her head pulsed as if she'd been carrying a basket of wet laundry around on it.

A grin snaked across her face. It was gone. After three years, the block was officially broken, disintegrated to dust or desert sand. Kellan knew somewhere her angels sang, trumpets sounded, and the creative gods she'd once banished had not forsaken her. A giddy elation swelled from her stomach up to her throat as she let out a laugh. Kellan had not experienced a high like this since Daryl Burleson kissed her in front of her entire third grade class.

"Thank you!" she shouted, rousing Riley from his slumber.

The sensation was pure joy, and it was short-lived as she felt a presence behind her right shoulder. Kellan spun her chair slowly around. Connor stood in silence, hands stuffed into his jeans. Again, he was as solid as any live person, but when she moved he shimmered as if he were underwater. The longer she stared, the clearer he got. His presence completely ruined her moment.

"I said I'd keep the gate closed," she said annoyed.

"But you won't tell him." His voice said in her right ear.

"No, I won't." Kellan shook her head. "You do not go to someone and tell them their dead brother talks to you, and oh, by the way, he didn't really jump to his death. No, some creepy Leech made him do it. Sure, he'd believe that. Even if he didn't think I was nuts, which I probably am, do you realize how horrifying that would be? I mean, what if he's spent years in therapy getting over your death, recently had a breakthrough, and finally getting back to living a normal life?"

"He's not," Connor said, emphasizing the not.

"If the gate appears again, I won't open it, but that's it."

Connor stared.

Kellan hated when people stared. "What if he doesn't want the life you think he should have?" She waited as he stared, unmoving. "No, I won't do that. I won't hurt someone, even someone I don't know. Not like that. It's too cruel. He would be devastated."

Connor remained steadfast. She could feel his desperation like a hunger, a need so great nothing would keep him from it.

"Go to your brother, Connor," Kellan said. "Hurt him and scare

him all by yourself."
"I already did."

* * *

Kellan looked back at her screen and looked for his reflection behind her. Connor was gone. She was talking to a kid in her imagination, right? Was this how Stephen King came up with his material? And what was the difference between real and imagined? How could she know if Connor was not just a figment of her imagination?

Her laundry had piled up, so Kellan continued to mull this over as she fed quarters to the washing machine, then ran back up to her desk to snatch her Webster's from the shelf of reference books. She started with the word imagination. After reading its willowy definition, she continued to words like fact, actual, true, authentic, and genuine.

When she had taken swimming lessons as a kid, her right side was much stronger than the left which made her swim in circles. She had the same feeling now as each definition circled back to the previous like a snake swallowing its tail.

Kellan slammed the book shut. There was no proof of what was real and what was imagined. If imagination was the forming of mental images, what if they were things she did not chose to see? Was it merely the function of the eyes to capture the image like a camera lens? She expected blind people the world over would probably be able to put up a good argument for what constitutes a mental image and how they determine whether it was in fact present.

Kellan knew a woman who wrote *Star Trek* novels who went to the Fan Fairs in costume. She had told her some fans took the Trek world so seriously that they were convinced it was real. Kellan snatched the dictionary back up and turned to reality, to no further satisfaction. The Webster's flew into the trash can with a great whomp.

Why should she care? So, there was the uncomfortable matter of the dark Leech and the dead kid, and the possibility of traumatizing a mysterious brother for life. On the bright side, this was a writer's paradise, a deep well of overflowing material. No need to determine what was real and what was not. She had only to embrace the world and the characters that appeared to her as Peter Rabbit had to Beatrix

Potter. They didn't send Beatrix to the asylum because she talked to her drawings as if they were real.

When she was finished, she'd have a book. A book was real, something solid to hold in the hands, present to the world and proclaim with mighty aplomb, I Am Author. See? Here is my book, neatly printed and brilliantly bound. That was real. The texture of the paper, the smell of the glue, the fabric on the board and the glossy jacket were the treasures she sought. No jewels, houses, cars or rare things in jars could equal in measure the worth of that treasure.

Kellan sighed. No one locked up Dr. Seuss either.

Chapter 7

When Anthony was a kid, he had a heavy globe that stood on the nightstand by the bed. He would spin it with his eyes closed, feeling the bumps and seams beneath his fingers like a blind man. When it stopped, he recorded the place under his finger in a notebook and resolved to someday travel to that very spot. He'd spend the next couple weeks imagining what he would find when he got there. In college, this list was transferred to a computer file. Copious notes were made whenever he could tick off a reached destination. Anthony made a point of going to at least one new place a year until he found a career that took him there on purpose.

Shooting film had become his life and he couldn't imagine doing anything else. Documentaries afforded him more time for in-depth stories. When he figured out that he wasn't the most seasoned cameraman in the business, Anthony pieced together a lucrative career from scraps no one else wanted. A twenty-minute piece on the mating habits of the Arctic puffin, a three-minute spot inside a hotdog factory, a ten-minute instructional on waterproofing leather, a video diary of a guy who attempted to date thirty women in thirty days, a half-hour video on metal shop safety, and too many commercials to count. No job was too tedious, insignificant, untimely, or inappropriate to hone his craft or pay the bills.

In twenty years, he had built a body of work that granted his name respect and enabled him to land larger projects. Decent work, but he craved pieces with some meat on the bone. That drew him to the underbelly of the world. Getting shot at was a bonus that played well on film. In places governments didn't want nosey reporters, Anthony had more wiggle room. "I'm making a movie," he'd say. Everyone wanted to be in the movies. While shooting choreographed performances, he could sometimes squeeze through cracks, breeze past guards, and step under police tape to bear witness to dirty little secrets. He'd often wondered if he might have made a good spy or private detective.

Alone in his hotel room, he turned on his HD camera to review the footage he had shot just hours before he had to button his borrowed tuxedo. He was wired from all the socializing and needed half an hour to wind down. He might get a couple hours sleep before his flight or work straight through, depending. His finger found the stop button, then play.

A middle-aged woman appeared in the handheld screen -- corporate bob, red nose, skin blotched from crying. Her eyes focused on a point out of the frame, unable to look at the prying eye of the camera. Her hands fumbled with a wad of tissue. Anthony's voice was louder, closer to the microphone.

"Take your time. You don't have to divulge anything you're not comfortable with," he said, off screen.

"Nothing about this is comfortable."

"This is just a way of helping people cope. To know they aren't alone in their pain."

She nodded, distracted, focused on the tissue in her hand. "He waited until I went to work." Then she straightened herself in her chair, the consummate professional.

Anthony had remained quiet, allowing her to move at her own pace. This was not a subject to be rushed.

"He usually left before me, but he said he'd overslept. I offered to write him a note so he wouldn't get written up as tardy, but he said no, his homeroom teacher wouldn't write him up." She shook her head. "Silly, I know. I should have called the school office anyway. But I had a busy day. By the time I got home, his body was. . ." She wiped her nose. "He must have done it as soon as I got out of the driveway."

The lens reached her eyes, spying on the soul of a mother who had lost her child.

She sobbed. "He wouldn't talk to me, no matter how many times I asked him what was wrong. All he'd ever say was 'nothing.' 'Gerry, what's wrong? You can tell me anything. I only want to help.'" Her face contorted as she tried desperately not to lose control. 'Nothing. I'm just tired, Mom.'"

She wept some more. Anthony hit fast forward, stopping when she reached for another tissue.

"Do you know what he took?"

She sniffed back some control. "Everything in the cabinet. I didn't even have anything serious. Just over-the-counter stuff -- antihistamines, pain relievers, sleep aids, some old cough syrup with codeine. He swallowed it all with a bottle of gin I used to soak raisins."

More quiet time, then she looked directly into the camera again.

"How do you help a child who won't communicate with you?" Her eyes pleaded then her voice grew louder. "A couple months before, I took him to the school psychologist. Gerry joked like he didn't have a problem. I knew something was not right. I couldn't pry it out of him. I would have. . .done anything."

She stared at the camera with penetrating eyes. "Do you have children?"

"No, ma'am."

"From the moment they draw breath you'd do anything to protect them." She nodded. "Anything."

Silence followed. He had wanted to ask questions but felt that he'd lost a connection not having been a parent.

"My son took his own life thinking I couldn't understand whatever was bothering him; that I couldn't possibly do anything to help him. Pray you never know what that feels like."

* * *

In 1988, Anthony had been an intern on a film shooting in a remote location in Wyoming when a state trooper came out to the set with a note that said to call home, it was an emergency.

"Come home now. It's your brother," his mother told him in a strained voice.

"I can't just leave in the middle of the shoot." Anthony had grown tired of his brother's being aloof and inaccessible. "He's not in trouble, is he?"

"He's gone, Anthony."

He thought her voice was off, but couldn't tell over the noise. "Gone where, Mom?" Anthony strained to hear over the hammering going on outside the only trailer for miles with a phone line. He plugged his other ear so he could hear.

"He jumped from the balcony."

* * *

Even on a bereavement ticket, he couldn't get a direct flight out of the dinky airport in Worland to any major city. When he finally made it to Cheyenne, he was able to get one to Pittsburgh. By the time he'd gotten there, he'd missed the last flight to New York. So he rented a car and drove. This had given him too much time to think.

How could he do it? How could he jump fifteen stories? What was he thinking? Was he drunk? Drugged? Anthony was frightened by the fact he thought about these things as if he would get to ask Connor when he got home. Never again would he be able to corner him and demand to know what was going on, why he was being such a brat, creating episodes for them to worry about. Did he bother to leave a note? Did he even consider what this would do to their mother? Did he care? How could he do this to her? How could he leave him alone to deal with her?

Guilt settled into him like a virus. He could feel it growing hotter as it worked his way through his system and it would have to run its course. Nothing could hurry it along, or prevent it from overtaking him like a tidal wave. He knew Connor wasn't right the last time he saw him. He was a little angry, odd, laughing at inappropriate things, and getting furious at things he would have ordinarily brushed off.

He should have recognized it more clearly, done something, anything. He could have taken him somewhere, just the two of them, deprogrammed him from whatever it was that had him unnerved. Stayed with him, watched and waited until he sounded like himself again. Connor'd split from his girlfriend. Who had broken it off? Was he broken-hearted? Did she do something to him? Was that what sent him over the edge? A phrase that he never imagined he would hear in the literal sense.

I should have done something, said something, asked the right questions, saw the yellow signs as red. I should have known, he told himself. *I should have known.*

* * *

Twenty years later, his search for answers continued, for no other reason than to reconcile how this would never happen to him. His brother appeared to snap. His autopsy showed no foreign substances in his system to cause any sort of misfire in his mind. He left no note or no clues, said no goodbyes, and had no consideration for anyone he'd left behind. No one in their right mind could do such a thing.

So that left one simple explanation; he was not of right mind. But what had made him that way?

So what would this little film do now? Wouldn't bring him back. Wouldn't fix anything. What was he hoping for here? A documentary filmmaker found detachment necessary for objectivity. But inside, the lost boy, left alone to assume responsibility for his widowed mother, felt insecure in not finding answers.

The project had begun as an attempt to fill in the gaps, find some solace, even if it was someone else's. The woman in the film had startled him with her question. *Do you have children?* No. He was careful not to risk any attachments so that he would never be faced with such a choice. He traveled too much to have a long-term relationship, much less be any kind of father. It was an excuse he clung to, knowing full well the reason had more to do with his feeling unavailable to protect anyone. He was on the other side of the country when his brother needed help. If he couldn't get to his brother in time, how could he possibly get to a child? Even if he had been near, he would not have known what to do to save his brother.

Which brought him to the unthinkable: what if Connor had some sort of mental condition? He had been seeing a therapist who hadn't been able to answer this question either. Could it have been hereditary?

Anger lingered inside him. Conner had left him here to clean up the mess with no warnings of what to watch for so that whatever it was did not find him too.

His chest seized and he clutched his left side beneath his collarbone; too much carbonation, too many potato chips, or not enough real food. He dug through his bag for a roll of antacids and chewed three of them down. He couldn't lie back down until the gas bubble stopped biting at his insides like a piranha.

He imagined the pain as a little angry man inside that prodded him to find the truth to one burning constant. Could whatever got Connor get me?

* * *

Kellan's chest hurt and she was finding it hard to breathe. This was so real it was creepy. But her mind had just latched onto Connor and his brother and conjured this stuff, right? Connor never told her his brother's name, what he did for a living, nothing. Wasn't she just taking pieces of things, memories or creative thoughts, and weaving them together? Or was her subconscious trying to plug into an invisible network in attempt to find logic?

Kellan paced behind her desk, hoping to spend some of the energy that was building into anxiety and fast turning into a headache. Then she remembered that Jade had told her to take a salt bath. She hadn't wanted to at the time. But what if she had some sort of psychic residue on her, messing with her mind? Or worse, what if she didn't?

Kellan shook her hands as if trying to get something sticky off them, then retreated back to her chair and commenced typing at a rate of speed she'd never known herself capable.

* * *

Anthony and his not so merry film crew packed the van outside the gates of a closed funeral home in Chicago.

"How does a piece on grave-recycling turn into a feature on the afterlife?" he asked his assistant producer.

A.J. looked more like a teenage boy than a thirty-two-year-old woman and had more tattoos than leather bracelets on her wrists. Her kinky hair was due to leave the eighties any minute now. "Connect the dots," she said, not looking up from her laptop. "They need a ratings boost and the network wants to ride the popularity of ghost hunting and talking-to-dead-people shows."

Anthony stared at his clipboard while his cameraman leaned past him to stow a heavy black case in the van. Ramon had a physique that turned the heads of both men and women. Anthony always felt a bit scrawny next to him, not to mention jealous that Ramon was a better cameraman than he was.

"They need sponsors. Airtime is not cheap, in spite of all the trashy reality shows."

A.J. peered over her sunglasses. She was probably the toughest woman he'd ever met. When she spoke, it was direct and decisive. No one questioned her. He was lucky other people found her uncomfortable to work with, or he wouldn't have gotten her on his team.

"We could put up a united front," she said. "Rally for the poison-water piece. We've got half the footage."

Anthony sighed. "We have a schedule to keep, regardless. How far away is the first interview?"

"Three-hour drive," Ramon answered.

"We gotta move." Anthony dialed his cell phone and listened. He closed his eyes as it went straight to voicemail. "Still not answering." Executives were never available when you really needed them, but always around when you didn't.

"We got a bigger problem than that," A.J. said. She motioned him to step away from the rest of the production team.

Anthony checked his watch and looked into the sun. "Where the hell is Elaine?"

"Yeah," A.J. looked away and talked to the air. "News station in Texas made her an offer based on her starting immediately."

"She's under contract," he said. He knew Elaine had shopped herself to every network in the country. An anchor position would buy her an attorney to break a short-term contract with minimal fines.

"She wanted to try her hand at serious television." A.J. patted his arm. "Easy come, easy go."

He pulled a roll of Rolaids from his pocket and popped a couple in his mouth. He had hired Elaine because she was available on short notice and a name from a semi-popular sitcom that had gone another direction. She could follow a script and deliver punch to his writing that would have kept an audience rapt. It helped that she was beautiful and did her own hair and make-up. His concerns about bringing such polish into raw and unpolished locales were overridden by the stark contrast it would visually bring to the screen. Always a cameraman, he still saw the world lens-first.

He'd been freelancing since returning to New York. Real guerilla filmmaking: no computer generated images, no green screen, no ridiculous tantrums thrown by people referred to as talent. No numbing his butt waiting for instructions from a third assistant director fresh out of film school. True boy meets world stuff. This was his first production assignment for The Discovery Channel, and for the first time in his life, he felt like what he did mattered. Now it was sliding sideways.

A.J. scrolled through her Blackberry messages. "I threw a line out. No bites yet."

"Tianna?"

"Reality series."

Anthony squatted down and linked his hands behind his head. Then he stood and searched the sky for a hand holding a billboard that might reach out with an answer. Nothing was coming but dark clouds.

A.J. moved alongside him. "You have two choices."

"Yeah?"

"Pack up and lose your ass."

Keeping to his motto "never bail," he shook his head and waved a hand for her to keep coming.

"Mike up a clean shirt." She didn't even force a smile. "Did you even shave today?"

"No, no." Anthony held up a hand. "I'm not. . . I don't. . . I can't."

"I don't care. If we have a prayer of bringing this in on deadline, we need to keep the shooting schedule. As it is, we barely have editing time. We don't have time to wait for some beauty queen's agent to call back. "Got anything button down with a collar?"

"What about you?" His voice faded the last word.

This got him the both hands on hips, chin down, and horns sprouted through her unruly frizz.

Anthony slumped.

A.J. softened. "Pussycat, a little cleaning up, you'll be great."

"I am not what the network expects here." Anthony pouted a little, knowing his fate was sealed. "And don't call me that."

"Fine, Pumpkin, you're writing it, so you'll know the material. You look at the little red light, pretend it's on the chest of someone you want to have sex with, and work your magic."

Anthony's seduction skills lacked committed practice and, if he knew anything, he knew the camera caught everything. How did this happen? He could make some more calls. "I don't have magic."

"Then you'll learn how to make some, won't you?"

* * *

Kellan read and reread what she had. Was it coming from her head or not? If not, did it matter that it might be coming from a dead kid? Let them try to prove it. She could not remember that last time she had been so productive and had quickly fallen into a routine: up at four, she wrote for two hours, walked and fed the dog, wrote until she had to shower and be at her first job, if she had one, walked the dog when she got home, then wrote until she fell asleep. For the first time, Kellan was writing like her life depended on it. Repeated phone messages from Gayle, Jade, and Stefan went unanswered or forgotten. Kellan found it difficult to force herself away from her computer to do the few cleaning jobs she had left. This was too good to be true, and she was going to ride the wave until the tide went out.

Chapter 8

"I hate to admit it, but psychics are part of the story," Anthony argued balancing his laptop while Eddie took curves with the van as if he were driving NASCAR. "Hate psychics."

A.J. did not yield. "This is about the afterlife, not psychics."

"I'm just saying there's a perception that psychics can contact the dead or know something regular people don't about what happens when we die. It's probably bullshit, but we might need a couple for perspective."

"Mediums," A.J. said. "The ones that talk to the dead are mediums."

Anthony looked at her sideways. "Charlatans."

This got him a scary look.

"You don't think a few of them might be the real deal?"

Anthony glanced out the window. "Maybe, a couple. Most of them are just looking to hustle the grief-stricken."

"Even the ones who help the police find missing children and solve cold cases?"

The flipside of A.J.'s attention to detail was that she could be a serious pain in the ass. He'd had a couple of so-called psychics try to tell him about his brother's death. One had actually used the word possessed. Anthony did not think much of psychics.

Anthony sighed and watched traffic fly out the window. "Try to get us there alive, Ed."

Eddie raised his eyes to the rearview mirror, flashed a grin. "Losing light."

"Losing lives, we can't afford."

"Write it out." A.J. tapped the laptop. "Focus on why people believe in some form of life after death. Where it comes from. Then expand it to spectral experiences, hauntings, spirit contact."

Anthony stared.

Eddie called from the front. "If psychics are real, how come nobody has found Jimmy Hoffa?"

"Thank you." Anthony high-fived him over the top of the

driver's seat.

Eddie and Ramon continued to pile unsolved mysteries to the list while Anthony's his mind drifted behind them.

"What?" A.J. asked.

He shook his head.

"I can hear the gears grinding."

The rest of the van fell silent and waited.

Finally, he spoke, more to himself than the group. "Maybe we should find somebody who has had a near-death experience."

"NDE," Eddie said. "My aunt had one during her gall bladder surgery." Eddie talked to him in the rearview mirror. "Saw the light, heard an angel tell her to go back. Now she hears stuff."

"What kind of stuff?"

"People calling her name when they aren't there, then they call on the phone a couple minutes later."

A.J. and Anthony mirrored interest.

"That's it?" A.J. asked.

"I don't know. She kept hearing news reports in the background, like if you were in the other room and the TV was on. But the TV wasn't on. Way back when that space shuttle blew up, the one with that teacher on it, Aimee called my uncle at work freaking out, all oh-my-god. But the thing hadn't even lifted off yet."

"That's a premonition," Ramon said. "My mom has those."

"Fascinating, but how does that tie to an afterlife?" Anthony asked. "Did she flat-line on the table and come back?"

"Four and half minutes."

"But she didn't see God, or the pearly gates, or Saint Peter?" Ramon said.

"An angel told her to come back. You'd have to talk to her."

"Because you weren't even conceived yet," Anthony said.

Eddie rolled his eyes.

"Give me her number," A.J. pulled out a corner of a sheet to write on.

Anthony sighed. "People are taught what to believe from authority figures. If our parents are Christian, we are too or we fall away completely. When it comes to God, nobody really has any original thoughts or ideas that can actually be proven. What if God was just a safe idea?"

"Where are you going with this?" A.J. said.

"What if there really is no God? What if we just use it as a crutch to not have to face our own accountability?"

"Then we're screwed," Ramon said behind a scowl.

"Why?" Anthony smiled, surprised that he'd touched a nerve.

"Without God, there's nothing," he said firmly. "There's a God."

"How do you know?"

"I know, all right?" Ramon turned away from him. "Darwin was right about a lot of things, but man did not crawl out of the ocean still wearing flippers."

"Darwin never said that."

"Okay, if we evolved from primates, why are there still apes and chimps? And how come the Missing Link hasn't been figured out yet?"

A.J. leaned over so she didn't have to shout. "So you think we came from Adam and Eve?"

Ramon fidgeted in his seat, clearly uncomfortable defending his beliefs. "I don't know, but wherever it was, it was not evolution. And I don't think God looks like a guy either. The whole 'created in his image' thing is metaphoric. People take the Bible too literally, which is a collection of stories," he fingered quotation marks, "designed to give us a guidebook to living a moral life."

Eddie mouthed Wow in the rearview mirror.

Anthony leaned closer to him. "So you believe in an afterlife?"

"I'm not sure I'd call it that. I believe the soul is immortal and we drop the body, but we can come back." Before anyone could ask any more of Ramon, he pointed to Anthony. "Don't incorporate me into this. I'm the cameraman, not a character in this story. But I can see why people go to war over this."

"Holy wars," Anthony thought out loud. "Suicide bombers."

A.J. rolled her eyes, "Doubt we can land an interview with someone who went into a mosque strapped with C-4."

"They believe they are sacrificing themselves for a God-cause."

"Because they will be rewarded in Paradise," she nodded.

"That would make them believers in an afterlife. We need to find out what makes a person believe so deeply that they are willing to sacrifice their life here for a possible life in Paradise."

"Brain-washing," Eddie said. "Nobody has ever been able to prove life after death."

Anthony understood his take. "We're not trying to prove it. Pull over and stop a minute." Then he dug for the maps in the seat pocket in front of him.

"What?" A.J. asked.

"Who would know more about afterlife beliefs than Native Americans? Let's find the closest Indian reservation, talk to a tribal elder. Where are we right now?" He asked Eddie, who looked at Ramon, who looked out the window at the never-ending fields, then started laughing. "What happened to the GPS?"

"Maybe in the audio bag," Eddie's eyes glanced around. "Or maybe still on that picnic table back in Dent."

A.J.'s mouth fell open.

"We don't even know where we are?" Anthony slouched in his seat. He'd lost complete control, yet for some strange reason remained oddly calm.

A.J. was slapped the back of Eddie's head with the production schedule.

"Somewhere in Iowa," Eddie said smacking her hands away.

* * *

Anthony stood squinting in the sun like a five-year-old waiting for A.J. to pin the back of the shirt he wore that was two sizes too big. He wondered if his father could see him from wherever he was now, if he watched him work. He had never stopped missing his comfort, consistency, and safety. Did he approve of his choices, or was he disappointed that he wasn't of more help to his mother, angry he wasn't close enough to his brother to save him. No answers came in dark moments. No strange dreams. No spiritual journeys. His father and his brother were just gone. There was no mystery. They were once here and now they were gone.

A.J. pinched his back. "Sorry."

"You work out a little, you'd fill it out more," Ramon adjusted the camera.

"I got it where it counts."

He heard snickers. A.J. stepped behind him to pull the excess shirt together to fasten it with a hair clip. "If you had any ass, never mind."

"We're not shooting my ass." He looked around at her. "There's nothing wrong with my ass."

"Nothing to it," A.J. smoothed his fly-away hair. "Man, you're a mess. Do you even use conditioner?" said the woman whose hair

73

looked like overused steel wool. She turned to shout to Eddie, who was near the van. "Grab my blue bag behind the passenger seat."

"You're not going to spit in it like an old lady, are you?"

A.J. ignored the comment and dove into the canvas attaché Eddie handed her, and moistened her fingers with lip balm.

Anthony ducked away. "You're not putting that in my hair."

"It's all I got. Probably not much different than the crap they make for hair." She reached for him and he caught her hand.

"We're outdoors," he fussed. "Hair's allowed to move outdoors."

A.J. stood her ground. "Am I going have to sit on you? See yourself through the lens. You want to look professional, or you want to look like some used-car hawker standing next to an orangutan holding balloons?"

He let go of her hand and dropped his head like a dutiful child. A.J. worked her fingers through the front and managed to smooth the wavers without leaving a greasy trench in his hair. "Man, are you going gray."

Anthony closed his eyes while she picked some more.

"Good thing you're starting your new career now," she teased, "before no one recognizes you."

He batted her away, cleared his throat a couple of times, and practiced looking directly at the camera. No, Ramon's finger, just to the side of the lens. He'd told countless actors that over the course of his career. This was so stupid. Why was he nervous? He didn't get nervous behind the camera. He didn't get nervous talking to famous people or anyone heavily armed.

"Three deep breaths," A.J. ordered. "Don't think. You think, you'll rush it. You rush it, your tongue will trip over your teeth and we'll have to do more takes than we have time for." She faked a smile that reminded him of Wednesday Addams. "But you will look like an amateur, which will be fun for us at editing."

Anthony breathed as requested. "I'm seeing a side of you I never knew."

"Get your eyes checked." A.J. moved back to stand next to Ramon at the camera. "We ready? Roll tape. Five, four," she stopped talking, using her fingers to count the last three. When she pointed to him, Anthony began his monologue.

"Oklahoma is rich in history. The mid 1800's brought a staggering number of Indian tribes here, rounded up and driven from their home territories like cattle. They brought with them their customs and traditions, and the belief that when they died, they would be returned to their family who had gone before them, taking their place at the Great Council fire."

"Cut," A.J. said. "Let's try that again."

Anthony held his hands out. "What?"

A.J. made her way to him. "Your words are fine. But your eyes are rolling around like a *Chucky* doll. Keep them steady and open, actually looking at the camera. When you look away, look immediately back to the camera. It's the president of Discovery, right here." She pointed to Ramon.

"I looked possessed?"

Anthony checked faces. Eddie frowned. Ramon forced a weak smile.

"Let me see the tape."

"No." A.J. stopped his retreat. "You, back on your mark. Cookie, we got rain rolling in and no cover. Now, I'm going to stand to Ramon's right. You look at me, like you're talking to me and nobody else."

"Who's running this?"

"I am," she snapped. "You can't direct yourself yet. K? Stay." A.J. pointed, then went back to take her place next to Ramon.

Anthony fidgeted like a kid on picture day and willed the cramp in his chest to relax. "You're getting that grave house in the frame?"

Ramon gave him a thumbs-up. Anthony needed reassurance that he was still in command. He didn't mind taking orders from A.J., but now he was self-conscious about his eyes. His brain would be telling his eyes not to move, then he'd look like a zombie. And if his hair was waving, he would look like a zombie-faced Muppet.

"Roll tape," A.J. said five more times. In the second take, he'd looked at the ground too often. The third, he'd turned away from the camera too much. The fourth, he'd swayed back and forth like a nervous prom date. And the fifth was what A.J. referred to as Vanna White hands. By the time they got a take she approved of, the gears in Anthony's brain had solidified from the dry heat, and the only thing he wanted to lubricate them with was alcohol.

How did people do live television?

There was a flicker coming from the other part of his brain. The right-sided optimist told him *I can do this*. He was better looking than Michael Moore, and not nearly as gray as A.J. pointed out. He could do this. His interviewing wasn't bad, and being in front of the camera didn't feel as strange as he had thought, just unpracticed. He'd look the tapes over, see his mistakes, and work it out. He would be fine out of the frame with the camera focused on an interviewee. A little time, a little practice, he'd be better than Michael Moore. Acclimate to the space in front of the camera. *It's just a ten-foot difference from where you usually stand.*

Tape was telling. "Let me see."

Chapter 9

"You've had a week," Gayle told her on the phone. "I'm twisting in the wind here."

"I told you I wouldn't be available much this month."

"You have to eat. Why don't you come over tonight?"

Kellan knew they were headed for the are-we-getting-married-or-not conversation, and she was not ready for it. She did not want a repeat of Dan who never understood her need to spend time with anything but him.

She went to Gayle's anyway, knowing she could not put him off much longer without a better excuse. By the look of his apartment, she was toast. Flowers stood in a vase on the dining room table that was actually set for dining instead of covered with mail, regulatory binders, and piles of gently used laundry. His hunting and racing magazines were neatly tucked into the rack next to his Lay-Z Boy chair.

Ruh-roh.

She'd never enjoyed the trappings of romance, finding them a commercial ploy and nonsensical waste of money. All the flowers, cards, and gifts in the world could not provide her with what she really needed: genuine appreciation and desire. Could be why she had never in her life been able to read a bodice-ripper past page three. Gayle's version of chivalry was letting her decide what movie to see or if they should have an appetizer before dinner. Those were within her comfort zone.

Any youthful designs that Kellan ever had about love had faded quickly after thirty. Almost forty, she was that in-between age men didn't quite know what to do with: too old to start a family, too self-reliant to need him to take care of her, and too young to trade the sport coupe for a large luxury sedan. So when a man remembered something she'd told him more than a couple days before, it meant he actually paid attention to her. That was all the aphrodisiac she required.

Now here he was, all slicked up, wearing a dress shirt and

cologne that clawed at her throat.

"Since when do you wear aftershave?"

He leaned on a dining room chair, one hand on his hip. "I needed a way to spice myself up for you."

She bit her lip, touched by how hard he was trying. "You don't need any spicing up."

He grinned. "Does that mean I can wash this stuff off? I think it's stopping up my nose."

She waved him away and he went into the bathroom. "What is that anyway?"

"Hugo Boss," he called back. "Hannah said Tommy wears it."

She was overtaken by snickering as she made her way into his living room pit. "You're taking advice from Hannah?" Gayle's middle sister was the only one in the family to have married more than once. Her second husband owned the local bowling alley and smoked as if tobacco might stop growing at any moment, which explained the need for cologne.

Gayle rejoined her, buttoning a fresh shirt. "So how's the writing going?"

"Great, actually, for the first time in years."

She opened a beer and held it out to him. He climbed over the back of the sofa to ease down next to her, arm over her shoulders, as if nothing had happened between them.

Kellan was not ready to have this conversation. She didn't want a life commitment yet, nor did she want to break up. He'd gone so far as to clean for her. That was huge. "You know, I would have given you a price break."

He sipped his beer. "Nah, lady down the way just swooped in and dumped it all into a box, stuffed it in that closet there." He pointed back toward the hall.

"The Polynesian lady?"

"She watches kids at her place all day," he said. "Got the feeling she enjoyed the quiet."

"You didn't have to clean up on my account."

"Well, I took an inventory of reasons you might not want to marry me, and my messy house was in the top ten."

Kellan bit her lip. "Your bathroom is always clean."

Gayle sniffed. "Well, I am civilized in some respects."

"Bachelors are my best clients."

He quieted. "I'm tired of being a bachelor." He looked at her with such certainty she had to break his gaze. "And I don't want to be one of your clients."

"Gayle," she shook her head. "I'm not sure I'm what you need."

"Why is that?"

"You don't know what you're getting into."

"I'm sorry about that morning," he said. "I never should have come over all twisted up, judging you."

Crap. How often did she get to hear a man apologize?

"Baby, I want us to be okay."

"I was just getting comfortable where we were," she said, unsure of how to continue. "Don't fix what ain't broke, you know?"

"It's called 'taking the next step.'" His tone shifted, and he put his beer on the coffee table. "You about to use that 'it's not you, it's me' garbage? Because I can feel it coming, and you're too old for that."

Kellan was a little taken aback. "Really?" He was bristling quicker than she had expected. "You know about my first marriage."

"And this is not about your ex-husband, or the mistakes you made in your past."

"No, it is, Gayle." He was about to pounce when she held up a hand. "Hear me out, now."

He sat back and folded his arms as if no matter what she said, he wouldn't believe it anyway.

"You are probably the most caring guy I've ever dated, and I don't want to lose you, but I'm not ready to remarry yet." Kellan paced around in front of his plasma TV, "especially under these circumstances."

"I know the timing wasn't the best, but it has been on my mind a while. I just couldn't figure out how to bring it up in any kind of way a woman would like."

"So you do it at a funeral home. Then at a cemetery."

"It wasn't the best laid plan." Gayle looked away. "Doesn't mean it didn't come from the heart."

"You know that your mother orchestrated this betrothal hoping that it would blow up in my face. She hates me."

"Momma does what she does, but what she doesn't get to do is chose my future wife." His ears were turning red and his jaw was set. "I did not propose to you because Momma thought it would save our reputation in the public eye."

"Fine, but there are other things to consider," she said. "When I

79

was married to Dan, I was writing after work, on weekends, and it didn't take long for him to not like it. He resented the time it took from him. So I actually felt bad, and starting doing things he wanted to do, even though I hated them."

Gayle cocked his head. "Do I make you do anything you don't want to?"

"No, but he would say that he didn't understand how I could spend so much time on something that didn't make any money. What's the point, right? When we split up, he came to get the last of his stuff, he actually said, 'I wish you would have sold something so I could have gotten half of it.' And he was the one who cheated on me."

"I'm not him." Gayle said each word with punctuated purpose.

"No, you're not. You're sweet, compassionate, and considerate. Hell, you're everything he wasn't."

His eyes searched the room for understanding. "But I have the misfortune of being a man."

Kellan closed her eyes. "You are the town hero, and every woman in this county would die to have you look at her. I know this. Don't think I don't appreciate you for everything you are. But I need to get a book published. I should have done it by the time I was thirty."

Gayle didn't move. "You think I'd prevent you from that?"

She sighed. "Not intentionally."

"But you think getting married would prevent you from that."

Kellan clammed up.

"Wow," he sat back into the sofa and drained the rest of his beer in one gulp. "Did you think all this up before you came over here or are you really that screwed up?"

Kellan slumped. "I have been trying to think of a way to tell you without hurting you." She found it hard to look him in the eye. "I can't afford to be derailed or distracted this time."

"Now I'm a distraction."

Kellan wished she could vaporize into smoke and spill out through the key hole in the front door. "I don't want to lose you, but I don't think I have what it takes to keep you."

Gayle stood and took his beer bottle to the kitchen, her eyes following him the whole way. Without a word, he pulled a bottle of Jim Bean from the cabinet over the refrigerator and poured himself a finger. He swirled the whiskey in the glass but did not drink it.

"My goal wasn't to just get married, Kellan. It was to marry you."

She stopped breathing. No man had ever set her as his goal in life. He was too good to risk ruining or hurting in any way.

The timer sounded when the lasagna Janie had sent over was ready. They stared at each other for what felt like an hour before Gayle turned off the oven. The silence was broken by his cell phone. He checked it and flashed a look at her that was all business.

"You need to go," he said raising the phone to his ear.

Kellan froze.

When she did not comply immediately, he said with a sharp edge, "Now."

Kellan was not sure how to take that, but quickly stood, grabbed her bag and left him answering a call that was probably from the firehouse.

Back in her own parking space, Kellan sat in her El Camino and cried.

Now she knew how Connor must have felt staying away from people he loved. Hopefully, Gayle would cool off, say there were was no rush to get married, the gate would stay in the darkness where it belonged, and she could focus on the story.

The phone rang and the caller ID displayed a number she didn't recognize. Kellan sniffed her tears back and cleared her throat for her professional phone voice.

"K.B. Cleaning, Kellan speaking."

Back in reality once again, she jotted down the address of a potential new client and set up a time to meet the next morning. Thank God, a reality check.

* * *

In her rearview mirror, Kellan could see the back of Connor's hair blowing in the breeze from the back of the El Camino. Ridiculous was the only word that came to mind. He was like a little kid riding in the back of a truck for the first time. And if he really didn't have a body anymore, how was it that his hair was blowing around?

Melissa McManus met her on the sidewalk out front. She certainly didn't look like any property manager Kellan ever met. She looked like Barbie's shorter friend, Midge; tiny, strawberry blonde, her height from heels and her pizzazz from layers of Liz Claiborne. After introductions, she handed her a card from a real estate company. A much better fit.

"My client has only been here a few months. Bought the property as a rental investment, but liked the area so much he renovated half of the top floor for himself."

Kellan surveyed the six story brick building that looked more like a college frat house than an apartment building.

"He's a dream client. Travels heavily, most of his contact is by phone. You might never see him, but I have to admit," Melissa leaned close, and Kellan tried not to back away from her feathery cologne that was already tickling her throat. "He's worth a look."

"Mr. Worth-A-Look have a name?"

"DeSantos." Then Melissa screwed up her face. "Even in a snapshot, he takes a very nice picture." She showed a digital print stapled in the file of a professional thirty something Latino with corporate hair, young eyes and an expensive smile.

"You take pictures of your clients?"

"Security reasons. Criminals impersonate property owners all the time. Can't be too careful."

Kellan cocked her head. "He reminds me of someone."

"A soap star, right?"

"I wouldn't know about that."

"Anyway, I never got a first name. All the paperwork is DeSantos, LLC. His signature is completely illegible." She flipped through a file nestled in a leather portfolio.

"Here, see? So male. A couple initials and a line, like he can't be bothered. Could be a P, could be an F, or an R." Melissa snapped it shut in Kellan's face. "Anyway, Mr. DeSantos needs someone to clean every week, stock essential groceries when he's in town and change the light timers and pick up mail while he's away on business, like he is now."

"Mind if I ask how you heard about me?"

Melissa grinned. "Your card was in my manager's file, so I asked, and he said you did a lot of Kay Van Kesler's friends."

Did might be the key word there. It would be interesting to see who she had left once the dust settled.

"So I called Mrs. Van Kesler to get a recommendation."

Kellan steeled herself. *Please let it have been before the séance.*

"She had nothing but nice things to say about your work."

Melissa smiled dental perfection. "You can trust her to do what you ask, she said."

Whew.

Melissa turned on her heel and headed into the main door, then stopped. "And when she mentioned you had a bit of a scare at a séance, I just had to meet you."

Kellan blinked, waiting for the shoe to drop.

Inside, Melissa dropped her already small voice to just above a whisper. "When I was a little girl, I saw a ghost in my best friend's house. No one believed me, of course. Then we were playing with her pet rabbit in the garage and found an old box with pictures in it. One of them was the woman I saw. Apparently, she had been the grandmother who didn't speak English, dead for years. Things moved in that house. Pictures would fly off the walls; things on the table in the foyer would get rearranged. Nobody ever saw who did it."

"You called me because. . ."

"I can trust someone who has seen a ghost. People might think we're full of it, but if you are anything like me, you tell it like it is." She smiled as if she were posing for a photo, and then motioned Kellan down the hall. Connor trailed behind, unbeknownst to Melissa.

A jazzy little number spilled from a piano on the ground floor. The music grew louder at an open door. The man playing held an unlit cigarette between his lips. The rest of the space looked like a sparse recording studio with a couch and coffee table across from the piano. A few guitars stood along the wall behind microphone stands and a shiny black drum set crowded the far corner.

"Ground floor is full of artists. No one complains about the music unless there's drumming after midnight." Melissa led her to the elevator that had seen better days.

"Nice landlord."

"He leaves details to me. The lady above them?" She nodded back to the open door. "Never wears her hearing aids unless she goes out."

The elevator dinged and they stepped in while Melissa went on.

"The whole building is like a layer cake. Artists on the bottom, hard of hearing and out-of-towners on the second floor, the next two are mixed bag, a couple seasonal rentals, a college professor, a pair of yoga instructors," another ding announced they had reached floor six, "and the top floor is Mr. DeSantos' suite."

Melissa arrived at the apartment door and opened it with a key. They entered, and Kellan made a point of shutting the door in Connor's face. Her work world had enough stress at the moment.

The first thing Kellan noticed was the scent that reached out and hugged her. Melissa inhaled too, but didn't comment. Everyone's home had a unique, personal scent, but this was nothing short of heaven. Sweet and sage smelling, it lightly drifted around the space. Room to room, it hung like morning fog. It erased all her ills: the women at the funeral home, the cemetery proposal, the séance, and the dead kid waiting in the hall. Catching this guy at home would be something to look forward to.

Mr. DeSantos liked things tidy, simple yet elegant, soft but modern. Earth tones, splashed with bold color in the form of throws and centerpieces, obviously done by a professional decorator. Large photographs of what looked like South American landscapes were the only adornments on the walls. There were no family pictures or mementos. A peek in his closet while Melissa took a phone call in the other room revealed a simple wardrobe: blue jeans, button downs, two sport jackets, one suit and a leather Bomber.

"Sorry about that." Melissa returned and produced a list of weekly instructions.

Kellan gave it a quick glance. It was pretty basic.

"If you find it acceptable, I'll give you a key, my numbers and his. Probably be good to call his home number before coming, just to double-check. Wouldn't want to walk in on a naked man sleeping off an overseas flight. Well, I guess you would, but he probably wouldn't."

Kellan grinned as Melissa's eyes flashed appraisal. Her mind was not hard to read. Compared to this life-sized doll, she might as well have been wearing coveralls and a bandana on her head. "I'll look this over and fax you a contract."

Melissa clutched a hand to her chest. "How I wish everything could go this smoothly. I knew you'd be right for this." Then she got another call, held a finger up, and tip-toed into the kitchen area to argue with someone.

Kellan took a deep breath and let her eyes rove. This was the apartment of a bachelor. The kind in detective novels who worked alone, never formed attachments, and could have any woman he wanted for the night. It would be most disappointing to discover he might work in some financial office driving a desk all day. Nah, not with one suit in the closet. No, Mr. DeSantos did something only heroes do.

Melissa returned flustered. "I apologize. Do you have any questions for me?"

Kellan wanted to ask her to describe Mr. DeSantos and tell her what he did for a living, but that was none of her business. She was a professional and need only concern herself with aesthetics. She shook her head. "Not that I can think of."

Melissa nodded at the card in Kellan's hand. "Fax number is above the cell. If you could get the contract over this afternoon, you could get started this week."

"Works for me."

"Great, so we're done?" Melissa smiled.

Kellan mirrored it back.

"So can I ask you what happened at that séance?"

Kellan saw Connor closely examining a remote control from a chair in the living area.

"Good question."

* * *

Connor appeared daily with his deflated look. Every morning, as soon as Kellan was outside walking the dog, Connor would approach from behind. Sometimes he'd just walk with them, always one step behind. He rarely spoke, even when she tried demanding. He hadn't offered much. So far, he would not own the Anthony from her pages as his brother, he would not tell her his last name, or what he expected her to say to his brother. She had a possible first name, a fictional story, and a dead kid following her around. And she had grown accustomed to it.

Kellan's emotions began erupting with regularity. She'd wake up wanting to cry or so angry she wanted to hit someone, having no reason for feeling either way. She felt like someone else more often than she did herself. It was growing harder to discern her own feelings from Connor's and she questioned everything. She needed a plan of action, something to do to get a handle on things. Sleep hid from her like truth and fatigue kept her from dealing with people. Maybe she had picked up his sleep problem. Was that even possible, since the dead don't appear to need sleep? What she needed most was to know she wasn't losing her marbles.

"Are you going to talk today or what?" she asked him.

He cocked his head like a dog who didn't understand.

"I need answers."

He would give her a puzzled look. Maybe this was all a joke. She hadn't believed him much anyway.

"If there is someone else listening right now, can you help me understand what is happening here?"

Nothing.

She sighed, closed her eyes, and rested her head on the back of the chair.

Moments later she found herself before a black metal door, devoid of character, but freshly painted. She stood in at heavy wool coat at the top of gray stone steps. Flakes of snow fell around her, and grew larger and heavier. A man came up the steps, head down, reading a folded newspaper, black bag slung over his shoulder. As he slid past her, he brushed her arm and turned to look back at her.

"Sorry," he said, and went back to his paper. Connor, looking more the young urban professional than the innocent boy she was accustomed to, trotted up the steps to the black door, and smiled back at her before letting himself in with a key.

Darkness enfolded her and she was alone.

When light came again she stood inside a vault-like room with water rising around her. She could smell the algae and taste the salt. Dark things bumped against her. The door had a big wheel over a hand grip that she tried to turn, but it wouldn't budge. She took a deep breath as the water engulfed her. Again and again she tried the wheel, but couldn't move it.

Then she tried pushing. No luck, and she was running out of air.

Panic grabbed her. She clawed to the top of the water for air. *Focus.* The water was nearly to the ceiling, but there were a couple inches left in the air pocket. She took three deep breaths then let the water swallow her down again. She kicked and pulled herself to the door. When she got there, she asked for help in her mind.

If someone is here with me, please help me open this door.

She gripped the latch firmly and it turned hard, but steadily. When the turning stopped she was able to push it open. The water rushed forward, sucking her out the opening with it. She rode the wave to the smooth wet sand into the ocean surf. Behind her the door was open only about a foot. Regaining her footing, she struggled back to it against the tide that clung to her and shoved it all the way open to see light beam through.

When Kellan turned around again, the enormous dark angel startled her to fall back onto the sand. He shrunk closer to her size right before her eyes.

"He mourns," Azrael said.

"Who?"

"Connor thought that when you removed the darkness he could return to his life."

"But he killed himself."

"He allowed himself to be taken."

"Did you let him through to me?"

"The doorkeeper decides."

"Wait, I thought I was the gatekeeper."

"The doorkeeper tends doors to the higher realms."

Kellan wasn't sure she liked being a servant to a lower realm. "Who is the doorkeeper?"

"There are many doors."

"So what is your function exactly?"

"I assist the departed and the grieving that remain."

"But why did Connor return after he departed?"

"To fulfill his contract."

"What contract?" Kellan said.

"Consult the doorkeeper."

Color shifted around her. Orange, yellow, brown. Where Azrael had stood was a tall, slender dark-skinned man in white robe and blue turban.

"You're the doorkeeper?" Kellan asked.

"I am Morin."

"Why did you let Connor come to me with that dark thing attached to him?"

"It was you I came to. You opened the gate."

"I don't understand."

He smiled and said nothing.

Kellan's head felt light as questions ripped through it.

"He needed a voice and you needed awakening."

"To what?"

"What you are. Did you not help him?"

Something dropped in her stomach.

Morin bent down, his nose nearly touching the top of her head when he said, "Can you not help him still?" He straightened to stand his full height. She felt herself sliding backward trying to look up at him. His smile gave her goose bumps.

Kellan wiped cold tears from her cheek feeling like she'd been asleep for a month. The beach was gone and she was back in her computer chair with shaking hands, sweat-soaked shirt stuck to her chest, and a resolve to take greater care in the future when she asked for anything.

Chapter 10

After her meeting, Kellan sat at the computer intent on getting a contract out to Melissa. A stabbing pain shot through the top of her right foot. So crippling was its force, she twisted round to pull her knee to her chest and rub her foot. As she struggled to breathe through it, her eyes found its source.

Leather bound feet startled her. Her eyes worked up the heavily blood-caked bare legs standing on her carpet. She caught her breath and slumped deep into the chair at the sight of a group of large, filthy, fair-haired men clustered behind the one who held the staff that poked her foot. Blue eyes grayed by death stared from behind long matted hair, unkempt beards, and vacant expressions. Clearly Nordic.

The staffed one wore a horned helmet and shouted, "Apn porten."

Kellan was stunned by the intrusion, especially to be surrounded by a group of savages that could only be from centuries past. Where had they been all this time? Even more frightening was the fact they were able to cause her physical pain. When she did not respond immediately, he jabbed at her foot with the staff again transmuting her fear into defensive anger. She didn't have to know his language to understand he wanted a gate opened.

She held out both hands. "Wait. Just. . .I have to find the. . ."

A mangled gate appeared to her right in front of the closet, but not the same one Connor had come through. Pitted with rust and framed in wood that suffered from dry rot, it waited. She had been given no instructions on how to open a gate, but then again, she had no idea how it just materialized either.

Mr. Horned Helmet was about to give her foot another jab when she stood to confront him. "All right, give me a second."

He leaned back and locked eyes with hers. Every hair on her body bristled with the creeps.

She focused on the gate and silently asked it to open. It complied. How or why, she had no idea.

The herd of more than thirty hustled through it while their leader appraised her like a juicy steak. With his eye contact came sensations and images, faster than a music video: fire, screaming, blood, combat, sex, gluttony, and murder. She clutched her chest. The staffed one showed his partially rotten teeth. She wasn't sure if it was an attempt to smile or growl. Then he turned and followed his band into the darkness.

The gate closed and vanished without a peep from her, and she made it to the bathroom just in time to lose the small contents of her stomach into the commode. Tears obstructed her vision and she broke into a cold sweat. She soaked half a hand towel mopping her face. Just as she wiped the last of her tears away and cleared her nose, her body shuddered again, and she cried harder than she could remember.

What do I do with this?

Half an hour later she crawled to the doorway, looked both ways down the hall, the creepy feeling still coating her skin like adhesive. She was alone. That was if she didn't count Riley who napped undisturbed on his bed. Her foot still hurt and she needed a diversion from the throbbing.

She went back to her computer and faxed Melissa the cleaning contract for Mr. DeSantos, then pulled up her writing file. She glanced around every two minutes as if expecting another wave of rowdy barbarians to materialize. This Gatekeeper business came with no manual, video guide, or any clue as to when to expect travelers. She had no one to ask about it and knew in her gut she could never tell anyone. Who would believe something that crazy?

She had a deadline and didn't have time to freak out over instant visitors, no matter how painful they might be. That stuff was from another world, and she was still in this one.

* * *

Screams woke Anthony. Her screams.

Sleep was something Anthony did in small increments. He had not had more than two consecutive hours of it since his mother found his father on the bathroom floor when he was ten. She had screamed again when she saw Anthony come in the door after he dropped off the rental car. His brother was dead by his own design and no one had any idea why.

Anthony hadn't known what to think or how to feel when he saw him in his coffin. He looked less like himself than his father had. One of his med school friends told him that when a body fell from a great height, the bones shattered like glass. The kid he'd grown up with had been reduced to nothing more than a bag of sand.

Guilt settled in deeper. He revisited that lunch a million times: the last time he saw him. Impromptu. Uncomfortable. They literally ran into each other outside a bookstore. They stumbled over the shock until words came. Words he couldn't remember now.

The pub was dark. The scent of fried fish oiled the paneling and furniture. The crowd eased their discomfort. They ordered beer. Anthony rarely drank but had a genetic taste for beer. Their food came. He couldn't remember what he ordered because he didn't taste it. He remembered the beer, not knowing what to say, wanting to ask a lot of questions, but feeling like a child for doing so.

Anthony had no idea that his brother was in the midst of a meltdown. He used to lead them on all their childhood adventures. But every year since their father's death, the wall between them had grown thick enough to bounce a wrecking ball. Conversation was strained, limited to work, old gossip, and the weather. Nothing significant that required them to feel anything but confidence. Anthony should have recognized that he was hiding something, having to talk to many people every day. Why couldn't he find words for his own brother?

He was the source of their mother's anguish and an ongoing worry, that's why.

What a shame, everyone had said. "He had his whole life ahead of him. What a shame." The shame was on Anthony for not being able to find tears for his brother. Or find the answer to the one question that remained. Could that happen to me? But he had no trouble finding blame in himself. Blame for the screaming. He would never forget his mother's screaming.

Unable to get back to sleep, he put on his running clothes and donned his earbuds. A radio station claimed it played music "from the seventies, eighties, and nineties." The first song he caught from their play list was Soul Asylum's *Runaway Train*.

Anthony pocketed his key, and ran into the darkness.

* * *

"Perfect," Kellan muttered looking through her peephole.

Betty Ann Schick looked back at her, purse clutched in both hands, spine straight as a steel rod. How did that woman find her? Stupid question. Betty Ann knew everyone in town. Gayle would never send her here. Betty Ann had claimed to have gotten past her being a Yankee divorcee cleaning lady, and nothing remotely deserving of her son. The fact that Kellan had not joined any church since her arrival was a bone of contention.

Gayle had not frequented church like his mother wished, but she badgered him into it whenever she could manage. Kellan had even gone with him, once. But they immediately began pushing her to join, so she pulled away, having never been a joiner, not even of a book club. The church seemed nice enough, but indistinguishable from others, apart from all the singing. Kellan didn't sing within earshot of another human and figured that if God knew everything, he knew church wasn't for her.

Now they each looked straight into the eyes of their nemesis. If there was one thing that would ensure she would not marry Gayle, it would be this woman. Betty Ann straightened her navy polyester skirt. She had a fifties style about her, but the hair at least made it to the nineties. At sixty-eight she was as fit as forty, which was not fair, seeing all the pies she made. Maybe she didn't eat any of them. With her baby blue blouse and matching silk scarf, she could have worked for an airline back when attendants were still stewardesses.

Kellan checked the front of her oversized sleep shirt for stains, having not yet changed from her pajamas. Betty Ann would never allow herself to be seen in such condition. Kellan smiled. This should repel her.

"He didn't send me," Betty Ann called through the door. "Just so you know. He wouldn't do that."

Kellan pulled open the door and leaned against the frame with her arms folded. "So what brings you by?" She had no intention of inviting her in.

"I'm worried, of course."

"Well, if it'll ease your mind, you don't have to worry about me infecting your son."

Betty Ann raised her head with defiance. "Duck can handle himself just fine. But he's miserable and worried you're gonna quit him for good because of me -- my opinion was his word."

Did she just hear her right?

"If encouraging your engagement made you feel like I was interfering, I am sorry. Certainly was not my intention." Betty Ann glanced down at her shoes waiting for Kellan's response. When it didn't come immediately, her eyes found Kellan's again.

"I appreciate your coming here to say that, but the timing is bad and I need some time to myself right now."

Betty Ann grasped the handle of her bag like a rope that needed tightening. "He got that stone two months ago. I told him not to rush things, but he was so certain. He was hoping to make it special, I know. He didn't mean to spring it on you."

Kellan looked away. She should have been enjoying Betty Ann's discomfort at trying to right things, but all it did was make her uncertain.

Betty Ann didn't move. "He's a good man."

"Look--"

"My son is upset, therefore I am upset." She fingered her scarf. "Don't take it out on him that I overstepped my bounds. I had his best interests at heart, and yours."

Oh, brother.

"Betty Ann." This was the first time Kellan had called her anything but Mrs. Schick and it clearly hit a nerve. "I had a terrifying and confusing experience that has the whole town thinking I'm infected by something, and that hasn't helped my business. And probably not Gayle's either, for being associated with me. If anything, it showed me that appearances in this town are no different than someplace like Hollywood. Only here it's not your body or your bank account that draw scorn, but your blood and beliefs or lack thereof. You never thought I was good enough for Gayle. I would have thought you'd be popping the cork on the champagne that you have evidence of it now."

"Come to church, Kellan. Talk to Pastor about what happened. He'll tell you even the strongest can be seduced by the Devil."

"I wasn't seduced by anything," Kellan said.

"The Lord tests us in many ways," Betty Ann said. "But my concern is my son and believe it or not, you. But if you have some problem, steps should be taken."

Kellan closed her eyes and willed herself not to raise her voice and let this woman goad her into losing her cool. "I agree, which is why I chose to take a step back."

Betty Ann took a step closer. "This is something you confront head on, Kellan. What if evil has you singled out? Cut you away from the herd so it can go to work on you?" Betty Ann's voice cracked.

"Nice metaphor," Kellan grimaced.

"The very idea that you took part in such a thing as conjuring the dead has me scared to death."

Death, huh? She wondered what Azrael knew about that. "I didn't conjure anything."

"Well, I pray for you."

"I don't mean to sound ungrateful, but if I'm okay the way I am, and I don't buy into the devil stuff, praying for me to become who you want is a waste of your time."

Betty Ann tightened her lips. "Well, I've made my offer."

"Thanks for stopping by." And she closed her door, only to pull it back open. She thought she saw Betty Ann jump an inch out of her pumps. "Maybe you were right all along. Maybe I'm not what your son needs. But that is still between him and me."

* * *

Sweat stole Anthony's comfort and he fidgeted, unable to sleep. Connor sat on the window sill and watched him. His brother climbed out of bed to play with the dial on the ancient air conditioning unit, already on the coldest setting, blowing barely enough air to dry a paper towel.

Connor placed himself in front of his brother, grabbed both his arms, looked into his eyes and shouted, "Tony!"

Anthony reached through him and snapped on a light. He paused for a moment to rub his arm, then reached out again, puzzled by the sensation.

Connor's heart leapt. His brother had felt him, he just didn't know it. The room was a muted yellow and smelled like stale cigarettes. The blood red carpeting was too filthy for bare feet and had more burn holes than a crack house floor.

The comforter had been kicked to the floor in hopes the sheets were actually clean. Not every town they stopped in had a Holiday Inn.

Connor was beside himself, desperate to get Tony to recognize it was him and not something to ignore. Nothing was working. With all

94

his frustration and power, he kicked the duffle out of the grimy corner chair so that it fell open onto the floor.

Anthony froze as he stared at the bag on the floor.

"Come on, you know it wasn't just sitting too close to the edge. I'm right here," Connor pleaded as loud as he could. "Why can't you hear me?"

Anthony's eyes worked the room before he picked up the bag and tested the chair to see if it wobbled.

Connor persisted. "Four solid legs, no sloped floor. How did it fall? Think."

He watched as his brother's gears worked about twenty more seconds before he abandoned the notion and pulled out his laptop. Waiting for it to power up, he stole a glance back to the chair, squinted, and returned to the computer screen.

Connor's effort was wasted again. He tried fruitlessly to move something else, intent on setting the room alive, but he'd spent all he had in that one motion and now felt himself being pulled away, fading back into his new world.

* * *

Kellan brought Jade up to speed about what had happened to her during the séance and what was showing up on her computer screen.

"See, I told you you'd get a story. Does that mean you're over being pissed at me?"

"Not completely. But I have to work with what I'm getting, and what if everything I've written was really coming from a dead kid?"

"Then you have something to validate, prove this kid existed. You should be able to find his brother." Jade sorted through a huge mess in her suitcase, placing clothes in separate piles that didn't make much sense to Kellan, since they were mostly black. "And then decide if you're really going to go talk to him or not."

Kellan hesitated. Not as if the thought hadn't occurred to her, but hearing it from someone else made it more real. She chewed on a straw from an iced coffee. "That's crazy, right?"

Jade put a hand on her hip. "Why would all this come up, if you weren't supposed to actually deliver the message? I mean, what if this guy has some huge destiny to fulfill that can change the world?"

"Let's not get carried away here. But say that's true; wouldn't this potentially give him a heart attack or, at the very least, unearth his grief all over again?" Kellan shook her head. "How could I risk that?"

"Maybe you just do the book and wash your hands of it. If he gets it and reads it, the job is done." Jade lit a cigarette.

"But how would I know if he read it? What if he gets it and tosses it on a shelf and never looks at it?"

Jade cocked her head. "For someone who doesn't want to do this, you have certainly given it a lot of thought."

Kellan slumped in her chair. The idea of approaching anyone with a message from a dead kid mortified her. "You can't just ambush a guy with this when you don't know what kind of emotional state he might be in, much less his beliefs. Most people believe the dead are gone, even with all the movies and the TV mediums. It's just not normal."

"And you know all about normal, don't you?" Jade said reorganizing her bag. "People talk to dead people, aliens, angels, and demons all the time. Hell, the Indians have been talking to their ancestors for centuries. And plenty of people act on voices they hear in their heads or from their dreams. I mean, how many times have you heard 'I had a dream that told me to do it?' Then they go out and make a million dollars on some invention, or magically meet their soul mate."

Never, Kellan thought. Okay, she'd read articles, but they could have been exaggerated to sell publications. "The Son of Sam acted on the voice in his head. Said his dog told him to kill people."

"This kid is not telling you to kill people."

Kellan was not really paying attention. "Those pudding people with the sneakers and purple shrouds? They thought killing themselves would take them another planet."

Jade waved her off like a gnat. "You're not trying to do anything harmful."

"You don't think telling Connor's brother this story could be harmful? It could undermine years of progress with some very expensive shrink."

Jade smirked. "The kid has asked you to deliver a message. That's all. You are not responsible for how his brother takes it."

"Can we change the subject?" Kellan said. "Something normal, fun. What's up with your Danish dude?"

Jade struck a pose, hand on hip. "He gave me a bootleg copy of one of his earlier albums, oh my God. It's so raw compared to their current material. They sounded so young, unpolished. They didn't quite have their sound yet."

"And where is Mr. Raw now?"

She checked her watch. "Probably halfway to Japan. Two weeks in Asia." Kellan watched her dreamy face as she drifted away to wonder how he was, what he was thinking. "They're here in the states the end of August. We're meeting in New York Labor Day weekend." She danced in her chair and squeaked. "Ritz Carlton."

Kellan laughed. "How old are you?"

"My heart is a mere twenty-two." She examined the skin on her arms. "If only the rest of me matched." Jade folded a handful of items and placed them in a drawer behind her. "So, you gonna get around to telling me what Betty Ann said when she came by or what?"

God, nothing was private in this town.

Chapter 11

Riley pulled Kellan down the stairs to the hydrangea. She squeezed her eyes shut and let the dog drag her around. She didn't need to see. He knew the way.

The blast of a train horn stopped her cold. Riley was on a vole hunting mission and didn't seem to notice. In the three years she'd lived there, she had never heard a train. Just when she was about to dismiss it as her imagination, another long blast came. Her mind segued to Connor. Where was the nearest railroad track?

Riley sometimes enjoyed romping through some of the manicured lots that surrounded the industrial buildings and offices nearby. A pristine lawn was not wasted on him. Kellan noticed a red-tailed hawk floating on a draft above them. They did their usual spin around the complex and up Beck Avenue. Kellan wished she'd remembered her sunglasses, as she was starting to get a headache from squinting. Twenty minutes later the same lone hawk passed overhead. Every corner they turned the hawk seemed to follow, banking turns, gliding in large circular patterns. Perhaps she was paranoid. Riley wasn't in the mood to dawdle and she was grateful when he turned around for home.

And so did the hawk.

* * *

"I need an outing," Kellan told the dog and headed for the door. Riley beat her to it, but she produced one of his favorite treats with a sleight of hand. "You stay here. Watch for weirdness." She hated leaving him, but didn't want any distractions.

Kellan needed to find the nearest railroad crossing, if only to satisfy her curiosity. She'd go, see if there was a rational explanation. She couldn't remember being stopped at a crossing anywhere in the area.

Taking Coliseum Drive, she crossed University Parkway, Patterson Avenue, and then plunged into the old section of town.

Homes once shiny and new sat decaying, paint graying from elements, stone crumbling with age, the earth that supported them strewn with rusting articles and discarded children's toys. Vehicles present were twenty years or older, held together with duct tape and Bondo. No mothers strolled small children, no gardeners pruned overgrown hedges or mowed weeds that had conquered the grass in a war of evil over good, and no one was out walking their dog. Life hid from places like this, fleeing in exile for a new land.

Brick buildings grew larger as she entered an industrial area. Painted signage once bold and bright had faded to ghosts. Then she saw it, just a hundred feet ahead: railroad crossing. Before she could cross the next intersection the red lights flashed, the hammer banged the bell a steady beat and the red and white striped gates descended. A train horn blasted short, long, short, short, long, loud and familiar. Until she had moved to Landon, Kellan had always lived near a train track.

Kellan eased the El Camino to the gate and watched, for what she did not know. She put the truck in park, letting it idle as the train's diesel engine strained slowly past. Her vision clouded for a split second and she found herself standing on the gravel below the track line in an entirely different place with more trees. Heat from the engine came in a wave as it pressed past with no cars attached to it. Up in the tiny front window, two small brown-haired boys waved down at her. Kellan's hand reciprocated before she realized she was waving at Connor and his little brother.

With a breath, she was back in her El Camino, watching a man wearing a New York Yankees cap rest his arm on the engine's window ledge. He didn't wave and she retracted her hand. No other cars waited at the crossing, yet she was not alone. Connor was in the back of the truck bed, feathered bangs over his right eye, his left eye met hers in the rearview mirror. Car carriers, cement-dust tankers and box cars lumbered through. The train took its time, five beats per car passing the gates.

The windshield wipers struck up by themselves. Her hand automatically reached for the switch to find it in the off position. Kellan dropped her hand. In a newer car, the relay switch might have worn out, causing a cross signal to trigger the power. This truck was forty years old. All electrical devices were powered directly from the wire to the battery. The wipers flopped back and forth, thumping and squeaking against dry glass.

"Oh, come on," she said turning the switch on and off, then hitting the washer button to spray fluid so the rubber of the blades would slide instead of skid. The train pressed on, flat bed cars picking up speed. She would have to drive all over town with the wipers scraping if she couldn't get them to stop.

Then they did.

She held her hands in the air as if a robber had her at gun point. *What did I do?* Across her windshield reflected white tractor trailer boxes secured on the flat bed cargo haulers, one after the other, after the other. Blue lettering spelled: Clarke & Co., Clarke & Co., Clarke & Co.

She stared, dropping her hands slowly, feeling a tug in her chest, and a dip in her stomach. "Oh, God."

She felt a hand gently squeeze her shoulder. Then she noticed he was dressed in banana and white striped shorts, white socks in white Nikes with soles like shark's teeth. A matching yellow sweater was draped over his shoulders, tied in front by the sleeves. Kellan bit her lip to keep from laughing. "Big croquet match later?"

Connor held up his arms and checked himself out.

"You look like," she searched for the right words, "an Easter egg." She pointed to the procession of tethered trucks on the train cars, too many to count and still coming. "Your name is Connor Clarke, isn't it?"

He didn't have to speak. She could feel the absolute certainty of it.

The thought that followed next was a little unnerving. "*That* Clarke?"

He smiled. Kellan wanted to melt into the seat cushion. She knew those trucks. Everyone did. Anyone who shipped nonperishable goods in the country knew, at some point, it would end up on a Clarke & Co truck. When she had worked in direct mail, her flats of envelopes always arrived by Clarke & Co. The US Postal Service leased those trucks at Christmas. This company was enormous.

She asked again, just to see a reaction. "It was you? The horn this morning?"

She felt his hand on her shoulder, always surprised by how solid it felt. The last of the train was through the crossing and growing smaller. The hammer pounded the bell again and the gates ascended.

Kellan's hand found the gear shift and put the El Camino in

drive. Her foot hit the gas as if she were in a street race. Her race driving was reserved for Interstate highways and country back roads. Yet she sped through the eastern part of town as if she were on fire or needed to blow off some steam. It had been a while, but it felt good and was also a little scary, as if she weren't herself.

* * *

The library downtown was quicker than going home. She didn't realize she was sprinting to the door until an elderly man gave her a startled look. Gathering her composure, she held the door for him, waited for him to limp out before sliding through the security portal. She found the computers occupied by kids. It was summer. What were they doing so diligently?

She drifted behind them to see what held their attention. Two surfed the internet, two played games. One was looking at a cellular-like strand of something vaguely pharmaceutical. She'd prey on the net surfers. Gamers were not easily distracted and motivated by the need to win. The chemist might be armed. She leaned over a chubby boy of about twelve and flashed him the ten dollar bill in her hand.

"I need to get online for twenty minutes," she whispered.

"Ten." He didn't look up. "Dollar a minute."

What, did his mom work for some 900 line? "Fifteen," she countered.

"Dollar a minute."

Little con. She dug in her jeans for her last two bucks. No Starbucks for her on the way home. Pressing the bills into his sweaty hand, she gave him a side nod.

He paused, tapped the keyboard to sign off his ID, and slid from the chair. A future import dealer, no doubt.

She signed onto the worldwide web, pulled up Google, the invasion-of-privacy engine of choice, and typed: Clarke & Co. Immediately a website for the industrial company came up. Pretty basic, no headquarters address, and a toll-free number she wrote down on a scrap paper with a pencil nub. There was a listing of hubs nationwide. What she needed was a history. She clicked on About Us and read.

The company had begun in the late 1890's as a transporter of lumber and building supplies by horse and ox drawn wagons. When railways connected both coasts, the company shifted to being a sort of shipping broker. Then it bought portions of the rail systems. Emmitt Canterbury Clarke became a giant in what was referred to as the "growth movement in America." Interesting factoid, but it didn't tell her about Connor.

Kellan closed the site and typed Connor Clarke. What she got was little, but enough. A *New York Times* archive from 1988 had a photo of his family exiting a church at his funeral. The caption underneath the photo read, Naomi Wilhelm and son, Anthony Clarke. Electricity shot up her spine. Kellan peered closer at his picture to see if he resembled Connor. It was a bad angle, his head turned away from the camera so his features were hidden. She'd need a clearer, more recent photo to tell if they were related. At the same time, she needed to settle her breathing that bordered on hyperventilation.

She skimmed the article, in the interest of time, knowing the boy she bribed would return with a higher figure in mind. Connor Vincent Clarke had indeed fallen to his death from a high-rise apartment in New York, ruled a suicide in black and white. Her head felt light and her stomach woozy. She'd taken that jump with him in the séance, or perhaps as him.

She willed her breathing to slow and quickly typed Naomi Wilhelm.

Butter cream flowed through her veins, the granddaughter of a German cellist who was the black sheep of some affluent family. Naomi did not fall far from the tree, sent away at four to study music with the notion of continuing the family legacy. When she was seventeen, a car accident crushed her arm. Four operations could not restore the wrist flexibility required for the violin. She took up the paintbrush, initially for therapy, but years later her skill transcended to her independence. Her paintings had become popular, which was saying something for a living artist.

She had done some modeling for other painters and a nude of her had hung in the Met for a while. Wow, talk about confidence. Naomi had fumbled through a couple of brief marriages before falling for Cyrus Clarke, grandson of Emmitt, the founder of Clarke Carriage, later renamed Clarke & Co. Cyrus flirted with being a novelist and though his short works were well received, his career never took root. He resigned himself to the real world and took the reins of the family business. He died of cardiac arrest, never having published his book. Naomi and Cyrus had two sons, Connor and Anthony, who had not reached their teens when their father died.

Anthony is really his name, she thought.

A whisper came from behind her. "Tony."

"Tony, right," she said aloud, prompting two of the kids to look at her then go back to their gaming. Everyone talked to their computers once in a while, right?

Kellan's heart fluttered. The bottom of the screen listed other links. One read: Naomi Wilhelm photos. She clicked on it. Most of them were black and white from the sixties and seventies. She was exquisite, gentle-faced and dreamy-eyed. The painting revealed a delicate figure and, being a view from behind, not too revealing. Tasteful, they would have called it. There was one with the entire family when the boys were small. She made a mental note to revisit it when she got home to her own computer and scrolled through the photos quickly, looking for the most recent. It didn't take long to find a photo of Naomi, arm in arm with her grown boys. It was taken at a benefit, the boys in tuxedos, mom in a long formal gown. She saw Connor's smile, his sparkling eyes, his mother's actually, and his mask to the world.

There was a whistling in her ears. Her stomach felt like a washing machine and her vision shifted. Kellan had to remind herself she was in a public place. No panicking, no passing out, and no calling attention to herself. But here was a photo of the kid following her around from the hereafter, and it overwhelmed her.

Snap out of it. Kellan focused on the facial features. He and his brother had different faces. Anthony's was narrower, sharper than the rounded sweetness of Connor's. His hair was parted on the opposite side. In a quick glance, they might have passed for bookends. Kellan couldn't move. Her mind ground to a halt. She was staring at validation that she was not imagining things. They were real people.

Nausea threatened to overtake her. She swallowed it back. Time was ticking.

Quickly, she searched for Anthony Clarke. He was not as prominent as the rest of the family and took a few clicks to find. He hadn't created an empire or a tragic headline. But she soon discovered Anthony had been a busy boy. After graduating from college with an eye for politics, he made a Bohemian career move to Hollywood. Not as a performer or musician, as one might have expected given his bloodline. Instead he chose to stay behind the camera, and had racked up a lengthy body of work. He'd made a move from film to television, doing commercials, a couple sitcom pilots, an HBO special and a documentary on prison reform. He'd even won awards for writing and cinematography, and had once been nominated for an Emmy.

Kellan clamped both hands over her mouth and leapt from the chair, the legs scraping loudly on the floor. She made it into a stall in the restroom fearing a repeat of the previous night. Nothing came, but little green starbursts popped before her eyes as she leaned her head against the cool partition.

Connor and his brother were real. Everything she'd written about Anthony had some semblance of accuracy. How was that possible? Her body shook and she broke out in a sweat. If they were real, why did everything about this seem so unbelievable?

* * *

Anthony hated leaving his crew behind to shoot exteriors and do research while he flew home for a day. He wished he could just cancel the appointment, but a friend had called in a favor, though she had not been asked, to get him in to see this specialist. Desperation could make a man do things he loathed.

He did not notice Connor walking next to him through the city.

"You've looked better," Connor said. Of course, Anthony didn't hear him. He didn't hear the women talking about his physical attributes as they checked him out, either. Good looking women, too. A little young, but Anthony wouldn't have noticed if they were buck naked and rubbing up against him. He didn't notice anything when he played with that little black contraption that said Blackberry on it. What could be so fascinating on a tiny little screen? He watched Anthony's thumbs work a keypad so tiny GI Joe would have had a tough time.

Connor noticed a couple bundles of magazines on the walk outside the newsstand. "Look out," he shouted.

Tony glanced up sharply and took a couple hops to the left managing to miss the piles.

Connor smiled wondering if he'd really heard him. He had developed the ability to manipulate physical things, yet he didn't think his voice was strong enough to provoke a look.

A jogger with a pulling dog headed toward them, the taut leash a recipe for injury. Tony walked head down. Connor yelled in his ear. "Heads up!"

This got Tony's attention just in time to dodge the leash.

"You heard me."

This got no response. Tony went back to scrolling the screen type.

"You can't see past that thing." He looked at the Blackberry with loathing, wondering if he couldn't mess with it somehow.

Four blocks later, Tony turned left down a few stairs to a green metal door. The sign didn't list tenants and he slowed his pace in the faded hallway searching for a number. The doors were a good five shades whiter than the eggshell walls. They reached number 108 and Tony shut his Blackberry off before pocketing it. He peeled the wrapper from a couple antacids and chewed them down before opening the office door of Dr. Ingrid Baumgartner, Psychologist.

Connor stared at the sign. "You can't be serious."

A few minutes later, he sat unnoticed on the corner of the woman's desk, staring at his brother with concern. Tony would not have approved of his eavesdropping, but he'd done a lot of things Tony would not have understood.

* * *

"You want to start with what is bothering you?"

No, I want to start with what is bothering the rest of the world, Anthony thought, wondering how he got here and wishing time would jump to the speed of sound so this would be over.

The good doctor didn't move. Anthony suspected she had been a traffic stopper in her younger years. Her dark blonde hair perfectly swept into a twist, seamless make-up and beige silk suit had her looking like a fashion critic or an art dealer. The reading glasses made her look more like a Supreme Court judge. Her accent was so slight he wouldn't have placed it, had he not been told she was Hungarian.

"Not really sure what is bothering me."

She didn't move, just patiently watched and waited. After a long period of silence she spoke. "Why don't you tell me a little about you, then?"

"What do you need to know?"

"The more the better."

"I'm tired. Can't sleep."

She lifted her chin ever so slightly and remained quiet. The silence grew louder.

"Mr. Clarke, I can't ascertain why you can't sleep unless I know something more about you."

"Right." He shifted on the surprisingly comfortable sofa. "I'm working on a project that is rather sensitive in nature."

"Is this project having some emotional effect on you?"

He sniffed. "Yeah, it's pretty personal."

"Can you tell me about this project?"

He nodded and rubbed his pinky finger. "It started because I thought other people might have answers. So I started shooting a documentary to ask people." He stopped.

He looked at her for guidance and got none. She waited. The woman was maddening.

It was a struggle, but he inched forward one step at a time. "I wanted to know what drove someone to take their own life."

She didn't blink. "Is this something you are considering?"

"No, no. I just, I want to know what could do that to someone. What somebody would find so unmanageable that they could just leave everyone behind."

"Who left you behind?"

The question was so direct it froze him. He opened his mouth and for a moment, nothing came out. He had to force the words. "My brother."

"I'm sorry." Then she made a note on a pad. "When did this happen?"

"Twenty years ago."

She cocked her head. "Did you seek counseling at that time?"

Anthony hung his head. "Talked to his therapist. Wasn't impressed. Guess I figured his success rate sucked." Half a laugh fell flat.

She leaned forward. "Now you decide to give therapy a chance?"

Anthony found himself looking at the ceiling above her. "I'm no closer to answers."

"Only your brother could tell you why he took his life, Mr. Clarke. It might be more productive to ask yourself better questions."

"Such as?"

"What would knowing his answer really do for me? What do I

want it to do? And can I attain that outcome without knowing his answer?"

He didn't like where this was going. What did he want it to do?

"What if he was schizophrenic?"

She glanced at sheet he'd filled out. "Any history of it in the family?"

Anthony shook his head. "Not that I know of."

"Schizophrenia has been proven to be genetic."

His heart did a flip and his gut twisted up. "So if he was, I could be."

"At your age?" she raised her left eyebrow. "Unlikely. If your brother was indeed schizophrenic, he might have passed it along to his children and grandchildren. Are you hearing voices that aren't there?"

"No."

"Have feelings of paranoia or think someone is conspiring against you?"

"No."

"Struggle with depression? Feel withdrawn from people?"

"I don't have time for depression."

"Mentally check out at inappropriate times, business meetings, social situations?"

"Not that I know of."

"You sound pretty safe." She pressed again in a softer tone. "Is it peace you seek?"   ·

"I don't know. I guess I want to know if whatever got to him could get to me."

"Twenty years and you're still here." She adjusted her recorder and sat back into her chair and crossed her legs. "Let's begin there."

Chapter 12

Still reeling from her library visit, Kellan spent time at home downloading photos and information. Her mind was too scattered to write, but she pulled her working file up anyway and stared at the screen. There was a paragraph at the bottom where she had stopped yesterday that she had no recollection of writing.

In April, I used to go to the Jersey shore. I liked to watch the waves come in. Sometimes they would roll in and sometimes they would crash in. Just like life. Sometimes you roll with it, then next thing you know you crash with it. The beach at night was so peaceful. I felt like I could stay there forever, just me and the ocean, the stars shining down on me, finally at peace with myself and the world. I would sit there in the sand and look at the stars, contemplating what to do with myself and my life. During the day, I felt so alone and confused, with nowhere to turn for answers. At night, I felt at peace as long as I was on the beach listening to the waves. There was something about the water that helped. Sometimes I would try to sort it all in my journal, hoping to find an answer or at least be tired enough to sleep.

Was this Anthony or Connor? Kellan's heart jumped. Journals were physical evidence people left behind of their thoughts, dreams, and fears. Did Anthony keep his brother's journal? If her writing was coming from Connor, perhaps his old journal could validate some things. And the only way to find out for sure would be to talk to Anthony.

* * *

The Journal of Parapsychology sat at the edge of the in-box and Anthony had to force his eyes from it. There was actually a professional journal on this stuff?

"Over eighty percent of Americans believe in some form of personal continuation after death." Professor Gerard Jessup from the University of Arkansas played with a pen while he spoke, turning it end on end. His complexion was as white as the paper in front of him and he had more red hair on his face than on his head. "It's biologically based because the human brain has the unique ability to comprehend other people's mental states."

A sticker on a file cabinet read: *We don't stop when we drop.* Anthony sat beneath the camera out of the shot, his team crowded behind him in the small gray office.

"I don't follow. How does comprehending other people's mental states support a belief in life after death?"

The professor sat back in a creaky, utilitarian chair. "As humans, we are unable to imagine not having some sort of psychological state. Any rational person knows that when he dies, his brain ceases to function. Since he's never been without logical thought, he has trouble with the concept that once the brain stops, any manner of thought stops too. And without a thought process, there would be no need to exist on any level, anywhere.

"Mental and emotional states drive human behavior. We are the only species that we know of with theory of mind."

Anthony leaned forward. "Theory of mind."

The professor nodded. "We have the ability to think about the consciousness of other people, which means we can consider the consequences of death, even for someone else. We have the ability to question whether consciousness continues after death."

"But just because people question it, consider it; empathize with someone who died, how does that convince people the afterlife is real?" Anthony asked.

"Belief in the afterlife is universal and natural. Our study focused on how people came to those beliefs. Each subject in the study read a story that described a fictional person's emotions, physical sensations, and his state of mind. At the end of the story, the person dies suddenly. After reading it, the subject had to answer a series of questions about the person's mental state. We asked the subject if they thought that person still experienced physical sensations like hunger and fatigue. We asked if they thought the person could still see things here: his body, people, his surroundings. Could he smell, touch, love, hate, things of that nature. We also asked if they thought the person still had desires."

Anthony took his time before proceeding. If it ran too long they could cut it down. "Everyone knows the dead don't need to eat because they are, well, dead."

"The physical state is separate from emotional and psychological states."

"So what were your findings after this study?"

"We separated people into categories: extinctionists or those who believed there was no consciousness after death, agnostics, reincarnationists, immortalists and eclectics."

"Eclectics?"

"They believe in both reincarnation and immortality. In both, consciousness continues after death."

"What did you discover?"

The doctor sat still as a statue. "They believed that physical sensations like taste and desire leave, but thoughts and emotions continue, mainly because participants found it too hard to imagine the absence of those things. Even extinctionists have trouble believing that when they die, they won't feel or think again. These people wonder if the dead know they are dead."

"Sounds like empathy," Anthony said.

"Exactly. We know we will die eventually, so we have that common biological ability to think about the minds of the dead. It's naturally related to how we connect to other people mentally, thereby embedding this belief into our DNA."

"So you concluded that a belief in the afterlife is partly biological, but does not necessarily prove it's real."

"It's real to the believer." The professor smiled.

"What do you believe?" Anthony mirrored his smile.

The professor shook his head and held up a hand. "I'm a scientist. I'm not supposed to believe in anything unproven."

"But?"

The professor twirled his pen around, and didn't meet Anthony's eyes at first. "I wouldn't mind coming back in a new body." He patted his paunch then leaned forward as if he was going to share a secret. "To a scientist, a hundred years is a toe in the water."

* * *

Real fear began to creep into Kellan. Of what, she had no idea. After taking the dog for a spin around the neighborhood and tucking him back into the apartment with a treat, she drove with no destination in mind. This was a habit she'd acquired since getting her license, but that was back when gas was still under a buck a gallon.

110

Prices had more than tripled with all the international upheaval, but old habits die hard. Driving had always soothed her, but lately she'd become a reckless speed-demon, rolling through stop signs, and taking curves on the edge of the tires.

Within minutes, Kellan passed acres ripe with grapes, field corn, and soybeans. She had no idea where she was. Rounding a bend, she crossed a tiny bridge over a river and a brown sign told her she was in Rockford, a historical site. There was a market in a white clapboard building that looked as if it belonged in a western movie. She pulled in, parked, and cut the engine. Next door stood a garage-sized house with a sign out front advertising antiques. The rearview mirror reflected an open seating area with a couple of benches. Concrete spread over to two brick fireplaces that were all that remained of a hotel that had stood during the war.

Inside the market, she found an assortment of candy from childhood. She didn't know they still made some of it. Produce from a handful of local residents filled bushel baskets, hoop cheese wedges chilled in the fridge, decorative tins and nostalgic signs and bottles lined the walls. The baked goods counter had fresh donuts, cookies and something she'd never before seen: fried pies. They looked like small calzones, but were made of biscuit mix with fruit filling.

Kellan reveled in the feeling she'd stepped back into the past, until a man in a Confederate uniform answered his cell phone. So much for illusion. She bought a fried apple pie and an Orange Crush and wandered up the street to check out the museum. The little building used to be someone's home. An outhouse painted to match was wide open in the backyard. She stepped inside the door of the museum onto bare wood floor grey with age. The walls were covered with photos of the first settlers, old maps, and flyers for re-enactments. A docent was telling the history of the place to an older couple who probably belonged to the Winnebago she'd parked next to.

Kellan saw Connor in the window's reflection, reading the historical placards and examining the blue uniform coat draped over a rocking chair.

History buff? she asked in her head. His eyes flashed her way and his smirk left no question. Now she knew why they were there.

The place was pleasant enough, and her mind eased a little. When she finished browsing, she wandered over to sit on one of the benches by the fireplaces. The sun felt lovely. She had not spent much time outside in the past couple weeks and sat quietly basking with her eyes closed.

The creak of leather and the blocked sun announced someone standing in front of her. Whoever it was smelled like a sweaty horse. Kellan opened her eyes to a dark-eyed man dressed as a Roman soldier, complete with stiff red plume on his helmet. If his outfit wasn't unnerving, his sudden kneeling at her feet certainly was.

"Got the wrong century, don't you?" She leaned back as far away from him as possible without appearing repelled. Apparently, he had no sense of personal space.

"I get that a lot," he said in a slight British accent. "I'm here for you, Kellan."

Alarmed at the sound of her name, she straightened and forgot to breathe. He was not a player in some historical re-enactment, but a Roman, with a British accent?

"You're not imagining," he said. "All you've been shown and told, all you've written is, for the most part, real."

Kellan was stupefied. First she sees a dead kid, now a Roman soldier? Was this how drug use started? "Who are you?"

"Does it matter?"

She recoiled. "Well, yeah, if I'm supposed to believe you, I'd like to know who you are."

"Well then, I've been sent to be your guide for the duration." His voice was laden with sarcasm.

"The duration of what?"

"Don't be snide. That's insulting."

"I thought guides were supposed to be gentle and kind."

"Well, that doesn't work with you, does it?" he countered. "You require more of a firm hand."

Her mouth fell open. No sugar-coating with this one.

"Connor is real - his brother, his pain, his need of your help, all of it. Stop doubting and do what is asked. Time is of the essence."

"Little pushy, aren't we?"

He cocked his head. "You should see who they wanted to send."

Kellan shrank like a child scolded for mouthing off. He looked as real as she did.

"Go on," he said. "Touching Connor didn't convince you, did it?"

She squinted at him. But her conscious mind needed validation.

Was he another dead guy or an actual guide? Could she tell? She reached a shaky hand to his face. His black eyes smiled as he placed his hand over hers. The stubble of his beard was only a day out and his face was warm as any live person.

Gathering both of her hands, he said, "Now, if you're going to be of service to unsavory characters without being ill or losing your energy, you must learn to protect yourself properly."

Kellan was uncomfortable being in an open area, having to beware of onlookers who might think she was off her rocker, talking to herself. "What, like the scissors? Where did those come from?"

"Primal survival manifestation triggered by emotional trauma of your ethereal body."

Uh, huh. She glanced around again to make sure no one else was within earshot. "So if I'm frightened, will they reappear if I need them?"

"Not necessarily." He removed his helmet revealing short wavy black hair. "You must learn to shield yourself so you will not require weaponry."

"Shield myself with what?"

"Your own energy field." He propped one foot up on the bench and leaned over her.

"And you're the Jedi master sent to train me?" Kellan tried not to smirk.

He was not pleased. "Woman, with that toxic attitude, it's a wonder you've survived this long on your own. Hold your tongue and broaden your mind."

Kellan hated taking orders from anyone, but if he was correct that she needed protection, it might be worth taking him seriously.

"For pity sake, what?"

"How can an energy field stop a thing like Connor had on him?"

"How can the roof of a dwelling stop the weather from getting inside?"

She rolled her eyes like a first grader. "It's built of weather-proof materials."

"So, you can reason. How delightful."

"Hey, take some of your own advice," she snapped, then fell quiet when the muscles in his jaw clenched.

He launched into detailed instruction on how to build an impenetrable shield of protection around herself with her own energy, imagination, and intention. To deceased souls or entities from other worlds, it would be as secure as the fences around any federal prison and filter anything harmful from reaching her. This included the dark feelings and illness she felt after each encounter. Kellan was relieved to learn that she actually had power in the astral world.

The soldier warned, "A strong shield draws them to seek weaknesses to breach. You must remain vigilant in reinforcing your shield's strength at all times. Especially when you think you are alone."

Kellan's stomach seized. "I wasn't alone when Connor first showed up."

"Which reminds me, when you are in the company of others, it is your responsibility to protect all who are present, including animals."

No wonder her stomach was upset. "They could hurt Riley?"

"Not as tempting, but yes," he said. "You can push the width of your shield to surround a houseful if necessary. With practice, you'll be able to keep yourself and anyone in range safe."

"What about when I sleep?"

He closed his eyes for a moment, with his head back as if he were enjoying the sun. "I will be watching over you, until such time you are strong enough to construct a shield with enough power to remain through a sleep cycle."

Kellan nodded as if she understood completely, which she didn't. "What's your name?"

"Why?"

"So I can call you when I need you."

"I'll know what you need before you do." He stood and replaced his plumed helmet. "But this position is temporary. You must learn to stand on your own. Practice and stop doubting. You're not mad, and you won't be imprisoned."

Her eyes widened as he touched on her worst fear. "Wait, you're leaving?"

"You should be alone when you practice," he said looking over his shoulder at the people sitting on the porch of the general store. "I shan't be far, as I am at your service."

"For the duration," she impersonated his accent. "Watching me sleep. But I don't see why you won't tell me your name."

His shoulders slumped. "Choose one, if it pleases you."

Kellan chewed the inside of her lip for a moment. "Well, you can't actually be from the century you're dressed for or you wouldn't have a British accent."

"Could I not have learned English from an Englishman?"

Good point. "Or you could have been an actor who played a Roman," she said. "You die in costume?"

He bristled and looked at the Confederate soldiers walking toward the battlefield. "This uniform of elevated rank provided me the authority to silence any woman for her insolence." His voice almost purred.

"Wow, you must really hate this century then." Kellan had no doubt that women in his time were not trained in any sort of protection.

He finished with, "Your ignorance with respect to Roman history is quite remarkable."

"You sound like a Trevor," she said, hoping it would provoke a reaction.

"As you wish," he sighed. "Now. . ."

"How did I get to be a Gatekeeper?"

"Honestly," he stiffened, "you were marked from birth, but closed to it when you were frightened by visions you saw in your eighth year."

Kellan squinted. "I don't remember any visions."

"Fear closes the door, you might say, on frightening memories." He finished with a practiced smile. "Go home, Kellan. Practice building your shield as often as possible. Add to it. I'll be watching."

Before she could speak again he was gone, and she didn't even think she'd blinked.

* * *

Kellan sat purposely in the middle of the couch, with Riley on the floor at her feet, hoping she could remember all the details of Trevor's instruction. When he'd gone, she'd made abbreviated notes on the brown bag that held her purchases and smelled of fried pie.

She read, "Feet on the ground, draw energy through the spine from the earth, through my crown, fan like umbrella." She sucked in a deep breath. "Right."

The energy began moving as she read, making her feel warm and strong. With her eyes closed she could see it was an odd shade of yellow, like the crayon that never got used. She focused on the cord that reached from the earth, through her spine and out the top of her head, jagged as lightning that wobbled. The cord inflated into a balloon that she could thicken and spread at her will. He said to give it a color, so she tried to see it as aquamarine. It vibrated, giving the appearance that it had grown in power. She imagined it to be like molten glass, easily blown to shape while hot, and pushed it to expand around her 360 degrees, from her head to beneath her feet. Then she pushed it wider to accommodate Riley, who had stretched out on his side without being disturbed.

There. Not so hard. She and the dog were encased in a bubble of aqua light.

Kellan made the next layer pink and another inside that green. For the outside structure, she could choose anything she desired. She thought a four-sided pyramid made of smoky quartz crystal would be solid enough for practice. And a shiny black hematite for floor protection.

Between the layers of light energy and the solid stone of the pyramid, she imagined coils of silver razor wire, and set the even-numbered strands revolving clockwise, the odd, counterclockwise. She added vertical strands to match, and filled it in with shrieking noises that careened around the corners of the pyramid.

She watched it pulse around her as though it had a life of its own.

Her stomach was warm and her spine tingled even though she had constructed it all in her mind. Trevor told her with practice, she would add emotions and feelings, so when she had them, it would instantly place the protective shield up and reinforce it when she felt threatened.

"Cool."

Chapter 13

"I hate this." Anthony chewed a couple antacids while watching raindrops dribble down the van window. "A paranormal investigator? What the hell is that anyway?"

A.J. did her best to smooth his ruffled feathers. "He said he had footage of a full-bodied apparition."

"How do we know--?"

"It's not dubbed in? Not an actor?" A.J. handed him a fax. "From the video lab who verified the footage is authentic, not doubly-exposed, and unexplainable."

Amid the technical language, Anthony read the words 'original recording' and "dimensional mass" but this did nothing for his heartburn. He washed down the chalky residue with a Coke that foamed on his tongue. "Full-bodied apparition," he said, in a bored tone.

"Let's try to be open-minded," A.J. said faking a smile. "Say it with me now, I love my job."

Anthony mumbled. "I love my job. I hate this assignment." He thumped his chest in attempt to move the burning sensation stuck there.

"You look a little green," she said.

"Too much pizza."

"Or too many Rolaids," Ramon craned his neck from the front seat. "Maybe you need to see a doctor."

"What I need is a real assignment," Anthony said.

"This is a real assignment, so don't be condescending with your questions," A.J. said as he cut his eyes to her. "From what this guy said on the phone, he approaches each case with the idea of debunking any paranormal activity."

Inside Anthony's chest was a small volcano becoming active. "I'm a professional."

Ramon piped up. "I say, let her rip. Conflict will be much more interesting."

"This is not reality TV," Anthony said.

"If a documentary isn't reality, what is?"

* * *

"You're a skeptic. I appreciate that."

Jeffery Margolis was the founder of Camden Paranormal Investigations or CPI.

The initials aggravated Anthony, who had to chant in his head, "Be objective." Jeffery had the thick neck and table muscle of a geek who spent too many years playing Dungeons and Dragons. Wisps on his patchy face proved that he couldn't grow a man's beard, and the unique skull tattoo on his bicep invited in-depth study. He seemed excited to tell his story in front of a camera.

"I was the biggest skeptic on the planet until a buddy of mine was remodeling his kitchen and stirred up a world of activity."

"What kind of activity?"

"Things would disappear--tools, materials. Paint would run like someone tossed a bucket of water on it. In one spot, the paint would not stay on the wall. Dude, my buddy would paint it, get up the next morning, and all the paint just dripped off onto the floor."

"Maybe it was just cheap paint."

"No, dude, he took it back to Home Depot. They painted a piece of sheet rock with it, let it set overnight. Nothing happened. Definitely not the paint."

Anthony was bored already. "And this got you past being skeptical?"

"No, not at all. I thought there was some extra heat source or moisture inside the wall, but check it out. I go over there to watch a Browns game, and I need the head just before half-time. So I'm walking past the kitchen and, in my peripheral vision, I catch this big black cloud over near the stove."

"Was something burning on the stove?" Anthony asked.

Jeffery wagged his head like a little kid. "We ordered pizza. The stove was never turned on."

Ah, football season. Anthony clenched his teeth to swallow a yawn. He had never been much of a ballplayer and had not grown into a fan.

Jeffery droned on. "I stop cold in the hall, back up slowly and whatever it was shifts, like it's looking at me, you know? Only it didn't have a shape really. Just like a cloud of bugs swarming around, but solid."

Anthony snuck a glance at A.J., who widened her eyes, reminding him not to nod off.

"So I turn, and it does, too. I get this creepy feeling. Every hair on my body is standing up. When I turned on the light, it flew right at me. I had to duck. Nearly piss--wet myself."

"How sure are you that it wasn't something natural?" Anthony asked.

"Like noxious gas, cigar smoke, aerosol sprays?" Jeffery did the exaggerated head wag again. "None of the above. Nobody was smoking. The smoke detector never went off. The oven wasn't on. We checked the dials, felt the burners. We even had a guy come in and check for gas leaks and do carbon monoxide readings. Nothing."

Anthony worked hard to maintain a serious face and pretend he was interested.

"We ruled out everything we could possibly think of. So then we set up cameras and tried to lure it out."

"How do you lure it out?"

"Provoke it. Call it chicken; tell it it has no balls."

"Did that work?"

"Unfortunately, no."

Imagine that.

"But when we made a huge mess in the kitchen, it got busy." Jeffery nodded as if he had known it all along.

"Busy how?"

"Moving stuff."

"You have that on video?"

"Yep." Jeffery slid a DVD into the machine behind him. The picture showed a couple cans coming off a shelf to hit the floor, seemingly on their own. A can of tomato juice bubbled and oozed in one tight shot. But to Anthony, these things could have a number of natural explanations.

"So this is what changed your mind?"

"Nope. I got pushed," he said, nodding as if they would understand what that meant.

Anthony waited him out.

"When we were cleaning up, something or someone hit me in the back of the shoulder so hard I pitched over, slammed up against the refrigerator."

He produced a Polaroid shot of a red mark on his shoulder.

Again, one of his buddies could have slapped him hard.

"I know, you're thinking anybody could have done that, but dude, I'm telling you, I was alone in that room when it happened. It was half-time and my buddy was taking the trash out."

Jeffery hit a button to skip ahead, stopping at a spot that showed him stagger, as if he'd been shoved, hitting the refrigerator, and reaching for a pain in his shoulder. The camera angle covered a good three quarters of the room from above. He was indeed alone. Theatrics? Maybe.

"So after that, you were a believer?" Anthony said.

"Not quite," Jeffery said.

Not quite the answer Anthony was expecting.

Jeffery pulled some paperwork from a brown accordion file and handed it to Anthony. "I did some research on the property at the courthouse. Back in the forties, this local fry cook ran the only restaurant in town. He was a pain in the ass, according to all the notes in his file. Always late with his taxes, never paid the full amount. Got thrown in jail a couple times for threatening a clerk."

Jeffery pulled the DVD from the player and switched to another while continuing his story. "So here was a guy nobody wanted to keep in jail very long because he was the only cook in town, and apparently a really good one."

"Is this house the restaurant?"

"After his actual restaurant burned down, he opened his house up to people until they could rebuild."

"Your buddy's house?"

"Yeah," Jeffery said, as he watched the numbers change on the digital display. "So whenever my buddy was home, he talked to the guy. His name was pronounced Ro-shay, which is spelled R-o-u-c-h-e-r. But when he said it, he purposely said it like it was spelled."

"Why?"

"To provoke him. And it worked," Jeffery glanced at the camera, "because he clearly heard the guy correct him. Practically shouted, Ro-shay! So this was definitely an intelligent haunt."

"As opposed to, what, an un-intelligent one?"

"There's what we call a residual haunting, where activity occurs without interacting with the living. It's similar to an imprint, which is kind of like a replay of the past event. But this cook was responding to him."

Anthony wanted to cut to the chase. "Okay, so what are we about to see here?"

"This is a different case altogether. And this, my friend, is the Holy Grail."

Of course it is. Anthony had to resist the urge to sigh heavily.

"This was shot at an abandoned asylum that closed in the mid-sixties. It was a kind of dumping ground for all the people they couldn't figure out what to do with. Like today, you got your manic depressives, bi-polar, ADD, autistic, and chemically imbalanced people they have designer drugs for. Back then you got locked up in a psych ward so you couldn't hurt anybody. It was an embarrassment to have somebody like that in the family, so you put them away and pretended they'd died, which they eventually did."

"Let's have a look." Anthony fought to maintain his patience.

Jeffery cued up the video, revealing a dark hallway drawn with graffiti, and some trash strewn about as if it had been used as a flophouse.

"This," he pointed, "is the hallway leading to Ward C, where the worst cases went. The owners still report hearing voices, laughter, crying, and thumping. Sounds like someone pounding their head against the wall. So we set cameras up in all directions.'

He pressed play. "Watch it first, and then we'll go back and do a slow-mo."

They all watched the hallway remain still for what felt like an hour, then a streak of light drew their eyes to a dark figure draped in a long cloak or dress that dragged the floor. What looked like a foot poked from the bottom of the cloak, before the whole figure vanished into a fold in space.

Anthony leaned in as Jeffery rewound it and played it again.

"See how solid it is?"

"How do you know it wasn't a prankster? A kid in a cape?"

"Who can walk out of one wall and through another?" Jeffery's voice was excited and he cued up a laptop to play another piece of footage. "We had a camera in the room it would have come into from the wall."

The picture showed an empty room with the skeleton of a bed frame rusting quietly in the corner. Nothing moved.

Anthony started rationalizing. "So this, whatever it was. . ."

"Full-bodied apparition," Jeffery corrected.

"Tell me this is what converted you from skeptic to believer."

Jeffery nodded. "This is what sent me over."

"And you believe this is proof of life after death?"

"As close as we can get so far. Because this guy," he replayed the shadow figure, "has been seen by many in different areas, but mostly in Ward C. We checked with the security company. They have cameras all over the perimeter of the building now because they don't want lawsuits from people getting hurt in there. Dude, they have some weird footage too, but won't release it to anyone."

Everyone was silent as he reran it several more times.

Anthony was one big question mark. "We know you had the footage authenticated, but you can't prove that this figure is not an actual person."

"No, we can't, but we have no explanation as to who it might be or how it can materialize out of one wall and vanish through another. I mean, who could do that?"

Criss Angel, David Copperfield, Siegfried and Roy, but those guys were pretty public about it. Anthony had to admit that it was interesting, but his mind just couldn't quite go that far. There had to be some logical explanation.

* * *

Kellan needed more information, so she called the only person who might have any clue: Jade.

"Know any demon experts? I need to know more about that thing. Why it would attach to someone. For what purpose."

"Well, most indigenous people believe in demons of some kind. But in this town, you'd be lucky to find any kind of expert. You might find come Cherokee to talk to up in the mountains, but you'd probably need to know someone to introduce you. They don't spill knowledge to just any ole' body."

Kellan fell back onto her bed, bouncing Riley awake. "There's nothing but crap online, speculation at best."

"You could try a priest. They do exorcisms."

"I'm a little leery of people who counsel on things they've never experienced, like marriage. Not sure many priests ever get to do exorcisms. At least, not often enough to know what they are dealing with."

"I thought there was such a thing as a Demonologist."

"They had one on that ghost hunting show, but he acted too much like a priest. I need someone who might know something about how a demon thinks, what motivates it."

Kellan could hear Jade's lighter click open. "Well, without being able to hear it straight from the horse himself, that's about all I can come up with in terms of experts."

Kellan sat up. "Well, thanks anyway." And she closed her phone before Jade could say anything else.

Who would know more than the actual Leech himself? It was one way of checking to make sure it was still safe behind the gate, right? Maybe it would talk, maybe it wouldn't.

What if it got attached to her and she couldn't get it off? It might drive her to jump off a building or lie on a train track. Then she would be trapped with It.

Kellan mentally turned it over. If she had produced the scissors before, she could do it again, somehow, right? With her new protective shield in place, she might not feel as exposed as the first encounter. Fear would not keep her from getting all the data she could.

The gate appeared at her request and Kellan looked between the slats into the dark void with apprehension. Connor's voice reminded her to keep it closed. The number two graced the center. She hadn't noticed that there before. No sound, no scent, no shadow reached out to her. Her protective shield securely in place, she breathed in some courage. Here goes nothing. She reached out, but the gate opened before her hand could touch it. The Leech had to be here or this gate would not have appeared, right? Was it still contained? Two steps over the threshold and the gate descended behind her.

Blackness enfolded her like quicksand. The smell of freshly broken earth teased her sinuses and the cold made her wish she'd worn warmer clothes. The flicker of a torch flame licked a wall that zoomed into focus from a distance. Behind her was black, before her was light. No question which way to go. A large cage housed something shifty beneath the flaming torch. The bars glowed like laser beams. Kellan felt herself drawn to it like a moth. The closer she got to it, the more her head hurt. The familiarity of the angry creature confirmed that it was the one chained to Connor. It wasn't nearly as frightening squashed down in a six by six cube. Still, inside her mind and her chest, she felt seething, burning anger. Kellan knew it ached to get at her.

"You," It spoke in a deep, hoarse grunt that reminded her of an old man with a three-pack-a-day habit.

123

"Who are you?" she asked.

"I have many names."

Oh, goody. "What is your purpose?"

"None of your business."

"Really? I guess I should just speak with whoever's in charge here then."

A moment of silence was followed by howling laughter that seized her stomach. "You are nothing that could stand before my master. He leaves your kind to me. I feast on grief, dine on despair, and drink the anguish of pathetic simpletons like you."

"Who is your master?"

"None of your business."

"Why were you attached to Connor?"

"He was r-r-ripe," It said as if he'd tasted him. "I have the power to manipulate emotion, unleash it at will."

"Why? I mean, what purpose could that serve?"

"It serves my purpose. Anyone I take serves me, so I may serve my master." Its tone was delighted, silky with pride.

"But why Connor?"

"He was an obstacle."

"An obstacle? To what?"

"Poor stupid little nothing. You have no answers."

"Connor was a child. He couldn't have known what you were."

The Leech laughed hard. "You nothings see only what you desire."

"If he was an obstacle, then you were after something else," she spoke more to herself than to it, "or someone else."

It shifted from dark to lighter. "She was mine, and he interfered."

"Who?"

"Her!" It paused. "I should have had them both."

Her who? His mother? Kellan's hair stood up. "You thought you would use her love for him."

"She would have followed if not for. . ."

"His brother," she said. "Why did you want her so badly?"

"She was mine."

"I don't understand. How did she belong to you?"

"She invited me to her."

"How? Was she a witch or something?"

It laughed. "Stupid little nothing, you. She was just the same. Stupid, foolish girl who played with toys she knew nothing off."

Kellan had no clarity on its meaning.

"He'll never believe you," It sang. "She told him herself I was not real."

"Who? Anthony?"

It sang some more. "He closed the door. He cannot see. She made him easy picking for me."

"Wait a minute. She told him what? Did he see you?"

It said nothing.

"If he was so easy, you'd have had him long ago." Kellan smiled. "His mother's love for him gave her the strength to foil your plan."

It whispered in a manner that chilled her to the bone. "They belong to me, still."

Blackness followed, as if the warden had turned the light out to signal it was time to leave. Kellan shivered with cold, but the Leech's last words through the dark froze her insides.

"And now, so do you."

* * *

The next morning she saw a hawk gliding overhead before she heard Connor's voice somewhere behind her.

"How could you be so stupid?"

Riley pulled Kellan to a tangle of overgrown shrubs that housed a cat.

"You went inside the gate? What were you thinking?"

She had taken a risk to learn something from it, and she had.

"It wanted your mother," she said. "You went to her house when you--" she stopped herself.

"I don't remember much until. . ."

"You were hanging from the side of a building by your fingertips?"

He fell silent.

"What was the real reason you went to your mother's?"

"Was just drawn there. It was home, where I felt safe."

"And did you?"

"When Dad was there," he said.

"You know what I think?" Kellan watched Riley stand frozen to wait out the cat. "I think you were taken there. Your mother was home alone. Your brother, the strong one, was out of the way."

"Safe," he said.

Kellan had so many questions she had to be quick. Connor's visits were short.

"He was safe, but you weren't."

"I could protect him." Connor's voice faded to soft breath. "I can't protect you."

Chapter 14

Anthony's mother believed in the supernatural - signs, mystical things no one could prove - but Anthony had never let himself climb down off the fence. His approach to any practice of faith was extreme caution. Anthony was a fact-finder with a deep sense of skepticism. He'd seen too much reality to blindly believe in anything. Now he was in Louisiana, where the unbelievable was so easily embraced, yet he'd had always been surprisingly comfortable here. New Orleans was one of the places on the planet he enjoyed revisiting. An interview with a voodoo priestess was not high on his list of gets, but he kept reminding himself that the food alone would be worth the trip.

Anthony sat in the back of the SUV, notebook in hand. Ramon sat behind him cleaning a piece of equipment while Eddie drove. A.J. rode shotgun turned sideways in her seat.

"Go," Anthony said, not looking up from his notes.

A.J. read from her netbook. "The voodoo practiced here is a blend of Native American shamanism, European folklore and Christianity."

"No conflict there."

Eddie caught Anthony's glance in the mirror as A.J. plodded on.

"This priestess practices a non-judgmental, positive form of voodoo, and she says Hollywood has completely distorted what voodoo is."

"What's her name?"

"Miss Terese," she said. "People claim she's up there with Marie Laveau."

"What do we have on Laveau?" Anthony said.

A.J. changed screens. "Born in 1794, raised Catholic, hairdresser by trade, did all her data-gathering in gossip, and her husband took off. When she found out he died, she shacked up with another guy and cranked out fifteen kids. They never married. She gave up hairdressing for voodoo and had secret ceremonies out at Lake Pontchartrain. Marie was said to be the most powerful voodoo priestess of the time. Apparently, there were quite a few back in her day. She's credited for adding the Catholic elements to the ceremonies, making them large carnival-style events. She prayed over a black coffin, sacrificed roosters, and danced with a 20-foot snake."

Anthony smirked.

Ramon looked up from what he was doing. "Hey, remember that picture with the model and that python from the eighties? What was her name?"

Eddie tried to help him come up with it. "Natasha something?"

A.J. wrinkled her nose and ignored them. "Laveau made big money off whites and didn't charge blacks. A rape case made her famous. Some wealthy white guy rapes a lower class girl. The father of the rapist goes to Laveau and says, "I'll give you my house if you can get my son off." So she does her magic thing, and influences the jury, who was probably afraid of her. Got her a house in the French Quarter."

"Sweet," Ed said, with a big smile.

"It gets better. The guy she got off rehabilitated, and wanted to marry the girl he raped. But of course, she wanted nothing to do with him. So he goes to Laveau who makes some charm bag, and he goes to church with it. The girl freaks and tries to run away, trips, and sprains her ankle. And who rushes to her aid?"

"Oh, come on," Anthony said. "She married her rapist because he was nice to her when she fell?"

"The next day," A.J. said.

"I am so getting a charm bag," Eddie said.

Anthony tapped him on the head with his notebook. "Folklore."

"Maybe," A.J. said with a grin. "Want another?"

Eddie was all over it. "Yeah, yeah, yeah."

"Some old guy wanted to marry a girl young enough to be his great granddaughter, but she refused. Her heart belonged to some young buck who was away seeking his fortune. But her father needed money and this guy was rich, so her Daddy tried to convince her to marry the codger, even locked her up, but she still refused. So he goes to Laveau who gives him some powder to put in her food, and gives the old guy a bag to make him, you know, a stud. Then she declared 'The wedding will take place.'"

Anthony shook his head. "They drug a girl into marrying a dirty old man and call it magic."

"Now, hold on," A.J. scolded. "So the girl succumbs, and the old guy throws a lavish wedding. Come time for the traditional waltz, he croaks right there on the dance floor, leaving her sole heir to his fortune."

They all laughed.

"She calls her true love back from his fortune hunt so they can live happily ever after off her new inheritance," A.J. said.

"And justice lives," Anthony said.

"So voodoo is really just fake?" Eddie said.

"Smoke and mirrors to manipulate a desired outcome by the sound of it," Anthony said.

"A belief system like any other," A.J. corrected. "When Laveau's popularity died, she returned to Catholicism, working with prison inmates. She retired, her daughter, also named Marie Laveau, took over. But the daughter did not possess Mom's warm heart, and she was more feared than loved. When Mom died, she went into hiding. Some people think she drowned in a storm, others say she lived a while longer. They say both women still haunt various parts of New Orleans." A.J. finished with a smile of satisfaction.

Anthony shook his head. "Everybody loves a good ghost story."

* * *

"Bridge been gone since Katrina." Their lanky Cajun guide pulled his boat closer to the dock. "Place been underwater, but she got her cleaned up quick."

The boat was small, wooden, and painted powder blue. The one-horse motor made a clacking noise that sounded like a broken toy. Arrangements had been made to meet Miss Terese at eight. The orchestra of frogs didn't mind the daylight. Mosquitoes did their fly-bys making Anthony itch. Much as he loved to travel, he was still a born and bred city boy. Nature was out of his comfort zone, especially when he seemed to be low on the food chain. His mother used to say bugs liked him because he was sweet. He hated being sweet. The buzzing made him nervous and the humidity helped sweat his DEET repellant away. But little details like those made his job adventurous.

A half-hour trudge through brackish water led them to a small land mass with a dilapidated stilt house that looked like a hunting shack. The gray and black wood had never seen paint, and the steps leading to the dry-rotted porch crunched. The tin roof had seen better days, but wasn't as worn as the rest of it.

Miss Terese was an elegant creature. Anthony had imagined a larger woman; the area's reigning voodoo priestess was barely five feet tall with the smooth sculpt of a dancer. She didn't wear the layered clothing and jewelry he'd expected of someone in her profession. Apparently, he'd seen too many movies. Instead, she shined in a simple white cotton sundress with tiny blue flowers at the hem. On her feet were simple sandals and her hair was wrapped in a scarf piled high enough to house a small pet. Her welcoming smile wilted when she looked directly into his eyes.

Before he could introduce himself, she took up his offered hand in both of hers; giving him the strange feeling she could see inside him. "Fixed you something."

Anthony threw a glance to A.J., who looked away casually. Ramon busied himself with senseless examination of the handheld. Terese motioned them to wait outside, and she pulled Anthony in. In spite of the many lit candles, the inside was dark as a cave. The place may have been crumbling, but it was meticulously clean. When his eyes adjusted, an explosion of bright color surprised him. Shelves were decorated with bottles capped with doll heads, painted gourds, and containers of what he assumed were herbs. Pictures of deities were nestled in the collection; some familiar and some plain scary. He recognized a tapestry of Mother Mary. A haze hung above them like the inside of a bar, yet he smelled a sweet floral bouquet and heat from the candle flames.

Terese let go of his hand and looked all around him. "Keeper of the Dead."

Anthony squinted. "I'm sorry?"

"S'what they call you." She moved silently, gracefully behind a raw wood countertop draped in red and green silk. "You travel with a crowd."

Anthony was about to rebut that a crew of three wasn't a crowd, but seeing the size of the place, she had a point.

"The dead work hard for you. Follow you like hungry dogs." She bent to retrieve a small pouch from a basket near the floor. "They protect you like a king, yet you do not see."

Anthony couldn't breathe. What was she talking about, and why was he feeling so uncomfortable?

"No matter," she appraised him, "they work their magic

anyway."

"Ah, magic." Anthony exhaled and had to force himself not to smirk.

"Brought you here, yes?"

He couldn't control his grin now. After all, an assignment and a bathtub toy had brought him here.

She tossed a handful of bones, small ones that made him wonder what they had come from, and if they had been acquired before the owner was finished using them.

"Yes," she said, and studied the scattering as if it validated her prognostication. "You don't believe in things you can't prove. But you speak the truth in what you can."

Anthony frowned at the bones. What kind of generality was that?

"You walk a tight rope between what was and what will be."

He shook his head. "I'm not sure I follow."

She raised her chin. "Release the pain you carry, so you may see again." Her voice was deep, flat, and eerily commanding. "Watch for a messenger."

His head dropped and he put his hands on his hips. He expected strange, but not quite so cryptic.

"Aren't you a messenger?" His voice was squashed by doubt. He noticed his crew had grown very quiet outside, listening to every word through the wood slats. His smile faded.

Terese cocked her head. "Listen, Smart Guy, and secrets long buried will be brought to light. But you have to be open to receiving."

"I see," he said, even though he didn't.

Terese knew, too. She smiled. "You were not always the skeptic you have become."

The woman was so far off she couldn't have hit a bug if it were on her nose. Anthony had never believed fortune-tellers, psychics, or anyone claiming to see into the future.

She tossed the pouch to him with something crunchy inside. "Your third eye is closed. You work on opening it."

"My third eye." He looked around, half expecting to see an eyeball roll across the floor. "Right."

Terese pointed to the middle of her forehead. "The dead have much to say. Put that under your pillow and *listen*." She smiled and looked away from him to a corner.

Anthony followed her gaze to a tall wood carving of a female fertility goddess in front of baskets laden with fabrics. He stared at it a moment, then rolled his eyes back to her. This woman was entertaining, if not crazy. Through a small window behind her, he noticed an overgrown graveyard. The filmmaker made a mental note to get a shot of it, but the child inside felt chills on the sight of it.

* * *

Connor smiled from the corner, a crowd of others standing vigil behind him, each a subject from Anthony's secret personal film project.

Miss Terese sobered when she brought her eyes back to Anthony, who watched her now as if she were mad. The tin roof ticked and the noise grew as the rain came hard. "Soon," she smiled, "you will see."

* * *

Cemeteries had always held great fascination for Kellan. The mystery of the life beneath the stone was ever so tempting to write. Her favorite stone garden was in Key West, where most of its tombed residents shared their sense of humor with the living on their markers. One of her favorites read, "I'm just resting my eyes."

Words did not pour onto the screen as they had the week before, so Kellan returned to her ritual of writing longhand in the cemetery. She held her pen over a pad, anticipating another installment of Anthony's story. Nothing came. Where was Connor? Half an hour later she wandered from stone to stone to regain the circulation in her legs. Small flags pointed out servicemen. Most were family plots. Each stone told of their relationships, how they would be missed, that they walked with their god or were spending eternity with their marriage partner.

Connor nearly startled her out of her sneakers. "Not one says 'Great at his job.'"

"For some people, work is their life, you know," she said. "Doesn't make them defective."

"Imbalanced," he said.

She frowned. "Yeah, you have stones to throw in that direction."

Taking advice on how to live your life from someone who appeared imbalanced before he took his own seemed pretty twisted.

She had to keep reminding herself that he had been taken, and it did result in the protection of his surviving family.

Connor went on. "When you read about successful people, do they ever say work was the key to their success?"

"No one says that." Even the rich and brilliant said their family was always the most important priority in their lives. Without their support, they would not be who they were. When asked of their greatest achievements, most replied, "My children."

What was her greatest achievement? Not having to file an insurance claim for breaking anything in three months? Kellan had never had children, and was grateful not to have damaged one in the divorce. She'd decided that if she didn't by the time she was thirty five, she wouldn't. At forty, she felt she'd done the world a service. Her kid might have been another mess for the world to clean up after. With her upbringing, she would have been a lousy mother, right? If kids learned by example, what would she have passed on to hers? Grocery shopping could be put off until you ran out of dog food?

This wasn't about her. Connor's brother probably had the world to offer his future kids, if he lived long enough.

"Your brother could still have children. Men never get too old. Tony Randall had one at seventy-five. No matter how old a man gets, he can rent some twenty-two-year-old with good genes and fresh eggs." Kellan shrugged. "By the time we get this message to him, he'll be chomping at the bit for a twenty-two-year-old."

This cracked Connor up. She could hear him as hearty and true as if he were alive. His laugh came behind a smile that could have illuminated a city street.

When he was done, he pointed to a black headstone in the distance. Everything around her went black for a moment. When light found her again, she was standing next to Connor watching Anthony work on his laptop. He sat at a round table lit only by the light of its screen. A fortress of boxes rimmed the room as if he were packing for a move. They were labeled neatly in black marker. She went to get a closer look. Anthony did not seem to notice he wasn't alone.

The first box she came to read Grief. It was the size of a refrigerator, with layers of tape on its seams. The one in front of it read Fear and was the size of a washing machine. Love was about the same size as Fear, and had about an inch of dust on top. The

Emotions box was big enough to place both Fear and Love inside. It was also covered in dust. Compassion was on the floor, the size of an entertainment center. It had been opened and closed so many times the old tape had lost its ability to stick to the scarred cardboard. The box labeled Isolation was the size of her first apartment, and wide open. There was a box the size of a grocery bag labeled Pride. The rest were smaller kitchen-appliance-sized boxes labeled Love of Mother, Love of Pets, Love of Friends, all partially open. She found a shoe box, lid askew, labeled Creative Writing. Two walls were stacked high with boxes of varying shapes and sizes, all labeled Work, all open and overflowing with stacks of scripts, rolls of film, and cassette cartridges.

Connor tapped her shoulder and nodded to a dark area. A pocket door was cut in the wall. He motioned for her to open it. It had a small brass handle that, when she tried it, slid the panel up. Kellan glanced over at Anthony, who didn't look up from his keyboard, then poked her head inside the opening. A huge aluminum duct jutted out before diving straight down. The floor was piled with discarded boxes. One big one labeled Dad was taped shut. There were many names of people she didn't recognize from his past. But the largest was balanced on its edge. Battered and abused, it appeared to be crushed in several places with layers and layers of tape covering the cardboard. This box was labeled Connor.

Kellan looked back at Connor who wore the look of the weary.

"He thinks I shut him out because I didn't love him."

It made her wonder. "Did you love your brother?"

"Of course. I couldn't condemn him to hell with me, could I? What if that Leech got him? I couldn't tell him I thought I was losing my mind."

Kellan held one hand up to calm him. They watched Anthony type a million miles into the unknown. "I'm sure he knew that," she said, feeling stupid after hearing it.

"He thinks I abandoned him to take care of Mom after nearly destroying her. I guess if the roles were reversed, I'd have thought the same thing." Connor took the seat across from his brother and stared. "I couldn't let him see his big brother be such a coward. Now look at him."

Kellan didn't think he looked bad.

"He spends all his time alone with machines. Has a job that keeps him running, always running. He was the golden boy I was supposed to be. Never shied from responsibility, always strived to make his way, never let anyone down. He thinks if he lets himself love somebody they'll just end up leaving, like I did. Like Dad did. To him we're just gone."

"We all go at some point."

Connor did not hear her. "He doesn't laugh anymore. Never does anything for himself. If you asked him the last time he did something just for fun, he'd need time to get back to you."

Connor studied him as only the dead would the living, with longing. "That's what I did to him. I left him alone when I was supposed to be his hero. His go-to guy, best man at his wedding, uncle to his children, partners-in-crime to the last, always a phone call away. That was who I should have been."

Kellan found it tough to find words of comfort after that. "I'm sure he has friends."

"Friends," Connor repeated. "They move with jobs, get married, have kids, and lives of their own. Some have married more than once, and he's never even come close. He begs off invitations, bails on vacations, and works all the time. Who will be there for him?"

Words escaped her. Her life wasn't so different, and the parallels were unnerving. Her friends had scattered all over the country with job changes; her ex-husband had remarried, she didn't have kids, and her father was retired. When she wasn't cleaning, she spent the bulk of her time in front of a computer. And she had just broken up with the best guy in town. Who would be there for her?

Stop it! This isn't about you.

She looked back down the hole in the wall at the boxes. There were larger unmarked ones on the floor beneath the battered one.

"What are those?"

"My stuff."

Kellan looked at him, alarmed. "He still has all your stuff?"

Connor nodded. "Books, music, stuff."

Keeping so many things that belonged to your dead brother couldn't be healthy. She didn't need to consult a shrink to tell her that Anthony had not faced his grief. But if there was something in one of those boxes unique to Connor, it might help her convince Anthony that she wasn't crazy.

"Poetry," Connor said, as if hearing her thoughts. "Couple songs."

"You were a poet?"

"Never let anyone read it."

"Is it in a. . ."

"Folder, loose leaf."

"Typed or handwritten?"

"Hand."

"Has he read any of it?"

"No."

"Weird." Kellan stole a glance at Anthony. "I would have wanted to go through everything looking for clues."

"Too dark for him," Connor said. "He needs to be seen pretty soon."

"Not everyone has the need to be seen," Kellan said. "Some of us just want to be heard."

"Seen by a doctor," he clarified. "He canceled a physical because he's too busy."

She was not his mother, conscience, or guardian. Anthony was a grown man, for Pete sakes. He should know when he had to see a doctor. "So what am I supposed to do about that?"

"Remind him," he said slowly, "of Dad."

Chapter 15

The next morning Kellan heard Riley digging on the couch and went to see what he was up to. She arrived in time to see him flop down with a smiling face and dangling tongue next to his new buddy Connor. Riley clearly enjoyed the extra company.

"Aren't you supposed to be somewhere, like your life review?" she said hoping for a reaction.

Connor didn't move. "How do you know about it?"

"Jade told me. You have to look at your life through the eyes of all the other people in it, feel what they felt about you. Things you said, things you did."

He ignored her.

"You're stalling." Kellan pointed at Riley. "And you are not helping."

"Look who's talking."

She ignored the comment, knowing it referred to her talking to Anthony.

"Fine," Connor sat up. "What if I go and you forget me? If I'm not around, it will be easy for you to avoid talking to him, and pretend I was nothing but your imagination."

Kellan felt her heart drop. "How in the world could I ever forget you? I haven't cried this much since diapers. And this entire thing with you has thrown a serious wrench into my life."

She could feel him sag.

Her voice shook. "As long as I've lived, I've never felt drawn to do something this illogical. I've never been so afraid to talk to anyone or so worried about what the information would do to him. Did it occur to you that I could actually give him a heart attack with this? The idea of causing him more pain, when he has been through so much," she gathered herself. "Even without the possibility of health problems, imagine how he will feel when he finds out that I got to spend time with you that should have rightfully been his. This needs to be done gently, with respect and diplomacy. Neither is my strong suit, by the way." She finished, embarrassed for shouting the

137

last part.

Connor fell back into the throw pillows.

Kellan composed herself. "He buried you. I can't bury him."

"He stopped living."

"Clearly, he's still here."

"Is he?" Connor said. "Married to the mystery of me?"

This kid was more frustrating than the living.

"When Dad died, I got weaker. Tony got stronger in some ways, but keeps everyone at arm's length, works himself into the ground. He has no Sam."

Kellan looked around. "No Sam?"

"Lord of the Rings?"

Ah, Sam, the faithful friend who always had Frodo's back.

"You think you were supposed to be his Sam." Did she have a Sam? *Cut it out.* "But isn't that his choice? He could find a Sam if he really wanted one." Kellan knew she was referring to herself.

"Until he lets go of me, he's just going to get worse."

"Speaking of letting go, why did you break up with your girlfriend?" she asked.

Silence.

"The real reason."

"She accused me of. . ." he stopped. "I would lose time and not remember things. I scared her. *It* scared her." Connor said. "All in all, I was never who people thought I was, who she thought I was."

"Did you hurt her, physically?"

"No," he said sharply. "But I worried that it could make me. She's safe now."

"And so is Tony."

"If you keep the gate closed."

"I don't think that thing can get loose even with the gate open."

"That's what It wants you to think. Don't let your guard down. You don't know for sure. You can't let It get to Tony. He thinks working out will make up for not eating right on the road and not sleeping. Three guesses why he doesn't sleep."

Kellan took her glasses off and rubbed her eyes. Doctor Connor. "He's a big boy. He doesn't need me to tell him that he needs to see a doctor."

"I'm his demon. He's angry, hurt, scared, and punishes himself for not having all the answers. He should get rid of my stuff, let go, and reclaim his life," he said in her ear, "believe there's something bigger out there."

"You mean God?"

"I didn't believe in anything, and look where it got me."

Kellan trod carefully. "You mean if you had believed, you would not have been taken?"

"I might have been able to put up more of a fight, and would have known to ask for help sooner. You have to ask for help. Nothing outside us can interfere with free will. Guides exist to help humanity, but I never believed enough to ask."

"So all Tony has to do is ask?"

"He doesn't know he needs help," Connor said. "That's where you come in."

Kellan wanted to be sick. He was placing all his eggs in her basket. "You know how big a long shot this is? I'm nobody, with zero credibility. He's never going to believe this if he's close-minded."

"You can't quit on me."

She closed her eyes. "You have to go."

"Raise your right hand and swear you won't quit?"

Everything inside her said not to, but her hand seemed to have a mind of its own. "I swear."

* * *

Anthony settled down into another hotel bed in front of the news after an exhausting day. The chaos of the world always made his problems small. Others suffered far more than he. Massive flooding swallowed the Midwest, forcing thousands from homes. Places he and the crew had driven through were underwater. A woman wiped tears from her face. They always got a shot of someone in tears, as if the roof tops peeking from the water's surface could not express the horror.

A few minutes later Connor watched his brother finally succumb to sleep. The flickering of the television screen splashed color across Tony's face as his mouth dropped open slightly in the steady breath of sleep.

Connor crawled up to his ear. "I know you can hear me, so pay attention."

Anthony's face relaxed. Without the dark crescents beneath his eyes, he'd have looked like the boy Connor remembered, worn out from a day at the beach. Connor's heart leapt at being able to see him, touch him, and smell him again. He took comfort in knowing he had an advocate working on his behalf. If she didn't chicken out.

A snuffle escaped, prompting Tony to roll onto his right side. If Tony had known he was being watched, he would have awakened from paranoia.

"I am so sorry for everything you had to deal with because of me. I didn't know what I was doing. Then I thought giving over to It was the only way to keep everyone safe. Who knows what It could have made me do to you, to anyone around me? It seeped in like carbon monoxide, pulling the strings. No one would have believed me, and I had no way out."

Tony sucked in a ragged breath and shifted.

"You probably did turn out for the better this way. Look at all you've done, all you're going to do, because of what I did. You were always the strong one. Now look, you're impenetrable."

Tony slept without response.

"But that's the catch. You're out in the world but keep yourself isolated. You won't stay still long enough to let yourself rest. You avoid attachments that could actually help you. There's so much for you to do to heal the mess I made."

Tony's hand twitched and his eyes darted in rapid movement.

Connor leaned close to his ear. "I know you're still angry. But you have to let go of me to save yourself." He sat back on his elbow. "I'm sending a messenger. Try not to scare her with your interrogation tactics. She won't have all the answers, and she doesn't want anything from you."

Connor watched him sleep a moment longer.

"See you later."

"La-ter," Tony breathed.

* * *

The beach was dark but alive. Anthony could feel the cool wet sand beneath his bare feet as he ran next to Connor. They chased each other through the sand giggling and waving sparklers while their father warned them to be careful not to fall. Huge pops followed big colorful plumes in the sky. Connor took his hand and they ran up the beach toward their reflection on the water. Sparklers danced with them into the promise of adventure.

Connor let go of his hand and ran too fast for Anthony to keep up. He kept going until he disappeared into the dark, and all Anthony could see was the tiny fizzle of his sparkler.

* * *

Connor was gone and Kellan felt his absence more than she had expected. Her writing had slowed to a trickle. Without much work to keep her busy, she had plenty of time to spend in search of facts that Anthony might believe. Her research yielded a copy of his cable documentary on a Texas prison with a radical warden.

She put the tape in and grabbed a notebook. It was narrated by an actor, but the only faces on camera were guards and inmates. Kellan watched the whole tape, learning more about prison life than she had ever desired. How anyone thought rehabilitation was possible by locking someone up was unimaginable. Yet it kept the bad guys from plundering and pillaging.

The film told her nothing about Anthony.

Her phone rang before she could find the remote and stop the tape. Credits rolled as she listened to dead air: no breathing, no static, no background noise. She hung up and dug for the remote, finding it had lodged itself between couch cushions. Just as she was about to press the stop button, a soft voice spoke, "So this is dinner, huh?"

The frame next to the crawl closed in on a sectioned cafeteria tray containing two slices of white bread, a glob of greens that looked skimmed from a neglected pool, and a puddle of brown lumpy liquid. As unappetizing as it looked, she was sure the millions of homeless would have been happy to have it. The camera shifted to a man with headphones around his neck, tucking a clipboard under his arm. He leaned over the tray to sniff the brown goop and made a wrinkled face.

"Smells like bug spray," he said to the camera.

Kellan pressed pause. His voice sounded slightly different from his brother's, but she could see Connor in his eyes. She rewound a minute, watched again, then paused at the spot where he glanced at the camera. So this was Anthony Clarke.

She moved closer to the television to study his every feature. He was handsome, but not in a scary way. Staring into eyes that didn't see her, she tried to imagine what those eyes would look like washed in the horror of what she had to tell him.

After ten minutes of memorizing his face, she let the tape run to see if there was more.

"Taste it," another man's voice said.

Anthony stuck his finger in the stew.

"That's not a real taste. Get a mouthful."

Laughter.

"I don't see you volunteering," Anthony said, as he broke off a corner of bread and dipped it into the brown gravy. He popped it in his mouth, winced, and spat it out in a napkin. "Aw, my dog wouldn't eat that."

He had a dog. Good to know. She could talk to a fellow dog person. They were usually social, easy-going, and open to talking with amiable strangers. Okay, it was a stretch, but a crumb she was grabbing.

Anthony walked to the camera, his shirt swallowing the lens. "Give me this. You try it."

"No problem."

"And get a mouthful now."

The camera bumped around, grabbing glimpses of the floor, the wall, the steel commode, and then righted to focus on the back of a dark-haired man in front of the tray. Kellan's head fell to one side. He looked sort of familiar. Then he turned so he faced the camera.

Kellan stopped breathing. It was him, Mr. Worth-A-Look. She was looking at her new client, Mr. DeSantos.

Plastic spoon at the ready, he said, "The lengths we go in search of truth." Steely faced, he loaded a spoon with a lump of the stew and popped it into his mouth. Chewing, he shrugged. "Doesn't taste like anything." Then he looked straight into the lens and smiled. "Needs salt."

"Your taste buds are fried from hot sauce."

Mr. DeSantos' hair was longer than the photo in Melissa's file. Kellan grabbed up the video case to search for the copyright. Four years ago. She rewound the credits to the beginning and watched for his name. Ramon DeSantos was buried among others. What invisible force had shrunken her six degrees of separation down to two? His mystery occupation had been revealed.

She checked the calendar on the wall. Shit, when was the last time she had checked his apartment?

* * *

As fun as snooping could be, it was against Kellan's code of ethics. People trusted her with their homes. They didn't give her a key so she could nose around their personal stuff, which was why she called the one person who could think like a snoop, and really dig this--Stefan. After bringing him up to speed on the Anthony situation, she picked him up, and brought him to La Casa DeSantos. He was dressed like a cat burglar in broad daylight, which took the edge off of her nerves.

"God, it smells fabulous in here," Stefan said.

Everyone's home had a unique scent, not just from products they used, but their own physiological chemistry. There were men who wore so much aftershave she could smell them hours after she'd left the place. This was not one of those places. The sage scent did not linger in her clothes as long as she would have liked.

"So what do we look for?" Kellan asked Stefan, who handed her a pair of latex gloves. She shot him an accusing look.

"You can never be too careful, lest you be framed by some psycho for being last in the room with the body."

"I'm the cleaning lady. My prints are on everything."

"The dresser drawer handles?"

"I knew you'd be the one for this," she said, pulling on the gloves.

Stefan glanced around the kitchen. "He has to keep paper somewhere, unless he carries everything with him in a briefcase, which would be reckless. Bag gets stolen. . ." He waved a hand. "So what do we know about him?"

"Raise your right hand and swear first."

Stefan cocked his head.

Kellan recited. "I swear that whatever I learn about Ramon DeSantos remains here, and will never be revealed to anyone outside of here. Ever."

He dropped his hand. "Ever?"

"Come on, now." Kellan put on her aggressive face.

He reluctantly raised his hand. "Fine, I swear. What we find here stays here."

"Okay, Ramon DeSantos is a cameraman who once worked with Anthony Clarke. He's very clean, and I haven't seen a single piece of paper or anything remotely personal yet. I don't really know what

I'm looking for. A business card, photos, correspondence, Rolodex, I don't know."

Stefan thought for a second. "Wouldn't it be easier just to contact the production company from the video, and ask how you could contact this guy? He's probably got an agent or attorney."

She gave him the why-didn't-I-think-of-that look. "You come up with this now?"

Stefan shrugged. "But we're here, so. You needed to change the timers anyway, right?"

Right. Kellan had a key. Ramon had asked her to come by to change the light timers and make sure everything was fine. All perfectly legitimate reasons for being there.

"Wait. The blinds!" He went to each set, turning the wands to angle the slats closed. "There could be some pervert or bored kid faking stomach flu watching the world through binoculars from the building across the street."

"Is that what you did when you were a kid?"

He glanced around like someone else could answer. "Once or twice, maybe."

"Now what?"

"Desk?"

Kellan shook her head. "No file cabinets either. One armoire, two dressers, four night stands, and an entertainment center."

"A hidden door in a closet wall, or a cut-out in the ceiling to an attic?"

Kellan shrugged and waved him off to find out. She started in the master bedroom, figuring she could just peer into each drawer at a distance, and only plunge her hand in if she spotted paper. That would be fast. That room yielded little information. The drawer in the nightstand with the phone held an open box of condoms next to a tube of breath spray. Nice to know he was considerate. A bundle of cheap pens with advertising fastened with a rubber band was in the middle, and there was a notepad from a Hilton in Detroit with nothing written on it.

Kellan could hear Stefan whispering to himself from the kitchen. "Anything?"

"He knows his wines," Stefan purred.

Wonderful.

She knew the spare bedroom would yield nothing but empty drawers, but went through it anyway.

Stefan called from the living room, "He's got a huge amount of foreign music, and a copy of every movie Nicole Kidman ever made."

Kellan sagged. "And how does that help me?"

"I'm just saying."

She did an eye roll and made her way to the kitchen that housed some unblemished appliances, and kitchenware with heft. Even the water goblets could be classified as weapons. The junk drawer was a catch-all and had the usual batteries, extra appliance lights, tape, chopsticks from Chinese takeout, menus, and an assortment of clips and loose change.

"If you find any notepads, rub them with a pencil to see what the last thing written was," Stefan said, picking through a stack of phone books.

Kellan headed back to the nightstand in the bedroom. She snapped on the lamp and tilted the notepad sideways. No impressions that she could see, her fingers couldn't feel any either, so she didn't bother rubbing a pencil over it. Where did he keep regular stuff?

The walk-in closet housed a small safe: a miniature version of an old-fashioned bank safe from the movies. It wasn't large enough to hold much: files, a pistol, some cash, maybe an heirloom or a Rolex watch. She moved the hanging clothes to the side to look behind them. Nothing.

"This is nuts. No one is this organized. Even if he pays all his bills online, there has to be something."

"I found a magazine rack," Stefan called from the living room. "*Time, Outside, Photography Today*, nothing exciting."

"Yeah, there's one in the bathroom too. I've been through them."

Stefan trotted past her to the master bath. She could hear him going through it anyway. "Mostly old newspapers and cable television guides. No *Playboy*, no *Madd Magazine*, and no bathroom humor books." Stefan sighed. "Maybe he has a wife and kids stashed somewhere, and this is just his play pad."

Kellan wandered back into the living area and fell into the leather recliner, marveling at how softly it hugged her. No piece of furniture in her apartment or Gayle's felt this nice. Gayle. A twinge of guilt ran through her. She had not given much thought to him or his proposal since she'd fully embraced the task at hand. What kind of woman can completely blow off a guy like Gayle for a dead kid? A stupid one.

The phone made her leap from the chair as if some security company was going to intercom in and tell her she had no business sitting in it. She froze while it rang. Stefan appeared in the doorway to stare at the phone that rang four more times.

"Answering machine?"

"Bedroom," she said, and they hurried to it.

A robotic voice asked the caller to please-leave-a-message. She and Stefan exchanged a glance, and then a less robotic sounding female voice complied in a staggered clip.

"This message is for Ramon DeSantos from Delta Airlines. Your flight, one four eight two, departing Wednesday, August twenty-seventh, at twelve thirty five PM, from Myrtle Beach, South Carolina, has been cancelled. You have been rescheduled on flight five four seven nine, departing Wednesday, five forty PM, August twenty-seventh, from Myrtle Beach, South Carolina, arriving Tampa, Florida, at seven thirty five PM. We apologize for any inconvenience. If you would like to hear this information again, press one now."

Kellan dove into the nightstand drawer for the notepad. Stefan recited the information to her after she freed a pen from the banded bundle. Ramon was going to be at the airport in Myrtle Beach on August twenty-seventh. Was there more than one airport there? She'd find out.

"Weird that they would call his home if he's traveling. Wouldn't they call his cell, too?" Stefan said.

"Maybe I should call him and say I just happened to hear it while being here."

Stefan shrugged. "Maybe his cell was off and it rolled to a secondary number."

"Right."

"Okay, so now you know where he'll be, but not the guy you need to talk to."

"Or if he's still in touch with the guy I need to talk to."

They stared at the now quiet answering machine that flashed the number one. "So what now?" Kellan asked. "Big deal. I know what time he's getting on a plane in Myrtle Beach."

Stefan mulled it over. "Well, you're too chicken to call him, and face time might be better for something of this nature."

"When he finds out I was here, listening to his answering machine on purpose, he'll have Melissa fire me, and call a locksmith."

He nodded. "But he might know your guy well enough to give you some pointers on how to approach him."

"But would he even listen to me?" Kellan pocketed the note and replaced the pencil.

"Timers," Stefan reminded.

She headed to the living room to change them.

"So, you go to Myrtle Beach--it's a good excuse to get out of town--and you explain the situation, get whatever you can out of him. If he wants his key back, oh well, you lose this job, which would be a shame because," he sucked in a breath, "the smell alone is amazing. But if he knows your guy at all, he might be able to give you some idea how he'll react."

It was a weak plan admittedly, a tightrope over a canyon crevice. But if she fell, it would be over quickly.

Taking risks had never been Kellan's fear, but feeling stupid and gullible made her nervous. Pursuing this quest seemed to fall in the category of complete and utter humiliation, with possibly a crushing emotional collapse for Tony. But the more she thought about his brother's persistence; she could not help but be drawn to do it. This was one of those things she couldn't seem to get out of, like oral surgery. She could put it off until the pain was unbearable, but inevitably it had to be done. If Mr. DeSantos wigged out on her, told her that it would be catastrophic for her to approach Tony, then she'd have to think of some other way. For now, this was all she had.

* * *

"Hello, Atlanta," Jerrik Rayner called into the microphone. "In case you hadn't heard, we're *The Ruined*."

Screams surrounded him. The fragrance of marijuana teased his senses and a cloud formed that filtered the light beams. A smaller venue than he was accustomed to, but he liked the intimacy. Six thousand seats filled mostly with women; blonde women. Who knew America had so many blondes? They all seemed the same somehow. Dyed hair, push-up bras or none at all, clothes two sizes too small, tattoos, too much face paint, and abnormally white teeth. They moved as one, flesh pressing flesh, arms in the air, swaying to his melody, singing along with the lyrics as if they shared some deep personal connection to the music. He felt as if he were watching a performance instead of being the performer.

That was how it was sometimes, looking over the throng of life trying to share his experience, as if he set the dominoes in motion with one cord from his guitar.

Once off stage, he sat in an open room with some folding chairs and fluorescent lights glowing a green. Soothing his raw cords with beer, he listened to the boys laugh, talk about select women from the crowd, what a great show they put on, and how grateful they were that the boss had planned the next day off so they could plot a little play before the bus pushed on to the next city. Jerrik felt completely removed, a ghost in the corner eavesdropping. His head throbbed, his throat burned, and his heart beat in his ears.

Instead of joining his boys, he rummaged for a pen and, not finding any paper, wrote on the back of an eight-month-old flyer pulled from the wall stained with smoke and moisture. Moments like these were excruciating but golden. When he was sure he couldn't think at all, ink would pump from his pen, blood from a severed artery, alive, spelling him out, exposing his secrets seemingly against his will. The chaos, the conflict, the shame, the guilt, the glee, the moments of delirium, then sanity, the screaming rush to silence, his shivering, his lyric, his voice, all for the judgment of the world. Only after a couple hours of rest would he begin to mine the jewel in it.

But there would be no polishing of a new song this night. No completion of the raw expression of what turned his stomach, shriveled his appetite, and stole his sleep. Jerrik put his pen down.

He had an appointment in the morning. One he'd been looking forward to and dreading all the same. It took some finessing of the schedule, giving the band a night off before pressing on. A filmmaker was shooting a documentary on those left behind by people who committed suicide. He had turned it down at first, but the guy was American, and he hoped the chances of the film reaching his native Denmark were slim, even if it became popular. Their publicist would have done everything to derail his doing it, but there was something about the idea of being truly honest on camera that appealed to him. Jerrik got a good vibe from the guy on the phone, and after two years of silence, he was ready to talk to someone.

He certainly couldn't go into depth with his new girlfriend about the loss of his old love. For an American, Jade was such a breath of fresh air.

This would either be good therapy or his own undoing.

Chapter 16

Jerrik smoked in a generic hotel suite while Anthony worked on attaching a microphone to his shirt and concealing the licorice cord. He gave his long wavy locks a shake and shifted in his seat. He'd only done radio to this point and wasn't used to people touching him.

"I like that it's just you and not a roomful," Jerrik said.

"Too personal." Anthony focused on adjusting the camera. "Caught your show last night. I think you're the only band I've ever seen with an ironic name."

Jerrik smiled. "Should've told me you were coming. I'd have got you back stage."

"Maybe when I'm shooting a piece on the rigors of the road," Anthony said, tightening the tripod knobs.

"Yeah." Jerrik lit a fresh cigarette, and stared at the camera. His stomach felt empty, probably because he hadn't eaten since breakfast the day before. Food was the last thing on his mind right now. "This is. . .well, how can people go on talk shows with a live audience and talk about this?"

Anthony eyed him. "Some people, all they want to do is talk."

"First for me." He sucked long and hard on his cigarette. "My mother wanted me to see a doctor after. . .you know. Get it out."

"I'm told it helps some people."

Jerrik watched him. This guy had a secret behind those bright eyes. "Do you any good?"

Anthony met his gaze. They sized each other up for a long moment. Jerrik won.

"Not yet."

"Who was it for you then?" He was busy, this one, making equipment adjustments, pretending to be the consummate professional.

"My brother." Anthony looked away.

"How?"

"Let go of a building."

Jerrik nodded, letting a moment of silence go by. "You telling it on tape?"

Anthony looked at the wall while checking the knob on a tripod leg. "Haven't decided. We'll see if it does you any good first." He snapped on a bright light that faced a screen to Jerrik's left.

Jerrik didn't want to look at the great eye of the lens peering at him, but he really couldn't help it now. He spotted a little green light on the side near Anthony's hand.

"We're rolling. You can begin any time."

Jerrik fidgeted. "Where do you want me to start?"

"Wherever you're comfortable. Some people start at the end and work their way back. Some start as far back as they remember. Others go right to how they feel now."

"Well, that's a mess, isn't it? Not knowing where it starts? Been so long, it's just one long middle. There is no end, not for us." He looked at Anthony, who sat on the loveseat opposite and fingered a pen on a stack of oversized index cards. "They get to leave, get to be done with it. But we're still here, and it's still going." His voice trailed off as he sucked on his cigarette.

Anthony nudged him gently. "Tell me about Mia."

"Mia," he said with nostalgia, as if he were having a chat at a bar. "Twenty-four, college grad, nice family, big dreams. She wanted to sing back-up but didn't have the range. We didn't use back-ups. No girls allowed."

Jerrik appraised the neatly-put-together filmmaker and wondered how broken he was behind that facade.

"She went on the road with us, summer of '06, always accommodating, didn't want to put anyone out, or get in the way. Never bitched about women making passes, popping out a breast for me to autograph right in the street. She just watched, taking it all in. She was so. . ." he cocked his head at Anthony, "lovely. Not a jealous bone in her body. And patient. Took her sweet time in everything." He exhaled streams of gray through his nose. "And I do mean everything."

That drew a tiny curl from one corner of Anthony's mouth.

"She seemed to be the one who could handle it all." Jerrik looked at the window, distracted by a car alarm going off outside. Anthony motioned for him to wait, and when the noise stopped he nodded at him to continue.

"Did your brother leave a note?" Jerrik asked.

Anthony shook his head.

"Mia left a note." Jerrik paused. "I ask myself all the time if it wouldn't have been better if she hadn't, you know? She didn't say why, how, nothing. All she said was, 'I love you more than you'll ever know.'"

Anthony remained stoic, probably practiced.

"What does that mean? 'I love you so much, I can't stand it, so I'm killing myself?' Or was it, 'I love you, but we're apart too often?' Was she showing me how much? You don't know what you have until it's gone, kind of thing?" Jerrik leaned forward and pulled another cigarette from the pack on the coffee table, lit it with the smoldering butt, and eased back into his seat.

"She left me wanting for a love I'll never have. I get to walk around wondering why. Why would someone who ardently loved me leave me in such a horrific way? Course they do it to all of us, don't they? How could she leave her family in such pain? Leave us all to wonder if we could have done something to prevent it. If we had seen a sign, a clue, something, could we have saved her?

"I second-guess myself all the time, have flashes of little moments. Was it something I should have said, but didn't pay attention to? Something I should have pointed out or questioned? Or was I too preoccupied? What if I'd asked the right questions? Demanded answers?" Jerrik looked as deep into Anthony as he could. "Do they have any idea how badly they destroy us? Or was that their purpose?"

Anthony hadn't blinked in a while. Any ambient noise in the room had silenced: the mini-fridge stopped buzzing, the air conditioner stopped humming, and the furniture held itself more still. Everything held its breath.

"I never stop asking myself, was it something I didn't see? Something I didn't say? And would anything I could have done mattered, either way?"

Past the ribbon of smoke that danced toward the ceiling, Jerrik saw Anthony as a delicate figure of hand-blown glass about to topple from the edge of his chair. He also hid his pain well, swallowing it down like a dirty secret.

"How did she do it?" Anthony asked.

"Hung herself from the chandelier in my dining room. Funny thing was that she was the one that picked it out. Said the one I had was ghastly."

Anthony looked down at his cards.

Jerrik risked a question. "How do you cope?"

Anthony blinked, recognizing the question had been directed at him. He waved a hand as if he were brushing away a bug.

"You work." Jerrik fingered a string dangling from bottom of his shirt. "I write songs, sing my pain. It's small release. Work makes time go faster, doesn't it? So you can look back and congratulate yourself that you made it all these months and years with so much guilt, and you're still here." He rubbed his knee and leaned back into his seat. "Thought I was past the guilt, until I met someone."

Anthony straightened. "You're dating again?"

Jerrik smiled. "You think it bad?"

Again, Anthony waved him off.

"Life goes on for us. Why should I continue to be faithful to someone who had no faith in me? Mia left in the worst way possible. But then the guilt kicks in again. Like it was me and what if I have that effect on someone else? Don't think I haven't thought of that." He smoked for a long moment, looking away. "Jade reminds me of Mia sometimes. But she's older, and life knocked her hard a few times. Toughened her up.

"I'm caught between those who tell me I need to move on, and my own conscience. You start listening to them after a while. Little thoughts work on me, like; do I deserve to be happy with someone else? Because I was halfway round the world when Mia died. I couldn't have got to her if I'd wanted. That makes me feel like I shouldn't let myself get attached. What good could I be if I was really needed?"

Jerrik saw it again on Anthony's face, the fear that he might turn to dust if he drew too deep a breath. Jerrik pressed on without direction.

"We take it on ourselves like it was our fault we couldn't save them when, really, we weren't even aware they needed to be saved."

A long pause passed between them. Anthony's eyes grew spooky.

Jerrik sighed. "I didn't anyway. What with recording, promotional dates, touring, writing new material. I had no idea. Mia was my sanctuary. She made all the bullshit go away. She just knew how to take it all and make me feel normal."

He sucked a cigarette that crackled so loudly he was sure Anthony could hear the flames inside it.

"They did some ridiculous survey--determined we Danes are the happiest people in the world, what with our government, housing, health, stress-free lifestyle." He laughed. It sounded fake, and Jerrik hated sounding fake. "Like we live in Disneyland, and no one could ever think of being miserable." He thumbed a hunk of ash into the ashtray. "We're only human, programmed to seek happiness and purpose. Well, I think we have purpose. For better or worse, might be wise to make the best of things."

Anthony turned over some cards and asked, "Do you think suicide is a crime? Or do you think it's a sin?"

Jerrik shook his head. "Don't believe in sin. There is only experience. Everyone's experience is subjective. We can only make decisions based on how we interpret our experience. It's a crime to those who remain. But who do we punish for it?"

Anthony didn't look at his cards. "Some would theorize that whatever drives a person to end his or her life might not necessarily be a choice."

"You mean mental illness?"

Anthony didn't respond.

Jerrik rubbed his stubble. "I suppose, but not with Mia, unless it was sudden like a knock on the head or an aneurism. I had a friend who knew someone he thought was possessed."

"You think that's possible?"

"Anything is possible," Jerrik said. "But nobody can prove it, can they?"

* * *

When Jerrik was gone, Anthony cued up a spreadsheet on his laptop to make notes of the recording. He added Jerrik's name to the bottom, and in the reason column he typed: unknown. Most of his list consisted of unknowns. Some offered speculations that included mental illness, substance abuse, depression, abnormal reaction to medication, financial ruin, exposed or unexposed secrets such as infidelity, sexual deviance, terminal disease, and murder. Things ate away at people, causing a psychological death perceived to be far greater than any physical one. For some there was no return from being a pariah.

What was Connor's affliction? Anthony had never known his brother to try recreational drugs, and none had appeared in the autopsy. No medication either, even though his therapist had given him a prescription sleep-aid. Anthony had not known Connor to overindulge in anything. Money had been a concern out of college, but there was no evidence of a gambling problem, or any situation that could generate enough fear. Everyone worried about not having enough money, didn't they? He had broken up with a girlfriend a couple months before, but had not exhibited such deep despair that suicide would have been suspect. With no mental illness in the family history, the only category left was secrets.

Secrets could be scary, and everyone had them. Whatever Connor's secret, he took it to the grave. Was he involved in something dangerous? Was someone threatening him, holding something over him? Did he witness something that had him scared? Anthony knew that *what* was not as important as *why*.

Anthony had to ask himself who he would trust with his deepest, darkest secrets. These days it was hard to trust anyone. Anthony had achieved a level of professional success that everyone seemed to want a piece of. People called it networking, but to Anthony it felt covetous. Had someone wanted something from Connor he hadn't been willing to give? Twenty years and no new clues had surfaced, no one had come forward with a great reveal, no former lover had come forward clutching to her breast his brother's dirty secret.

So why, after all this time, did he still wonder about an answer he would never have?

Chapter 17

"That's your answer?" Gayle stood on the sidewalk holding a crate of bleach while Kellan shoveled out the El Camino.

"I'll only be gone a couple days."

"But where are you going?"

Kellan did not want to have this conversation. Gayle was behaving as if they were still a couple and she owed him an explanation.

"What are you, my dad?" Kellan said, opening the passenger door.

"Just a question anybody would ask. One my fiancée wouldn't have had a problem answering."

"I'm not your fiancée. You deserve better. Ask anyone in this town."

Gayle went to the driver's door and leaned on the roof. "You know, things were going great until you went to that stupid séance. Now everything has been shot straight to hell."

He had a point. "It wasn't the séance, but what it brought out of us." Kellan scooped crumpled food wrappers, hair bands, and wadded up napkins from under the seat.

"Kellan, talking to a dead guy is not normal for anybody. You can't just expect me to pretend it doesn't bother me. But I've been willing to stick by you until you can get past it and be yourself again."

She backed out of the car and faced him over the roof. He was under the impression that this was just a temporary situation, a fascination that she would outgrow. Basically, he didn't believe her. Her understanding of his point of view didn't make it any easier.

"I don't know if it's possible to get past, Gayle. I'm a believer now. I will never again tell anyone who has lost someone that they automatically go to a better place." She stuffed her trash into a small shopping bag.

"Baby, I don't care if you believe that stuff."

Kellan took a pause. "Gee, thanks."

Gayle straightened. "I just don't like you letting it interfere in your life, is all."

"No, you don't want it interfering in *your* life. So now it won't." She opened her white tailgate, in contrast with the navy paint that covered the rest of the El Camino, and started digging through the milk crates. Gayle was not going away and stepped from the curb to hover over her. "This whole thing has changed me."

"What does that mean?" His voice was low.

Good question. How did she answer that? "Remember when you found out you were good at tracking down engine noises on tractors? You told me you could pinpoint exactly what it was so you could fix it?"

He screwed up his face.

"Well, maybe this is what I'm good at. I have to find out."

Gayle's face lightened as he stared at her. "Find out what?"

"Who," she said. "It's a who."

"Sweet Jesus."

She held up a hand. "I know how it sounds, but I've been over it a million times, and I know most people won't understand, but. . ." she sighed, "I have to see a guy. . .about a dead guy."

Gayle stepped back as if she had just burst into flame. "Tell me you're joking. Come on, you're not seriously going to tell some poor bastard you see his dead brother."

"Not if I can avoid it, but there are things he needs to know," she said, repacking a crate with cleaning supplies.

"Just avoid it then. Why in God's name would you even consider doing something like this?"

"I was asked to."

"Well, I asked you to marry me, but you're not doing that," he raised his voice. "Do I have to be dead, too?"

"Not fair." Kellan put her hand on her hip. "I don't want to hurt anybody with this, and I don't expect you to be supportive here. But I have to see this through to the end."

"The end of what?" Gayle was heated. "What good can come of this, Kellan? You're going to scare the hell out of this guy. And he's just going to think you're nuts."

She snapped at him. "The whole town thinks I'm nuts. What's one more?"

He pulled the crate from her reach and grabbed her by the arms to face him. "Listen to me now. You cannot do this. Baby, you're only going to hurt an innocent man. No good can--"

"Can come of this, so you've said already." Kellan pulled away. "I can still hear the living too, you know."

"Can you? Or it is just me you don't want to hear?"

She met his glare before she grabbed the crate and slid it into the corner of the truck bed by the wheel well. "Cut it out. This has nothing to do with you."

"Really? The woman I planned on marrying has turned into somebody I don't even know. She is going off to completely derail a stranger's life - make a fool of herself - and won't listen to anything I have to say about it. But that has nothing to do with me?" His voice was higher than she'd ever heard it go. "I am asking you to think this through. If you ever cared about me, don't do this."

"How is this about you?" Kellan snapped. "This is not subject to your input. This is not a decision that you are even part of. I didn't even ask for your advice."

Hurt washed over his face as he gathered himself. "No, you didn't. Now I know where I stand, don't I? I only wanted to protect you."

"You can't. People getting mad at me is not a new experience."

"I meant, protect you from yourself," he said slowly. "Tell me something, why this guy? What is so damned important about this guy?"

Kellan didn't answer. There would be no point.

He took a step back. "God's honest truth, you got me starting to wonder, maybe a dead kid isn't all you picked up."

"You think what you need to." She slammed the tailgate shut.

"Fine, you're going to crash and burn. I think you are in for a serious fall." He hung his head and sighed. "And I'm not going to be the dumb ass who sticks around to pick you back up."

"I don't need you--" She stopped, struck by how ugly it sounded. An uncomfortable silence vibrated between them like a high voltage power line.

Gayle snapped out of his shock and leaned in to whisper, "Well, I don't need you either." Then he walked to his truck, climbed in, and left without looking back.

Kellan's stomach lurched. He was just trying to protect her. Truth was Kellan liked him wanting to protect her. It felt warm and safe. Her heart was completely deflated. The sense of belonging to someone was appealing. Gayle was wonderful in so many ways, but she had learned the hard way love wasn't enough. The kindest thing she could do for him now was walk away. Free the nice church boy to find a nice church girl his Momma would approve of. Didn't mean it felt good.

Kellan waited until his truck was out of sight before curling up in her driver's seat for a good self-pitying sob. She was alone again. There was no one to prevent her from heading down a path paved with humiliation.

*　*　*

Anthony tapped away at his laptop in the dark of his motel room. The eleven o'clock news played on the television with the sound turned low. Tragedy abounded. A man had leapt from the fourth floor of a burning building. The baby he had thrown before him had been caught by neighbors. He had not been as lucky. At least he'd had a reason for taking the leap.

His mind reached back to Connor. What could have been going through his brother's mind for him to do such a thing? Then Anthony tried to remember details of his face: the serious brow when he was engrossed in conversation, the dimples in his smiling cheeks, and the flashing eyes when he was messing around. Connor had known he was witty and charming. Anthony remembered how apparent it could be in his voice.

Yet there remained so many unanswered questions. Why did Connor go to their mother's to jump? Why not just do it in the privacy of his own apartment? And why didn't anyone pick up any warning signs?

Anthony had visited Connor's therapist before the funeral. The doctor had returned a journal he'd asked Connor to keep. Neither it nor Connor had been revealing.

"I can't help what I can't see. Connor had trouble sleeping. I tried to get him to open up." The doctor had finished with a sympathetic head shake.

Connor's ex-girlfriend couldn't offer anything more than, "He got moody sometimes."

The rest of his friends were equally bewildered. No one knew what had prompted Connor to take the leap.

Anthony opened an empty file labeled with his brother's initials. Dr. Baumgartner suggested trying to "productively expressing anger" in an ongoing letter to Connor. What a ridiculous waste of time. Hadn't Connor's therapist already proven that technique ineffective?

Why didn't you leave a note? What were you afraid of? Why didn't you ask for help? Anthony shook his head, but typed nothing. *Why didn't you come to me? Why did you think ending your life was the only way?* So much for expressing anger. Maybe he didn't have any left. Anthony had half a dozen projects going, and didn't have time for someone who didn't bother thinking of him. He typed: *You left me here, Asshole.*

Anthony needed to get back to work. Vacations bored him. What did normal people do? How could they find happiness lying on beaches, stuffing their faces, and sucking down boat drinks? What could possibly hold their attention while they were doing it? Anthony had never been a good tourist. When he traveled, he wanted to get dirty, venture into the dregs, and photograph the dark corners. His eyes never stopped searching for the perfect shot, that right mix of light and shadow that delivered a complete story in one perfect image.

If he wasn't shooting, he was writing. Everyone had a script, but Anthony had stacks. So much to tell people willing to sit in a safe, clean, climate-controlled environment, to open their eyes to a world they had missed by never venturing far from comfort. But his ideas had proven too depressing for the entertainment industry.

"People want this, they can watch the news," they told him. "They want to leave the theater happy, uplifted. They get plenty of reality at home."

His stories weren't oozing with sweet success and happy endings. They were based in reality, and Hollywood dealt in box office, not reality.

You're always working.

Work was the oxygen he couldn't live without.

* * *

Kellan didn't do much night driving but wanted to reach Myrtle Beach in plenty of time before Ramon's flight. But what would she do when she arrived? Camp inside the terminal like a stalker and try to talk to him there? Casually bump into him as if she just happened to be in the same place? Walk up to him and just blurt it out?

"You know that guy you worked with on that prison documentary? Well, I need to get him a message from his brother. Yes, the one that died twenty years ago."

This was why she didn't write mysteries. Her brain didn't work in covert ways. She was thinking too hard and thinking something to death was one of her talents. Kellan could turn a thought over in her mind like a rotisserie chicken until it fell from the bone. And there was always a greasy mess to clean up after.

Both she and the El Camino needed fuel, so she exited the highway to find the Sheetz that was displayed on the blue highway sign. Sheetz was the perfect all-in-one stop. Open twenty-four hours, it always had clean restrooms. Gas was reasonably priced and hot sandwiches were made-to-order. Clarity might come with an empty bladder and a full stomach. She filled up first then pulled into a space in the side parking area away from the pumps. Inside she ordered a hot turkey and cheese with double meat to share with the dog. She hit the ladies room while the sandwich was being prepared. The wind had picked up outside. The radio weather report told her a cold front was on the way and she was glad she'd remembered her sweatshirt. Summer was ending.

Back in her truck, Riley inhaled pieces of sandwich picked off for him. Kellan had learned that eating while driving was a bad idea as the slightest wrong move on her steering wheel sent the El Camino off-road. She was fatigued and didn't want to think of the task ahead. Kellan had no clue about what to do when she arrived. Not a one.

Something blew by the rearview mirror that drew her attention. Her eyes searched around to spot the silhouette of a man stepping from the rungs of a ladder that reached to a lit marquee. The white board above the gas prices advertised specials. She watched as the man retrieved sheets of pliable plastic and re-climbed the ladder dragging a staff hooked to the back of his pants. Letter by letter he spelled out BOGO cupcakes. Instantly she was back in her kitchen before the chocolate cupcake, blowing out the birthday candle that she was convinced had set this whole mess in motion.

The rational part of her said things like, "A candle on a cupcake did not create your problem."

The not-so-rational, grasp-any-straw part said, "What have you got to lose?"

Kellan finished her sandwich, hit the overhead light, and pulled out a 2004 Road Atlas from beneath the seat. Main highways probably had not changed much in four years. She placed her finger on Myrtle Beach and back-tracked while searching for the most direct route. Near Florence, South Carolina there were two possibilities. Kellan measured the distance of both with a pen and chose the shortest. Now she had to come up with a plan of attack. Okay, poor choice of words, but true all the same.

Gathering her trash, she climbed out into the wind to head inside for her cupcakes.

"No birthday candles," the kid behind the register said. "We got emergency stick candles."

"Too big," she said. "Any stick matches?"

He picked around behind the counter, and then tossed her a plain white book of flat ones. "All we got."

Good thing there wasn't a birthday emergency. She pocketed the matchbook, and went back to the El Camino where Riley wagged his tail in anticipation. He'd have to settle for one of the peanut butter biscuits she'd brought from home.

Back in the truck, she placed one of the two cupcakes on the dash and crumpled up the top of the bag with the other. Riley homed in on the mound of sugary goodness. Might as well have been a live cat. If he had known how to use The Force, it would have been down his gullet before she got the door closed.

"Don't even think about it, Bud."

Entranced, he continued his vigil and started to drool, completely ignoring the biscuit she'd placed on a napkin for him.

Kellan pulled a gray paper matchstick from the pack and planted it in the frosting of the carrot cupcake, telling herself not to be superstitious it wasn't chocolate. One had to work with what was available. The match might burn for forty-five seconds before melting in a pool of sugar, so she had to be quick, clear, and concise. Nothing could be left to chance.

Now, what did she want to happen here?

She really wanted to be home, writing a fictional story that had nothing to do with any real person. She wanted to be the cleaning lady who spoke English, not the one who talked to the dead. She wanted to have Gayle over for dinner and a movie like they used to do before her life was churned up like a pond full of silt. But there was no rewinding the events that brought her to this moment. No wishing away the past. Kellan could only wish for the future, to be able to deliver Connor's message without his brother dismissing it completely.

After rehearsing the words, she struck another matchstick to light the one on the cupcake. "Please let me find a way to tell Tony. Let him be open to hearing Connor's message for the truth of its intention. Let there be a peaceful resolution for everyone involved. For this, I will be grateful."

And she blew the matchstick out.

Chapter 18

"If you died tomorrow, would you go to Heaven?"

A pair of conservatively dressed African-American women stood proudly before the camera holding their wallet-sized leaflets.

A green sweater clung for dear life to the heavier woman while she adjusted a severe set of rhinestone studded glasses and tried not to smile too big. "Only those who live by the Word and fully accept Jesus Christ as their Lord and Savior go to Heaven."

Her shorter, slightly older companion in a periwinkle pantsuit nodded throughout her friend's statement.

Anthony knew he had to be careful here, but he needed to ask. "What about indigenous people who don't know anything about your faith, who might worship things like the sun?"

"Well, the sun would be a false god. But if they don't know about Christ, it's not their fault. They're uneducated in the ways of the Lord and He looks into their hearts."

"So God gives them a pass then?"

The ladies looked at each other for validation before answering. "The Lord looks at their deeds and their thoughts, then decides."

Her companion nodded like a bobble head.

"What about children in this country, say, not brought up in a religious home? What happens to them if they die?"

"If they're baptized, they go straight to Heaven."

"And if they aren't?"

"Well, those go to a purgatory where they can learn and earn their way to Heaven."

"Learn and earn." Anthony looked over his shoulder at the camera then back to the duo. "So I'm assuming you believe in some form of life after death, if you believe in Heaven."

"When God calls you, you go to the light to live with Him in His Kingdom."

The nodding one spoke. "Praise Jesus."

"The Kingdom of Heaven is the ultimate reward. Do you believe in the Word of God, Mister Clarke?"

Here we go. Anthony glanced at A.J. who tapped Ramon--his cue to stop taping.

"In this project, we are documenting the belief in an afterlife, not necessarily individual faith. It's our job to gather data and ask questions without infusing our own personal views or ideas."

The nodding one was slightly indignant when she said, "A good Christian lives the Word in all that he does. Not like the folks taking prayer from the schools and 'under God' from the Pledge of Allegiance." With that she turned and marched away, leaving her sparkly companion to do the nodding and waving.

"Thank you, ladies," Anthony called after them, "for your time."

A.J. watched them go. "Lord, have mercy on our souls."

"We heard back from Eddie's aunt?"

Eddie piped up. "I got a message from my mom. Amy's in Ireland for two weeks. Pub tour."

Anthony sighed with envy. A pub tour would not suck right now. He grumbled to A.J. as she pulled the microphone clip from his shirt. "Have I mentioned I hate this project?"

She checked her watch. "Not in thirty-six minutes."

Eddie wound the microphone cord. "Maybe you should ask what they think is going to happen to them when they die."

Everyone paused to look at him.

"You know, instead of asking if they believe in an afterlife or Heaven. That way it won't sound like you don't."

Anthony watched him resume packing up equipment. He felt self-conscious now and looked at Ramon. "I sound like I don't?"

Ramon gave a shrug. "Well, you don't so."

"When did I say that?" Anthony asked.

A.J. walked past him. "You're kidding, right?"

Anthony's stomach growled. Maybe he was hungry, or maybe the idea of his father and brother sitting on a cloud somewhere, eating popcorn, watching him as if he were the star of his own reality show, disturbed it. "This is stupid. Nobody really knows anyway. There's no proof of life after death. It's probably something misfiring in the brain when we're on the way out. Like a battery dying."

Ramon picked up the camera case and fell in step with him. "Maybe that's why you got this assignment. So you could figure out what you believe."

"You a God's Plan man?"

"Nope. I think we make our own plans."

"But you believe in reincarnation, which is another term for afterlife, right?" Anthony said.

Ramon snapped the latches down on his hard shell camera case. "I figure, having to work with you on this, I owe you big for some past life misdeed." He smiled. "Maybe I knocked up the daughter you were hoping to marry off for territorial rights."

"Thanks, man."

He patted Anthony on the back. "I owed you."

Van loaded, they were on the move. A.J. sat drumming her pen on the clipboard in her lap. Anthony checked his email on his Blackberry but could feel A.J.'s repressed energy.

"What?"

She chewed a thumbnail. "What?"

"You're gnawing on yourself."

"So?"

"So, what?" He looked over his Blackberry at her.

"Before those women," A.J. pointed, not meeting his eyes, "studio called. They want to see where we are."

Network suits. Yes, they financed the operation but really didn't have much of a clue about field work. Anthony felt his gut flip. "Did you stall?"

Her accusing look said it all. "We have enough."

Anthony rolled his head back on the seat. He met Eddie's eyes in the rearview mirror. "They'll hate it. It's too impersonal. We need a personal experience, not religious rhetoric, or shadowy video. Ed's aunt swearing that she's seen the face of God, and not on the side of a building in New Jersey."

Ramon looked back at him. "We got two hours to the next stop."

Anthony took a deep broken breath. "Let's find some food, piece together a teaser, facts only. Stay with the cardiologist and researcher. Leave the paranormal dude out for now."

Ramon and Eddie shared a look. "He was the only one with video."

Anthony ignored them. "Are we headed east?"

Eddie saluted him in the rearview.

Anthony looked out the window at the never-ending sprawl of green fields. He didn't want to think anymore.

"Give me a few minutes to think?"

Eddie raised an eyebrow. Everyone exchanged glances as

Anthony closed his eyes and slouched down in his seat.

A couple deep breaths later Anthony felt plush carpet on his bare feet as he tip-toed down the stairs of his parent's apartment. He was conscious of the rustling of his pajamas, and the need to purposely quiet them. Light and shadow licked the wall. The flames came from candles in the dining room. Anthony held his breath down each stair and strained to hear what the adults were saying. His mother had guests. Anthony had chosen not to invite his brother, whose sense of propriety would have interfered with his mission. Guilt crept in his stomach. His father would not have approved of his spying either, and Anthony wished more than anything he would be there to snatch him up by the shirt and trundle him back to his room. But his father would never be there again.

Something solid scraped against the table. The sound lured Anthony further down the steps until the group was visible. Finally, he saw the four of them, arms outstretched, sliding an upside-down bar tumbler around the table. Weird. What did they think they were doing? Naomi sat across from a short, plump woman in a peacock feathered jacket. Next to her sat an older gentleman he recognized as one of his mother's artsy friends who didn't seem to like children. A woman sat with her back to him so he could not see her face, and he didn't recognize her long brown hair.

"Yes," the woman in the peacock feathers said. "Someone is here."

His mother whispered, "Cyrus?"

The scraping sound came again as they slid the glass to the other side of the table.

"No."

Anthony leaned as far into the banister posts as they would allow without crushing his skull.

"Please state your name?"

More movement of the glass.

"H."

The scraping continued for what felt like hours until they spelled out the name Howard.

"Howard who?"

Anthony had grown bored and sleepy through the painfully long letter-by-letter process. He wondered if his father had found this as excruciating as he, or if he was forever asleep.

Movement startled Anthony, as if someone had thrown a big

black blanket at him.

When he found light again, Connor was grown; looking exactly as he had the last time Anthony had seen him alive. Connor crouched on the floor in front of him looking so real Anthony reached out, and jerked awake. The only thing in front of him was the back of the driver's seat. Next to him A.J. tapped at her Blackberry. Up front, Eddie and Ramon lip--synced the words to the Van Morrison song on the radio: *Into the Mystic*.

* * *

Kellan had pulled into a state rest stop so Riley could have a sniff and stretch. The radio kept her company while she searched the map to assure that she had chosen the best route. After checking the door locks, she closed her eyes for a short nap. A familiar old Van Morrison song took her to the past, but not her own.

Connor picked at an acoustic guitar, teaching himself to play by ear, and wasn't half bad in the pieces he repeated. He stopped, made notes on a small pad, and resumed strumming without noticing her presence.

Kellan moved to the shelves that housed a turntable and a sizable collection of vinyl LPs. Eighties covers flashed before her eyes: The Ramones, The Clash, Quiet Riot's *Metal Health*, The Cure, Fleetwood Mac's *Rumors*, and Van Morrison's *Moon Dance*. Quite a mix of rock and punk, but one stood out like it didn't belong--Neil Diamond.

"How do you go from *Metal Health* to *The Jazz Singer?*"

Connor, oblivious to her presence, plucked out a staggered melody.

"Your make-out music?" she grinned. "Gift from a girlfriend?"

Judging by the size of his collection, music was high on his list of priorities. She looked at the notepad on the ottoman in front of him.

His handwriting was a very small and messy cursive. While she debated the ethics of getting close enough to actually read it, the sound of a tractor trailer releasing its air brakes pulled her back to her own world.

* * *

168

Kellan was smart enough to figure out that ambushing Ramon at an airport terminal would be a stupid move.

Jade's advice had been brief. "Call him first. See if he'll meet you somewhere." She had nothing more to offer in terms of what Kellan should say to him. "When the time comes, you'll know what to say. The words will just come out."

Sure, they will. Kellan made the call, but could not remember what she had said. Ramon sounded tentative and, after being reassured that nothing had gone awry at his apartment building, agreed to meet with her.

The IHOP on State Road 17 was easy to find. Kellan sat in a booth watching the TV overhead run highlights from a US Open tennis match. Kellan would have traded anything to be sweating her butt off on a tennis court. How did she get here? Kellan had no idea how to sell Ramon on putting her together with Tony or better yet, volunteer to tell him for her. Yeah, that'll happen. She resigned herself to losing him as a client but it wouldn't matter. Her cleaning business seemed to be drying up. Having uncovered his mystery occupation, Kellan wished their meeting was to talk of the many places he had worked. Asking a man how he'd feel about her giving a message from a dead kid to a colleague would never have been on her list of topics for discussion.

Kellan's heart skipped when a tall, hard-bodied Latin man glided in, pulling off a pair of Oakley's. This was the guy from the picture Melissa had in her file. He was definitely worth a look. Ramon DeSantos looked even better than his apartment smelled. His faded jeans and tight black T-shirt painted all his muscles, which only made what she had to do even harder. His approach was cautious, nervous even, but his smile was cordial as he extended his hand.

"You Kellan?"

Kellan took his hand hoping she didn't look terrified. "Mr. DeSantos, it's nice to meet you. Thank you for coming. I know I didn't give you much of an explanation, but it's not the kind of thing you discuss over the phone."

"Nice shirt." He nodded at the Grateful Dead T-shirt she wore for his easy identification. "How do you know Anthony?"

"I don't," she said, studying his reaction. "But I met his brother."

He sat back. Was he doing the math in his head? Did he even know his co-worker had a brother?

"How well do you know him?" she asked. "I mean, obviously

169

you've worked together."

"Still do. Ten years, maybe."

She could see he was unsure of where this might lead. Might as well just come out with it. "I need to talk to him about something rather sensitive, and I was hoping you might be able to gauge his reaction, help me determine how to approach him."

He sucked in a breath. "Okay." Ramon sat back sliding his hands from the table into his lap: a sign of discomfort. As she was about to spit it out, the waitress came by and they ordered coffee. Ramon's eyes never left Kellan's.

She swallowed, hoping the turmoil in her stomach wouldn't decide to cause an eruption. "At the risk of your thinking I'm crazy, and losing you as a client, I'm just going to lay it on you and hope for the best."

He didn't move.

Rubbing the top of her legs like magic lamps, Kellan steadied her breathing as best she could. "Anthony's brother died twenty years ago."

He glanced around as if his memory was just now catching up with him. "I knew that. Killed himself."

Kellan drew herself up. "At least, that was how it appeared."

He didn't move as she waited for him to fully absorb her words.

"What do you mean? He was murdered?"

"Not in the traditional sense, but. . ."

"Wait, wasn't his mom there?"

"She saw him go, but not what made him do it."

Ramon squinted one eye. "What made him do it?"

Kellan was careful to keep eye contact. Here was the tricky part. She spoke very carefully. "Something dark, not of this world."

Ramon shifted in his seat and glanced out the window as if he wished it would open so he could fly out. "What?"

"Did you see the movie *The Sixth Sense?*"

He furrowed his brow. "*I see dead people?*" It took a moment, but then it was all over his face. "You see dead people?"

She stared, hoping that if she didn't blink no tears would escape.

He sputtered out a laugh before his smile slowly melted away. "And you think you see Anthony's brother?"

She sighed. "Actually, I hear him a lot more than I see him."

He laughed hard and tapped the table with both hands. "You're screwing with me, right?" He looked around at the other patrons as if he expected Ashton Kutcher to reveal that he'd been *Punk'd*. "This is payback for New Orleans, isn't it? You and Anthony set this up."

Okay, he wasn't screaming from the building, but he wasn't buying it either. This was bad. Kellan searched the nicks in the resin tabletop for answers. His laugh faded when the waitress appeared with their coffee. It took a minute to pour them both a cupful and set down the plastic pot.

"Have you decided?" she asked.

Ramon sobered when he saw that Kellan was not laughing with him.

The waitress looked to Kellan who waved her hand. The moment the girl walked away Kellan leaned over the table and lowered her voice. "I know how crazy this sounds. But before Connor showed up, I had never heard of these people. Imagine my surprise when I connected him to you."

"So you called someone at the network, found out Anthony's assigned to a piece on the afterlife, so you thought you'd get on TV, right?"

It took her a moment to process his accusation, but when she got it, she was mortified. "No! God, no. You think I want to be on television with this? I'm already losing my business because of this."

"Then a little free publicity wouldn't hurt right about now."

"Hold on, Tony's doing a show on the afterlife?" Kellan's mind flew back to typing the first scene she'd typed out about Anthony and his crew being reassigned from a story on grave recycling.

Ramon frowned and slid to the end of the bench. He wasn't buying her ignorance.

"Wait, please. You're my only connection to him."

"You're nuts, lady." He launched himself from the booth.

"He's having chest pains."

Ramon stopped.

Kellan tapped her chest. "He's eating antacids like candy, thinking his problem is too much junk food. He doesn't sleep much either."

It hung in the air like a gunshot. Ramon examined Kellan hard. He eased back onto the edge of the bench leaning over the table as if he was ready to grab her by the neck.

"You some kind of stalker or something?"

"Five minutes is all I ask."

He gestured for her to get it over with.

Kellan rubbed her cup handle not knowing what to say.

"When you see something unimaginable, there's nothing that will convince you that what you saw wasn't exactly what you know you saw."

His face was one big question mark.

"People who have seen a UFO, the Loch Ness monster, Big Foot, go to their graves absolutely convinced that they know what they saw, no matter what any expert tells them. Just because there is no scientific evidence to prove it, doesn't mean it's not real."

Silence passed between them. Ramon shrugged for her to continue.

"I don't know how or why, but I've got a twenty-three-year-old kid named Connor following me around, showing me things from his childhood, and wanting me to talk to his brother. I said, no way, I didn't want to risk hurting anyone. I almost had myself talked into this being my imagination. But then I found out Connor actually existed, and he has a brother still living who once worked with you. Now, if you were me, what would you do with that?"

Ramon gritted his teeth. "Get my head examined." He sat back and looked away, but didn't get up to leave. Finally, he spoke again. "He'll want some sort of proof. His work is about exposing truth. That's what documentaries do. They document facts, point the finger of accountability, if necessary. Hold people to the facts." He bit down hard on the last word.

"The truth is out there." She smiled for a nanosecond. "*X-Files.*"

He stared at her like she'd spoken some form of Pig Latin.

"Truth," Kellan swallowed, "is subjective. Everyone's truth is different. Look, I don't have any proof. No documentation. No photos, nothing physical, but I do have a lot of information that I've been writing down. What if he can verify some of it? What if they are facts for him?"

Ramon stared at the table, the muscles in his arms tensing as if he were trying to suppress the urge to pull her out of her seat by her hair.

Kellan continued before she lost him. "I mean, I've never met either of them. How could I possibly know that when Tony was six he split his lip open Christmas morning by the train set, or that he kept a list of places he wanted to travel to based on where his globe stopped under his finger, or that he and his brother got in trouble for putting a tree frog in their cousin's bed at some beach house?"

172

"Anthony," he corrected her. "Nobody calls him Tony."

"Connor does. Did."

Ramon's face darkened. "Even if you're right, what good would it do to tell a guy that his brother's ghost knows he's having chest pains? I can't believe I just said that out loud."

Kellan shook her head and reached a hand across the table. "No, no. I wouldn't tell him that and risk it becoming a self-fulfilled prophesy. I can mention he's been tired, not getting enough sleep, and maybe could use a vacation."

The look on Ramon's face was grave.

"Connor's not a ghost. Well, I don't know what he is, but he didn't even know he was dead." Kellan kept going. "Maybe if Anthony knows his brother is still around, he won't feel so isolated. Maybe he'll deal with stuff he hasn't all these years."

"How comforting." Ramon shook his head and sat back. "Your dead brother, who killed himself, is worried about you. Rational."

Kellan didn't like how it sounded either.

He pointed at the table. "And how is he isolated? The guy is out there, chasing stories all the time. From what I've seen, he's pretty well-adjusted."

"We all wear masks. He got addicted to work to avoid facing his grief. And he's got suppressed anger lurking around his subconscious."

"You're a mind reader now?"

"Hey, do I look thrilled here?" Kellan raised her voice. "You think this is fun for me? You think I woke up this morning and said, 'Hey, I know, I'll turn a perfect stranger's life inside out? Pour salt in an ancient wound because I just don't have enough excitement in my own life?'"

Kellan noticed how quiet the restaurant had become by her outburst. Ramon shifted in his seat and looked down his nose at her.

Kellan surrendered in a lower tone. "I know we've just met, and I have no right to ask you for any favors here. But I'm out on a limb, and I'm being totally honest, no matter how psychotic it sounds."

He leaned over the table. "Lady, I don't know that you didn't huff so much cleaning fluid the functioning part of your brain is fried. Or maybe you slipped in the shower, took a blow to the head."

"Right," she nodded in defeat. "Fine, will you just think about it, please? There has to be some way you can put us together without him thinking badly of you. He wouldn't even have to know we know each other."

"We don't know each other," Ramon snapped.

She was embarrassed now. "I have to talk to him whether you help me or not. But he might actually listen if he had someone he trusted--" she stopped. "Forget it. Sorry to waste your time."

Kellan threw five dollars on the table for the coffee and stood. "I can understand your not wanting any involvement here, but I would appreciate your not warning him away before I can talk to him."

Ramon waved a hand and turned away.

Chapter 19

Ramon's head hurt as he stared out the window at the parking lot. The chick who cleaned his apartment thinks she sees dead people. And not just any dead person, oh no, Anthony's dead brother. How could she sit there and pretend not to know anything about what they were doing? She just happened to know he'd be in South Carolina? The lengths the whack-jobs will go for attention. He pulled out his phone to search for his realtor's number. They needed to screen their subcontractors better. And to think he was considering asking Melissa out. She was probably best friends with the whack-job.

Ramon stopped scrolling through his calls when a tiny little detail flickered in his mind. "He's having chest pains." Anthony had been massaging his chest, eating antacids like mints, and mentioning heartburn. How did she know that? Was she following them around with binoculars? But what if those regular little episodes actually added up to something?

Much as he hated the idea of saying anything to Anthony, he hated not warning him more. If he kept his mouth shut and Anthony dropped dead of a heart attack, he would hate that even more. Then *he* would be the haunted crazy person.

Anthony had ignored him when he'd suggested seeing a doctor. What if his condition was worse than Anthony thought? Then it wouldn't matter how the cleaning lady knew. It would only matter that she knew. And so did he.

* * *

Kellan got in her El Camino and tried hard not to cry. She'd made a complete idiot of herself, and now sat in a parking lot in the middle of nowhere shaking like an alcoholic who hadn't had a drink all day. What did she think she'd accomplish by bringing this guy into it? There was no reason to, and she was no closer to knowing

175

how to approach Anthony than she was before leaving home. Her new client was repulsed by the idea of her talking to him. Maybe she shouldn't. Maybe Gayle was right; no good would come of it. This was a disaster.

And where was Connor now? If he showed up she could tell him, *Tough luck, pal. You're on your own.* This was too much to ask of any live person. Tears rolled, which only made her madder at herself. She pulled off her foggy glasses and dug around the console for a couple Wendy's napkins to dry her eyes. Riley licked the right side of her face. He wanted out.

Yeah, me too. How did I get here?

Kellan checked her face in the rearview mirror. If she had to take Riley out, she didn't want to alarm any passersby. Her nose was a little red, but her eyes weren't bad. She hooked Riley's leash to his collar and climbed out, paranoid that she'd see Ramon leaving the restaurant. Who was she kidding? He was probably already gone, or making the call to Melissa about replacing the psycho cleaning lady.

Get it together. Nobody said this would be easy.

The dog pulled her down a row of box shrubs that cordoned off the parking lot. The entire country had turned into one giant strip mall with chain restaurants out-parceled in the front. Gray clouds slid over the sun coloring her mood. Perhaps a heavy rain would wash all her fears and obstacles away.

After a few minutes of sniffing around, Riley lay in a spot of shade beneath a Bradford pear tree. Kellan sat at the curb's edge wondering if she should just go home and pretend nothing had ever happened.

Anthony was doing a piece on the afterlife, and Ramon still worked with him. A burst of energy shot up her spine. Was Anthony here? So what if he was? Ramon DeSantos was not going to help. How would she track Anthony down? She could get online; see if he had an agent or manager. So what if she could find him? What if this kind of news sent him into cardiac arrest right there in front of her?

Riley stood and walked to the end of his lead. Kellan sat stunned to see Ramon walking toward them. His gait didn't appear cautious, but he didn't have spring in his step either. She started to climb to her feet, but he motioned her to stay put and stopped in the shade a few feet from her. Riley commenced sniffing him from stem to stern.

"You're right about one thing," he sighed in resignation. "He's been eating Rolaids like candy. He gets heartburn all the time lately."

Kellan wished she could see his eyes behind his sunglasses.

"He might be addicted to work, but when you love what you do, you can't count that as a character flaw."

"When was the last time you saw him?"

"An hour ago."

Her stomach did a flip, and green globules formed before her eyes. Good thing she was sitting down.

"You really didn't know?" His voice was still unsure, but slightly softer.

She focused on her breathing. "I was going for feeling you out, seeing if you knew how to get a hold of him. I didn't want to wait until you came back, and I couldn't risk you hanging up on me. So. . .I had no idea he was here."

"We're taping at eleven. Probably take most of the afternoon." He bent down to pet Riley, who rolled over to assume his favorite scratching position. "Doesn't mean I'm buying into any of this, and I'm definitely not introducing you."

She couldn't blame him. Waiting him out, she picked at a lace on her sneaker.

"Got your cell?"

She pulled it from her waistband and showed him.

"I was never involved," he stated strongly.

"You're not involved," she nodded, and tried not to sound relieved.

Ramon checked his watch. "I don't want you talking to him until we've wrapped for the day. I'll call you when we're a half hour from the hotel, but I won't speak. Just watch for my number. We're over at the Beach Hilton. How you run into him is on you. But I can't promise he'll even go out again once we get to the hotel."

"Thank you."

He still wouldn't look at her. "You know what he looks like?"

"Unless he's drastically changed in the last four years."

He gave her a weary look. "Well, if I'm around, we've never met, because I'll deny ever having laid eyes on you."

"Okay." Kellan thought she might come out of her skin. She had a few precious hours to figure how what to say and how to say it. "I'm just trying to prevent him from working himself to an early grave."

He looked over at her as if she'd actually said something that made sense.

"What?" she asked.

"Work is all he ever talks about." Ramon leaned on her truck and faced her. "Ten years and he's never talked about anything personal. He jokes about himself, but I only knew about his brother because our production assistant told me."

"What about the afterlife? Think he believes in that?"

Ramon shrugged. "I don't think he knows what he believes." He watched a motorcycle rumble past, and then looked down at her. "So what's in this for you?"

She squinted up at him. "You'll think I'm--"

"I already think you've got a marble or two stuck in a corner. But you're not just playing good Samaritan to some guy you've never met. I doubt he's going to pay you for this kind of information."

Kellan's mouth dropped. "I don't want money. I don't anything from him, all right?" And she didn't like how defensive that sounded.

Ramon waited.

How could she explain the influx of unsavory visitors to a man who thought she was crazy? "You've heard the expression 'closing the book' on something?"

He didn't flinch.

"I guess I'm hoping that if I do this, it'll 'close a gate' for me." Kellan slumped. "And that the truth might matter to somebody besides me."

"Truth?"

Kellan shot him a look.

Ramon looked away. "What if it doesn't?"

"Then I might need a lobotomy." Kellan sighed. "Look, it doesn't matter what you think of me, or what he'll think of me. All that matters is that Anthony gets Connor's message. It will either ring true to him or not. His call." She started to offer to clean Ramon's apartment for free, but thought better of it. He'd never want her near his apartment again. "I really appreciate your help. If I'm right--if Connor is right--you'll have done a really good deed."

"Or an incredibly stupid thing," he said, and walked away without a backward glance.

* * *

The Beach Hilton was pretty swanky. In the lobby, there were plenty of plush blue seating clusters available with a clear view of the front doors. A huge white canopy of netting hovered overhead. The natural light was brightened by white marble floors and pillars, making it perfect to draw or read by.

Kellan would have liked to have asked Ramon if they always frequented such hotels in their line of work. She had imagined them huddled together in one room at the local Motel 6, but she guessed their network could afford better.

With plenty of time and a lot of nerves to calm, she investigated the hotel as though she were a potential guest. Opposite the reservations desk, she found the obligatory gift shop, the world's smallest Starbucks (Hallelujah!), and a tiki bar at the entrance to the pool area. She walked through the glass doors to the patio where a handful of sunbathers waited for clouds to get out of the way of their savage tans. Most were probably companions of the many Southern Energy Conference attendees.

The Atlantic backdrop was a mixture of grayish green and turquoise. One lone fishing trawler had nets out a couple hundred yards from shore. An idyllic setting for a writing retreat: sand, surf, lounge chairs, bar. Low tide had smoothed a sizeable path for easy walking along the water's edge. A couple with their dogs took advantage of the hard-packed sand. She wished she'd thought to ask Stefan to keep Riley for her. Poor buddy would be stuck in the truck most of the day. She'd have to take him for a swim later.

Kellan took a deep cleansing breath of salt air. Then another. How in the world was she going to do this? Her hair flew in the breeze as she watched the edge of the water softly lick the sand. She'd need to clean up a bit, look presentable. She checked her jeans and polo shirt. Good grief. Not serious enough for the occasion. What should one wear to a civilized ambush? Checking her watch, she figured she had at least four to five hours, even though Ramon had given her no indication of when their day might end.

Two men in white button downs and Dockers stepped out on the patio for a smoke. Business casual would be the way to go, but girl clothes might be more approachable. There had to be something reasonably priced nearby. She'd pick up a simple frock, some sort of skirt maybe, camp in the lobby formulating her speech in hopes that the same mystical force that had brought Connor into her life might also bring some verbal clarity.

Approaching the reservations desk, she was a little disappointed to find it manned by an older gentleman. She would have preferred to ask a woman where to find women's clothes, but when in Rome.

He looked up with a welcoming smile. "How may I help you ma'am?"

"It seems I arrived a bit unprepared. Would you be able to direct me to the nearest department store or mall?"

"Certainly," he said, producing in one gentle motion a single-paged street map of the area surrounding the hotel in one gentle motion. "Any preferences?"

"I need something business casual."

He gave a nod and drew circles and arrows to a plaza containing a Stein Mart and a Marshall's. She had to grin. He had been well schooled in sizing up one's wallet while not looking down his nose at one's current state. He could just as easily have directed her to a Saks or Bloomingdale's.

"Anything else?" he asked.

She shook her head, but remembered, "Doggie Day Care?"

Riley was not enthusiastic about his being dropped off at a place with chain link fence and lots of barking, but she couldn't very well stay focused with him in the car all day.

She gave him a hug, promised him an ocean swim, and told him to enjoy the canine company. His ears wilted behind a dirty look. The attendant took him through a door, and he leered one last time before it closed. More guilt. Just what she needed. At Marshall's, she couldn't bring herself to try any of the gaudy print dresses, and the separates were far too young and skimpy. She did manage to find a smart pin-striped blouse and a navy blazer that would go well with the tan cotton slacks she had stuffed in her duffle. For a moment Kellan considered hitting a cosmetic counter for some professional war paint, but didn't want to go overboard with her misrepresentation. Instead, she chose lip balm with color from a drugstore. So it wasn't actual lipstick. Who could tell? Compromise was one thing, but crossing over completely went against her grain. A roll of Certs and a shiny barrette to keep the stragglers at bay would make her presentable enough. Besides, once she was done shocking the poor man, he wouldn't notice her horrid hair or lack of make-up.

By 3:20, Kellan had returned to the hotel, pleased with how well she'd cleaned up. She camped in the lobby with a notebook ready to write out what she should say. Focus, she told herself, time is running out. Her notes so far were pretty sad.

Mr. Clarke, I was asked to find you and give you a message. But first I need to ask, do you believe in life after death?

What if he says no? No one has ever been able to prove it.

Do you believe in God? Well, that was just none of her business.

Do you believe you go someplace else when you die? Connor was definitely not in a better place when she found him, and it would be the last thing she shared with his brother.

When you were six, did you split your lip on Christmas morning?

This was stupid. Kellan couldn't remember anything she did at that age. He'd want to hose her down with a can of Raid to get her to go away.

Hello, Mr. Clarke, I have a young man who claims to be your brother following me around. Yes, I'm aware that he's deceased, but he feels bad that you thought him ill and distant, but he just wanted to protect you. And he didn't actually kill himself.

She dug the page from the pad. How did John Edward do this? He didn't, Stefan had told her. His clients came to him wanting to know. What she would have given for a peek at his notes when he was writing his book.

Kellan's eyes widened and she sucked in a breath, keeping as still as possible to allow the fluttering idea to land like a butterfly. Once it settled, she hustled to the reservations desk, cell phone in hand.

"Peaceful Energies. This is Opal."

"Opal. Kellan. I know your Mom is out of town, but I need a huge, huge favor right now."

"What's it worth?"

Kellan rolled her eyes. "Fifty. I need you to find the key your mom has to my apartment, go boot up my computer, and email me a file."

"A little cloak and dagger?"

"Another fifty not to read it."

"Aw," Opal moaned. "Must be juicy."

"Not even close," Kellan said, checking her watch. "Got a pen?" She gave her an email address for the hotel, the file name, and instructions on where to find it on the hard drive.

"Wait, what if Mom has the key on her?" Opal asked. "She's in Chicago."

181

"The manager lives downstairs. Apartment one. I'll call and have him let you in."

"What if he's not home?" Opal asked.

"Ever the optimist," Kellan sighed. "Okay, if he's not home, break the window over the kitchen sink."

"And risk arrest for breaking and entering?"

"I'll bail you out, but call your Mom. And I need you to do this right now. Can you lock up, or have one of the techs watch the front for an hour?"

"A hundred bucks? I'll lock them in."

Chapter 20

The next thirty five minutes were the longest of Kellan's life. The apartment manager had been home, so Opal didn't have to break a window. Just as the desk clerk found the email and saved the file to a compact disk, Kellan's phone rang. Thinking it was Opal again, she answered and heard background noise and talking, but no one spoke. The words "shower" and "beer" were the clearest. The display read: DeSantos. Then it disconnected. They were thirty minutes away, or less. Her stomach gave a lurch and her breathing quickened.

The desk clerk handed her the disk in a paper sleeve. A flash drive would have been a more convenient size but, hey, who's complaining?

"You can check it over there."

Kellan followed the direction of the woman's finger. At the workstation, she pulled up the file to the messy first draft of her novel slash journal. She wished time allowed for tidying up. If anything on those pages had actually come from Connor Clarke, Tony would be the one person in the world who could recognize it.

She'd give the file to him, and hope he would read it all the way through. Even if he didn't, his accepting the disk would complete her contract, right? Message delivered. So why didn't she feel relieved?

Kellan closed the file, retrieved the disk, and headed to the ladies room to adjust her clothes, re-apply lip balm, smooth her hair, and lie to herself how this would be quick and painless.

"Doesn't matter what he thinks, if he believes a word of it. What matters is that he gets the message. What he does with it, or doesn't do, is on him. Then you'll never have to see him again." She nodded, sighed, and checked her teeth in the mirror. "You can do this."

The more she stared at herself, the more the fear marched across her face. Her breath was ragged and her chest cramped as if she were having an anxiety attack. Great. They'll find her sprawled on the bathroom floor, unconscious in a puddle of sweat. No irony there.

Three minutes later her phone rang. Thinking it was her partner in crime, she answered it without looking at the display. "Hello?" she said quietly so it wouldn't echo with the acoustics in the bathroom.

"You haven't done it yet, have you?" Gayle said.

"Gayle, not now."

"I'm asking you to reconsider what you're doing." His voice was deep, quiet, and deadly serious.

"What do you care what I'm doing to some stranger?" Boy, that didn't come out right.

"Maybe I don't want some other poor bastard to get stomped on this week," Gayle said. "And have you even thought about what he might do to you? What if he takes a swing at you? What if he's armed?"

Kellan closed her eyes. "I can't do this right now." She snapped her phone shut and cursed herself for not looking at the ID before answering.

Ramon had known Tony for ten years. He would've warned her if the guy was a snap risk, right? *Anthony. They call him Anthony.*

Her arm couldn't find the sleeve of her jacket. She felt sticky and disheveled. The last thing Kellan needed in her head was Gayle's voice or his guilt. Clipping the phone to her waistband, she yanked open the door, hustled down the hallway, around the corner to crash into a human obstacle.

All Kellan saw was floor and legs as she slammed into her victim so hard they both could have lost a limb. Her lungs struggled for air. She didn't see that whoever hit her had fallen against a table. The unmistakable sound of glass breaking on the marble floor happened at the same time her funny bone announced her impact was certainly not.

Still breathless, Kellan managed to sit up and stare directly into the eyes of Anthony Clarke, who reached toward her with a bleeding hand. There was movement around them both, other people, she couldn't register. She could only push her glasses back up so she could stare into eyes so blue they belonged on a velvet pillow under glass. Then green spots threatened to wash them away.

"I'm so sorry. Are you all right?" Anthony said, noticing his bloody hand and tucking it away before looking back at her. "Can you hear me?" He looked up at someone behind her. "She's turning gray."

Kellan opened her mouth but nothing came. No sound. No air.

"Stay still." Ramon's voice came from behind. "You just got the wind knocked out of you. Don't panic."

Good advice, because panic was all she wanted to do.

The lovely desk clerk who had downloaded her file jogged over. "An ambulance is on the way."

Ambulance? Her lungs fought to reach oxygen. It was slow, but gradually her chest moved, and she sucked in a small breath. Tony did not appear to be as big a guy as Ramon, yet had felt like he'd played point guard. Was this the universe putting up barriers? Was Gayle right? She turned to look at Ramon, whose face gave her nothing to go on.

"You're okay. Try to take small breaths."

Kellan followed his instructions as a woman with fuzzy hair and freckles wrapped Tony's hand in a towel. The desk clerk announced that paramedics needed to check them out, as per the hotel's policy.

"I'm fine," Kellan wheezed, when really she was horrified. Here she was supposed to be helping this man, not hurting him or breaking him. Oh my God, I broke him! "I'm so sorry," she breathed to the man who seemed more concerned about her than the pint of blood soaking the towel.

And Kellan wasn't the only one to notice. There were five people buzzing around him, guiding him to a guest chair, insisting he keep the hand above his heart.

Kellan barely heard a voice ask her if she was all right. Her eyes found a young blond man who looked like a surfer but seemed to belong with Anthony's group. He tried to stop her as she climbed to her feet.

"Maybe you should just sit there until the paramedics get here." The blond guided her into a wicker chair. But she was busy watching Tony's face, hoping he didn't pass out from blood loss. Paramedics appeared with red flashing lights, leaving their truck dieseling in the entryway. When they got to Anthony, he pointed to her, insisting that he was fine. It was an odd feeling seeing him look at her, into her, as if he could see her secret, but couldn't decipher the language in which it was written. She was being paranoid now. For all he knew, she was a guest at the hotel.

One of the two paramedics approached her. "I'm fine now," she told him.

Ramon told them, "Got the wind knocked out of her."

The paramedic looked in her eyes with a pen light. "Are you having difficulty breathing, ma'am?" He was very young, slightly

185

overweight, with a mustache that was barely there.

"I'm much better, really." She leaned past him to check Tony. "He's bleeding pretty badly."

"Jimmy's got him. Let's get you a shot of oxygen, have a look at your blood pressure," he said, opening his orange tackle box.

Ramon bent down behind her. "Subtle."

"I was coming from the restroom," she labored. The paramedic looked at her. "I never saw him coming. Not with that column there." Kellan nodded to the structural support that stood in an odd spot.

Kellan didn't dare look at Ramon with any familiarity.

"Her color is coming back," Ramon said to the paramedic, who handed her an oxygen mask.

"Take three slow breaths of that."

She complied, her eyes glued on Tony, who was reluctant to get on a gurney. What had she done? A blood pressure cuff tightened on her arm.

"One-thirty-two over ninety," he said. "Looks good. You hit your head or feel pain anywhere?"

Her insides had melted, and her arm was sore. "No, I'm fine, but he's--"

"How did you fall exactly? What part did you land on the hardest?"

"My elbow and my butt," she said, embarrassed.

"Let's stand you up. See if you can walk all right," he took the oxygen mask back and helped her out of the chair. Kellan performed a modified roadside sobriety test while they loaded her victim into the ambulance. Once inside the truck, Anthony talked to the frizzy-haired woman who stood outside the door and nodded a lot.

"You look better," the paramedic said, handing her a clipboard with a form to sign. "But if you have any signs of dizziness, blurred vision, headaches, anything out of the ordinary, get yourself looked at again, all right?"

"Sure," she said, checking his name tag. "Thanks, John. Could you find out about him for me?"

"Well, if he's in the wagon, he either needs sutures or x-rays."

Kellan couldn't help but think Anthony was getting away from her, just like the rest of her life. And no matter what anyone said, she couldn't let that happen. She'd come too far to bail. This was the only thing she had any command of right now. Ramon wasn't going to be any more help. Anthony's hand was cut badly or possibly broken, and it was her fault. Just like her previous client's vanity mirror, solarium door, and serving platter that had raised her insurance premium. She should at least offer to pay for whatever his insurance wouldn't.

No matter what happened from here on out, Kellan had broken Anthony Clarke.

The frizzy-haired woman looked tough, a fellow tomboy to the last. No make-up, T-shirt and jeans, hair stuffed into a big clip, sunglasses on her head, and her left arm half covered in leather laces. Part of a tattoo reached from beneath the neck of her shirt collar. She joined Ramon and the blond guy while Kellan strained to hear what she could.

She picked up pieces about cleaning up, eating, he'd call when he was done. All in all, the woman didn't seem too concerned, so maybe Anthony's injury wasn't so bad, or maybe nothing fazed these people. Maybe they had seen too much on the job to be bothered by a little blood or a few broken bones.

The group headed to the elevators and Ramon breezed by to look polite, she supposed. "Sure you're all right now?"

Kellan gave a nod. "What about him?"

"Probably needs stitches." He maneuvered so his back was blocking the view of his comrades as he whispered, "You've done enough damage. Go home." Then he headed to the elevator the others were holding for him. Once inside he shot her a final dagger, no surprise.

Kellan wilted. Of the many ways this meeting could have gone wrong, she had never anticipated physical injury. Hurting Anthony emotionally was all she'd prepared to do. Any right-minded person would have told her the same thing Ramon just had. Go home. Get your head out of your ass for some much needed oxygen, and rejoin the land of the living.

The tinkling of glass pieces drew her attention back to the crime scene. A uniformed maintenance employee was already cleaning the wreckage of the broken vase, along with some cattails and blue and white silk flowers. The glass table top stood completely intact. Anthony must have cut his hand on the vase.

Kellan eyed the man sweeping up: if he lived around here, he'd know how to get to the hospital.

* * *

187

The parking lot looked like an SUV dealership. It took several turns to find a parking space that was half a mile from the building. Kellan didn't bother to wait for a golf cart to pick her up, and jogged to the double doors under an overhang that read Emergency. Her first step onto the rubber matting triggered the doors to open, and managed to grab her shoe, sending her to her knees. You've got to be kidding. Twice in the same day? A desk clerk barely glanced from her work through the cutout. They probably got a lot of drunks through there.

Kellan climbed to her feet and straightened her clothes, again. If she fell once more today, she'd have a legitimate reason to be there. At the desk she waited to be acknowledged by the desk clerk, and soon concluded if she continued to wait, she might be admitted for old age.

"I'm here for Anthony Clarke."

Her lavender scrubs were pushed to their limit. Without a word, the clerk rolled her eyes to Kellan, who wanted to pinch a wrinkle or two in her creaseless baby face.

"Bloody hand? Came from the Hilton?" Kellan said impatiently.

The clerk's eyes returned to her computer as she mumbled. "Turn right at the end of the hall. Double doors on the right."

"Thanks."

No questions. No metal detector at the door. So much for security. Kellan followed her instructions and stopped short of the doors. It hit her that she was about to face Tony with no idea what to say. This was not the environment she would have chosen to do this in. The passageway flowed with foot traffic. An older woman with Q-tip hair rolled past in a wheelchair pushed by a decrepit man who looked worse than his passenger. Kellan stepped back into a corner to give them the right of way, and dialed Jade on her cell. Mercifully, it did not go to voicemail.

"Where are you?"

"Myrtle Beach," Kellan said, feeling tears creeping up on her. "I broke him."

"Who?"

"Anthony Clarke."

"What is he, a horse?"

"I knocked him flat in a hotel lobby. They took him in an

ambulance with his hand bleeding like a headless chicken."

"You jumped him?"

"I didn't even see him coming."

She could hear Jade laughing quietly. "So you cut a flipper. He's got a spare."

"Oh, my God, he's never going to listen to me. What do I do?"

"Apologize. It was an accident, right?"

"Yes, but I still have to tell him. How do I tell him?" Kellan pleaded.

"Wait till he's good and drugged."

Kellan's mouth fell open. "I don't want him drugged when he hears this. God!"

"Take a few deep breaths, center yourself, and plunge right in."

"That's your sage advice? I put the guy in the hospital, Jade."

"Where he's surrounded by others and won't make a scene." Kellan could hear Jade light a cigarette. "You're there to make sure he's okay."

"Right."

"So be polite, make small talk, feel him out, and see if the timing is right."

"Not like he can avoid me in here," Kellan said, disgusted at how it sounded.

"If he flips, they can give him something to calm him down."

"Thanks for that. I'm totally winging it."

"Sometimes it's the best way."

"Jade, wait," she said. "Just. . .tell me I'm doing the right thing here."

"Well, maybe not there. Back corner booth in a dark restaurant maybe," Jade said. "Is he cute?"

Chapter 21

Anthony sat on one of a dozen beds in the large exam room. On his far side, blue curtains were drawn around another patient. Kellan was grateful Anthony's back was to her. He was occupied on his cell phone in spite of signs posted not to use them in that area. She passed a young shirtless guy platted in roofing tar, blisters on his chest. Poor guy was riding a wave of some intravenous painkiller. The old couple from the hall was positioned next, talking to a big man in scrubs.

As Kellan inched cautiously closer, she could hear Anthony firming up a schedule, working as if nothing had happened, his damaged hand wrapped in a blue ice pack and a towel.

"So watch for the fax, and if you have any questions call A.J., otherwise, we'll see you at ten thirty," he paused, listening. "Yeah, great, all right then." He ended the call and commenced checking email. Connor wasn't kidding. He worked, no matter what.

A slender woman in green scrubs stepped past her without questioning Kellan's presence. Here she was stalking a man she knew only from a photograph and a video crawl. Anthony was close enough to touch, and Kellan felt sick. That moment he must have picked up on her energy and glanced over his shoulder.

"Hey," he said. "You get checked out?"

Her brain didn't process that Anthony had asked her a question. She just spit out words. "Did I break your hand?"

"I doubt it." But his face said otherwise.

She clutched her chest with both hands. "I am so sorry. Really, you have no idea."

He waved his good hand. "It was an accident."

Kellan twitched. "Partly."

That got his full attention.

Maybe if she kept talking she would keep from throwing up. "I mean, it was an accident that I flattened you, but I was waiting to talk to you, actually."

He sampled this a moment. "What do you need to talk to me

190

about?"

A high-pitched tone muffled the hearing in her right ear. This was the moment. Whatever came out of her mouth now would either help him in the long run or mess him up even more.

"I was asked to deliver a message."

Anthony stared. "Okay."

Little white specks buzzed around her face while Kellan told herself, You can do this. You can do this. Just tell him. Look him right in the eye and spit it out.

"From your brother." And there it was, hitting the ground like a boom that had snapped off a towering crane. She sucked in a heavy breath as the color drained from Anthony's face. "Connor."

His stare said he was not completely registering the information. It was broken by a plump, winded nurse's aide rolling a wheelchair to his side.

"All right, Mr. Clarke, I'm taking you to X-ray. Hospital policy says you get a chauffeur driven ride, so please don't put up a fuss. My shift just started and I'm stronger than I look." She secured the wheel locks on the front before spotting Kellan. "Oh, ma'am, you can wait in the waiting room down the hall to your right."

Anthony didn't seem to notice the aide. His eyes were glued to Kellan. "You've seen my brother?" His tone was accusing.

"He claims to be, but. . ." she finished in a whisper, "only you can tell me."

He shook his head slightly. "That's impossible."

Finding words was a struggle. Breathe, she told herself. Just breathe. Then she saw it in his eyes. Pain, and she was the cause.

"I really don't mean to cause you further pain."

"What are you doing?" he said, his body tightened, bracing for resistance.

Knowing that she had no physical evidence beyond what she'd seen and heard, she swallowed hard. "Keeping a promise."

"My brother's been dead for twenty years."

The aide had stepped back, her eyes flitted between them as if she watched a tennis match.

"I know," Kellan said. "Please, just. . .you can decide for yourself if there's any truth in it. Then I'll go, and you'll never have to see me again."

Time stopped and silence ripped through the room like a north wind. She looked at the aide standing stock still, not interfering, but not leaving either. Kellan held up a hand and took a step forward. Anthony looked at her as if she were a skunk about to hose him down.

"If this kid," she shook her head at the reference, "if he's really your brother, he said you didn't fail him."

Anthony was pretty pale to begin with, but grew more ghastly by the second. She kept going before he could stop her. "And he said that it wasn't his idea, the reason he let go of that building. It wasn't *him*. He wasn't on drugs or mentally ill."

Anthony had stopped breathing. She forced herself to talk faster, before one of them passed out cold.

"You chose a job that keeps you moving because you're afraid that if you're in one place too long, you'll form attachments you'll end up losing. You search for truth because you don't know the truth about what happened to him." She lowered her voice. "He didn't consciously take his own life. He never meant leave you alone or hurt you."

The aide pulled her hand to her breast as her mouth fell open. Anthony recoiled as if he were going to crawl under the covers to escape a monster.

The deed was done. Now what?

Anthony's brow furrowed into deep creases. "Who *are* you?"

The aide's swung back to Anthony. "You don't know this woman?"

"Nobody. I mean, I'm just a messenger. And until now, I've never done anything that mattered much to anybody."

His gaze penetrated every cell in her body.

"All right now," the aide advanced. "Time to go."

Kellan dodged her. "It's not important you believe that it came from Connor. Just ask yourself if it applies to you."

"Ma'am, you need to leave right now, before I call security."

Anthony sat as if he had been zapped by some alien device that stopped time. He needed someone to push his needle out of the groove.

"That's enough." The aide got right up in Kellan's face.

Kellan pulled the disk from her blazer pocket and reached it around the woman. "It's a long story, and it's a mess, but it all came from him."

The aide snatched the disk from her hand. "This could be dangerous. Have some virus on it. Crash your computer." She held the disk by the corner of the sleeve with two fingers and dropped it into a waste container as if it were a dead mouse.

Anthony stared at the waste bin, and a fresh wave of shock hit him.

"It's what came out," Kellan's voice cracked.

"Out!" The aide shouted at a painful volume. "Shaun, I need you down here!"

Kellan held up her hands. "I'm going," she squeaked, and darted through the doors only to pop back in. "Wait, there's a password."

Anthony looked at her with nothing but shock.

A large linebacker of a man in navy blue squared his shoulders and put his arms out to block Kellan from coming past him.

"Holly," she called, before retreating through the double doors.

* * *

Anthony imagined he was in a wind machine full of fluttering razor blades, each a fragment of data from his past. What just happened? How did she know those things about him? Did she go to school with his brother? Wait, his brother's death was well publicized, but that was twenty years ago. Why bring it up now? Was Connor's girlfriend's name in one of the articles in the paper? He couldn't remember.

The aide returned to him. "Mr. Clarke, I am so sorry. Are you . . . oh, you're shaking." She put a hand on his shoulder.

Anthony didn't notice until she pointed it out. "I want that, please." His hand was clearly trembling as he pointed to the trash bin. He slid off the bed and took the ice packs from his swollen hand.

"Mr. Clarke, what are you doing?"

"I just. . ." He looked at the doors. Big Shaun sauntered back in with a wave to the aide. "Is she still out there?"

Shaun shook his head. "Nah. Got out the front and took off running."

Anthony stood shell-shocked. The urge to go after the woman fought his common sense not to. He steadied his hand and picked the disk from the trash. There was a business card in the cellophane window of the sleeve. K.B. Cleaning?

The aide reached for it. "Here, we can put that. . ."

"No," he snapped, and worked at stuffing it into his shirt pocket. Its size fought him. "I'm sorry," he said. "It's. . .I'd prefer to. . ."

193

"All right then," she held a hand up. "You feel up for some X-rays?"

All he could do was nod, not really caring about his hand.

"If you'd rather lie down and relax a bit first--"

He straightened and cleared his throat. "I'm fine."

The aide got him secured in the wheelchair and resumed her normal tone. "We get some crazies through here, but we'll have security take you on out when you're through, just in case. You might want to rethink putting that in your computer. Have some kid check it out, make sure it's safe. My nine-year-old nephew can navigate a computer faster than an FBI agent."

Anthony said nothing, his mind a roulette wheel that wouldn't allow the ball to land. Down a corridor, up an elevator, through another corridor he hunkered down inside himself. As he passed through the door labeled Radiology, thoughts randomly poked his brain. Messenger. He didn't consciously take his own life. *You didn't fail him.*

"The messenger will bring secrets long buried to light," that voodoo priestess had told him.

He touched the disk in his breast pocket. Maybe this woman was crazy. Maybe he should take his shrink's advice and just stop wondering and accept that he would never know the answer to the only honest question he had in twenty years. Maybe the disk would crash his computer or maybe it would have nothing at all.

But what if it did?

Chapter 22

Kellan had kept her promise and taken Riley to the beach for a swim even though she was deflated. It was low tide and the water barely stirred. Riley didn't mind that she was a zombie, as long as she tossed the tennis ball as far out into the water as possible.

Her cell phone did not ring again last night. In a Days Inn, she had lain awake, a wet cloth over her swollen eyes. Kellan stayed all the next day, in case Anthony might want to talk with her. Apparently, he did not.

Ramon DeSantos did not return her calls either.

Kellan reluctantly decided she would head for home when Riley was sufficiently exercised, having done what was asked, and feeling the idiot, as predicted. If she were a bug, she would have flown into a windshield and ended her misery. No irony there. What had she done to that poor man? And who was she to have done such a thing? Kellan never intended to play God, just try to help because Connor had chosen to redeem himself. Now she wanted to disappear just as he had.

She would head west into the sunset, the anti-hero: The Great Wound Opener. Kellan plodded up the sand watching Riley run toward another dog that looked like a Boxer. The drive home was five hours and a good romp would have him sleeping the whole way. At least one of them would get some rest. Kellan had not felt this small since her ex-husband had come clean that he'd cheated on her.

What would happen to Anthony now? Could he validate anything or had she just imagined it all?

"Release the outcome," a familiar British voice reached from behind.

Trevor picked up a piece of shell to skip across the flat water.

His presence wasn't even startling, but did ignite anger. "How can I know I did the right thing, if I don't know how it turns out?"

"You did the right thing," he said dryly. "There. Feel better?"

Kellan wanted to kick his bare shin. "Were you watching? Did you see his face? He was horrified, as I knew he would be."

"Well, no one would take that sort of thing well, would they?"

"I thought he would at least give me some sign that he recognized something, anything, so I could know."

Trevor grinned. "Ah, you think you deserve a reward."

"No! But shouldn't I know if I got it right? I did just seriously derail my life and my business."

"Your business?" He shot her an amused look. "As a servant?"

His attitude did not help Kellan's mood. "Everyone thinks I'm nuts."

Riley galloped up to Trevor and deposited the ball in his hand. The soldier threw it for him, much farther than Kellan could have. "Poor creature," he said. "You got exactly what you asked for, did you not?"

She stopped walking.

"You asked for a story, which you received in less than thirty days, when you had nothing at all to start with. You fulfilled your contract--a bit whiney--but as honorably as someone like you could possibly. You did not accept the proposal of a man you knew could never be able to accept you for who you truly are."

"Well, I should have. If I did, I wouldn't have just made a complete ass out of myself, torturing a man who has suffered quite enough."

"You think so?" Trevor grinned. "You think Connor would have let you ignore him? Watch you sweep him under a musty carpet in your cluttered little mind?"

Kellan trudged past him before she could say something she'd regret.

"In death, Connor works to reclaim the power he was robbed of," Trevor said.

"Bully for him. Is that what you're doing?"

He made no response.

"Well, that's just dandy for you two. But I'm stuck here, and I had a life before that stupid séance."

"Is that right?" Trevor mused. "I didn't see you engaged in one."

Kellan turned to glare at him.

He softened, but only slightly. "Oh, stop wallowing in whatever ridiculous notion you've latched onto, and get on with it."

This, from a spirit guide?

"You did what was asked, didn't you? You got a glimpse of how private the death experience is. You learned you have an aptitude for something rather specialized. And now," he spread his arms wide, "you walk a glorious beach in the company of the handsomest man you've ever had the pleasure of entertaining."

Kellan clenched her teeth ready to spit nails at him.

"Not bad for a little nobody like you," Trevor teased.

If there was anything Kellan loathed, it was an arrogant man, especially one with a British accent. "For a guy in such a short skirt, you certainly think a lot of yourself."

Trevor pretended not to hear her.

"Don't I at least get to know if the guy lives longer? Finds a little peace? Someone to look after him?"

He cocked his head and threw the ball for Riley again. "Well, that's up to him, isn't it?"

Mouth open, she watched him march past her. "That sucks."

"Why?" Trevor glanced over his shoulder. "What happens to him now is his choice. His business. Accustomed to having everything turn out like an American movie? You really could do with some live productions. See some Shakespeare."

"Yeah, no dead people in Shakespeare." She kicked at a shell but it was too stuck in the sand to move. "What was the point of my interference if it doesn't help nudge the guy in the right direction? I mean, his life was his choice all along. He didn't need me to barge in and stir the pot."

"Didn't he?" Trevor grinned. "And here I thought you a free will advocate."

Kellan wanted to punch him out. "So I'm supposed to go home and, what? Apologize to people for going sideways on them? Let them think I was stressed out? Having some allergic reaction to cleaning fluid? Pretend it didn't happen?"

"You want a tidy ending?" Trevor said, as he took the ball from the dog again. "Write one."

Kellan was rendered speechless for maybe the second time in her life.

"You've got a fair bit. Fashion it to please you." He placed the wet tennis ball in her hand. "Finish the story you wished for."

Kellan didn't like his mocking finish, but recovered. "I can't do that. These are real people, with expensive lawyers and credibility."

"Honestly, woman, must I hold your hand every step?" Trevor frowned. "A good turn here and there. . .did you know, Hamlet's mother was warned by her lady-in-waiting about the plot to kill her king? But the lady was duped by the king's brother, charged with treason, but never tried, mercilessly tortured to death in the courtyard, then never seen again. William didn't write that bit. But he knew that it was not Hamlet who saw the ghost of his father, but his fair Ophelia, who saw him as clearly as you see Connor. That was what drove her mad. But you, my charge, have a bit stronger constitution, don't you?"

Trevor touched a finger to her nose and was gone when she looked up.

* * *

Trevor was right. Kellan could not allow this story to drive her mad. Instead, whether it was real or imagined, she would use the material to achieve her original goal. She'd been writing nonstop undisturbed by anyone living or dead for a week now. Kellan surfed the wave of satisfaction, clicked the save icon, pulled the flash drive from the port, and shut off her computer.

Riley's ritual of bone-before-bed completed, they settled in for the night. There was nothing all that interesting on television so she stopped on her usual Discovery Channel. *The Deadliest Catch* crew battled heavy seas in an episode she'd already seen. Kellan rolled onto her side and closed her overused eyes.

"Do you believe there is life after death?"

Kellan pried her eyes back open to see Anthony Clarke standing before an odd looking graveyard. Short little sheds clustered the grounds amid regular gray tombstones.

"There are those who don't just believe, but claim to have actually traveled to a place they considered to be the afterlife."

She grabbed the remote to turn up the volume.

"The Egyptians weren't the only ones to bury their loved ones with everything they would need to continue in the hereafter." Anthony turned and motioned to the yard behind him. "Right here in Oklahoma, Native Americans used to build grave houses over the burial site, filling them with clothing, gifts, even food for the spirits of their ancestors who passed before them, certain they too would continue to another life after this one."

If only he believed that. Kellan fell back into the pillow and pulled another over her face and let out a dull groan. She might have broken Anthony Clarke, but she hadn't buried him yet.

Chapter 23

Riley was the first to hear the beeping. Kellan sat bolt upright. In the dark they listened. Four short bips sounded from the smoke detector in the hallway. Kellan checked the clock. 4:02 AM. *Come on!* She finally had a sound sleep going, and the battery in the smoke detector decided to breathe its last.

Kellan flung off the sheet, grabbed her glasses, and stumbled to the closet to pull out the plastic step stool. The best she could do for tonight was take out the battery. She didn't think she had another nine volt in the junk drawer.

Bip. Bip. Bip.

Kellan turned on the bathroom nightlight, not wanting to blind herself with the full set over the vanity. With each bip from the smoke detector, a bright white light twice the width of her thumb flickered. Kellan put the stool beneath the device and her mind flashed back to the night she saw Connor in the parking lot of Starbucks. She had not replaced the batteries in the flashlight that failed that night.

"Spirits need energy to draw from to manifest," Jade had told her. "Batteries are the first thing to go."

This thought kicked the remnants of sleep from her.

"Connor?" Kellan called, doubtful. He never used to announce himself with anything but a circling hawk.

Quiet. The bips and lights stopped, and there was no response to her question. If the battery was truly dying, the beep would have remained continuous until battery was dead or removed from the device. She steadied her breathing and listened for at least two full minutes, hearing only Riley's panting. The smoke detector remained silent.

"If there is someone here--someone besides Connor-- can you do that again?"

The detector called out sharp, shrill, and alive, three times longer and stronger than the warning beeps, with a fully fired light. Her mind sifted through possibilities while the light faded, casting her into the dark. Kellan waited to see if it would beep again. It remained silent.

"If you came for a gate, there isn't one here right now, so, bad timing."

The hall was blacker than normal. Her eyes needed a few seconds to readjust to the dark. A shadow moved at the bathroom door partially blocking out the nightlight. Kellan remembered to project her energy field, thankful no prickling followed in her spine.

She backed against the wall, eyes searching frantically for a shape. Just enough light cast a silhouette of the top portion of a man close enough to touch. As he neared her, his bright eyes twinkled in the shadows. She expected him to wink at her as if he had a secret. He felt strangely familiar.

"Saw your light on," he said in a soothing tone.

Kellan glanced at the nightlight.

"Not that." He pointed past her. A pale blue stream crossed the floor of her office and reached out the window like a shimmering extension cord. Her eyes followed it down from the window. It stopped at her feet.

"Connects you to us like a telephone line."

Fabulous. Kellan looked back at him, the man in the white shirt. "You're Connor's father. I saw you at the funeral. You brought him."

"And you brought him back."

"But. . ."

"My boys needed help. I was given you."

Regret sucked at her chest. "I may have helped one, but I hurt the other."

"Anthony hurts himself."

Cyrus put his arm around her. She could feel his lithe frame, solid, and true as any father should feel. He smelled of Ivory soap and pencil eraser. She managed to keep her tears at bay as he held her like one of his own. When he let go, he backed into the bathroom where the golden nightlight enfolded them.

"Why did that thing take Connor?" she asked.

Cyrus's voice was quiet. "I don't have all the answers."

"So, you probably don't know how I got to be a Gatekeeper?"

"Sorry. But you won't have to be much longer."

"Really?"

"Gatekeepers don't usually have other talents."

Kellan wanted to ask what hers were, but was more relieved at the prospect of no longer being exposed to marauding murderers and other vicious members of humanity.

Cyrus's gentleness enveloped her. "I appreciate your not giving up. I know it caused you a bit of anxiety."

He pulled something gleaming from his pocket. She watched as he fingered an empty gold money clip.

Kellan shrank. "You're not here with another message for Anthony, are you? Because the only way he'd ever talk to me again is through Plexiglas. Surprised I haven't been issued a restraining order."

Cyrus smiled, and slid the money clip back into his pocket. "I came to show you something."

She grew dizzy as the room shifted and brightened a bit.

The two of them now stood inside a room lit by candles. Four people huddled over a table, arms outstretched to a glass tumbler that they shoved around. Three women and one man were spelling out something on a large Ouija board. Kellan tossed a distressed look at Cyrus, who stood with his arms folded and head cocked.

"Does that really work?" she asked.

"A crude and primitive tool, but yes," he said, with resignation. "Imagine opening a door to a huge crowd while wishing to admit one particular guest. The bigger, meaner bullies shove their way to the front. Who do you think gets through that door first?"

She had a good idea. "Who were they hoping for?"

"Me," Cyrus said. "Naomi paid the so-called expert in the feathers twenty-five hundred dollars."

"She was a charlatan?"

"Inexperienced." Cyrus turned to look into the shadows.

Kellan followed his lead and could barely make out someone crouched on the staircase. Her focus zoomed in on a brown-haired boy, face blank with boredom, staring down at the table. In the faint candle light, it was difficult to see him clearly.

"Anthony is almost eleven, as he would put it," Cyrus answered her mental question. "Connor is asleep."

Kellan's stomach tightened. Anthony had watched his mother have her own little séance to contact his father without having any understanding of what she was doing. A shadow drew Kellan's eye back to the circle. Necks craned to find the letters the glass slid to, oblivious to the black Leech that had flowed into the room with them. Seeing the Leech touched the nerve that had Kellan automatically adding layers to her energy shield and notice that there was nothing protecting the circle. Or Anthony.

Cyrus placed a hand on her arm. "You're witness to the past, not present."

"I don't trust It either way."

The Leech drifted around the circle unnoticed, then flew toward Anthony, who leapt from his post, and scurried up the stairs. Kellan's mouth dropped open as the Leech pursued the boy.

"He saw It? Oh, my God, he saw It."

The light faded. Kellan and Cyrus were in a hallway outside a closed door. "He's under his pillows gripping a toy sword."

Looking down the hall toward another door, partially open, Kellan could feel her heart slam against her breast bone. Cyrus did not have to tell her that the room belonged to Connor.

"Why would It go to Connor instead? A door like that won't stop It."

"He has a soft soul and a tender heart."

"Anthony doesn't?"

"Anthony possesses a built-in defense mechanism similar to your shield," Cyrus said, pushing the door open to reveal the blanket of black hovering over the sleeping Connor, his face and pillow were wet from having cried himself to sleep.

If Kellan wasn't horrified by the sight of It, she certainly was by Its voice.

Daddy's home.

Kellan had to cover her mouth not to cry out. Twelve-year-old Connor stirred, his eyes popped open, then he sat up, listening to the darkness.

I have a secret.

Connor heard the whisper. "Dad?"

Yes, I'm home. But you have to find me.

Connor mopped his sleepy face with his pajama sleeve, slid from his bed, and searched the room. "Dad, where are you?" As any child would play hide and seek, he began under the bed, then went to the closet, then behind the curtains, while the Leech slithered into shadows behind him.

"Dad?"

Nothing.

"Dad, come back," Connor pleaded.

If I do, you can't tell anyone. It must remain our secret.
"But Tony will--"
Tattle to your mother. Your brother is too young to understand.
"Are you going to stay?" Connor asked the darkness.
Do you want me to stay?
"Of course! Don't ever leave again."

Tears rolled down Kellan's face as she stood powerless to interfere. She was bearing witness to Connor's sealing his fate with a simple invitation. No one was the wiser, except his little brother.

Kellan looked to Cyrus. "But if Anthony saw it, how did he grow up to be such a skeptic?"

Cyrus reached a hand to Kellan. When she took it, the scene in which they stood changed.

The sun cast a spotlight through the windows of Connor's bedroom onto an army of red and blue painted soldiers positioned on the floor. The boys were engaged in war, complete with sound effects, the felling of troops, advancing of cannons, and breaching of fortress walls. All seemed normal until Connor began yelling and throwing metal soldiers at his brother, along with anything else he could get his hands on.

Anthony covered his face with his arms, begging Connor to stop. When he didn't, Anthony scurried to the door. "Cut it out. What's wrong with you?" Then he watched an enormous dark shadow rising behind Connor like a tidal wave about to overtake him.

Connor practically growled through gritted teeth. "You don't know anything about conquering the enemy. You're too stupid to know how to fight. You're small and defenseless. Get out of here, you coward. Get out now!"

Anthony did as commanded, more frightened by the lurking shadow than his raging brother. He ran down the stairs calling for his mother, who was in the kitchen with the housekeeper.

"Mom, Mom," he said, out of breath. "Something's wrong with Connor."

"What's wrong?" Naomi asked, half-heartedly.

"He's acting crazy. It's that big black thing in his room."

"What thing? What are you going on about?"

"There's this huge black shadow in Connor's room. I think it's making him mean."

This got Naomi's full attention.

"What?"

"He was throwing things at me, when we were just playing. He went crazy, yelling at me, and that black thing made him do it. It's evil."

"Puberty can do that." The housekeeper interjected. "Connor's coming on thirteen. Getting testier every day. Losing his father. . ."

"No!" Anthony grew angry. "It's that black thing doing it. It was climbing up behind him, and--"

Naomi grabbed up his hands. "Stop it, right now. There is no evil black thing in your brother's room. Why must you make up such things? I won't have you lying for attention, young man. This is not the sort of behavior we expect of you. Your father would have been very disappointed."

Anthony wilted. "I'm not lying."

"Is it not enough that I have to deal with everything by myself now that Daddy's gone? You think you're helping, making up stories?"

"I'm not making it up." Anthony glanced at the housekeeper for help, but all he got was a look of pity.

Naomi pulled her wrap tighter and folded her arms. "You will not tell another lie like that again. Do you hear me?"

Anthony scowled. "It's not a lie. You have to see it. Just go look in his room."

"Fine, show me this evil thing then."

The housekeeper shook her head as Naomi followed Anthony up the stairs to Connor's room. Once inside, Anthony was mortified to find the floor swept of the soldiers and Connor sedately lying on his bed with a book. Anthony searched the room. No evil black thing loomed.

Naomi, hand on her hip, looked down at him accusingly. "Well, where is this evil thing you're going on about?"

Anthony went to the closet. Nothing. He checked under the bed. Nothing. He glared at his brother, who wore such an innocent look that even Anthony questioned himself.

"You were throwing stuff at me, and you kicked me out."

Connor's eyes registered nothing but question. "You haven't been in here."

Anthony was dumbstruck.

"To your room, now. And don't come out until you are ready to admit you lied."

Anthony gave Connor a hard look before doing as he was told.

His mother followed him, and he slammed his bedroom door in her face.

Naomi shouted, "You pick now to behave like this? My nerves don't need this, Anthony. You stay in there and you think about the consequences of being a liar."

Cyrus spoke softly. "The boys grew apart. Connor kept to himself, at the evil thing's command. Anthony put doors between them, focused on becoming self-reliant, and decided he didn't need to trust or confide in anyone."

Or believe in things he couldn't prove. "Poor kid. What if she had believed him?"

Sympathy flooded his eyes. "One of the ladies at the séance that night saw it, too. Naomi wouldn't hear of it, of course, and didn't have any further contact with the woman. Even if she had believed, what could she have done?"

Kellan searched her memory and came up blank.

"Your kind were underground at that time."

The carpeting changed to white tile and the nightlight washed them both a soft canary. They were standing in her bathroom again.

"My kind?"

"Those who see what others can't." Cyrus took a step into the darkness.

"Wait, what do I do now?" Kellan wanted to grab him and hold on tight.

"Finish the story," he smiled. "I'd like to see how it ends."

It was then she remembered that Cyrus had wanted to be a novelist. He was the dead writer her first wish landed on. Before she could say another word, Cyrus Clarke stepped out of the glow of the nightlight to dissolve into the darkness.

* * *

He was in dire need of a haircut and shave. When he lit a cigarette he reminded her of James Dean. Kellan's eyes refocused on The Gate behind him. If he needed that gate, he had been a very bad boy.

She strengthened her protective shield with an extra layer of rotating razor wire along with a layer of blue flame.

"I gotta show ya, right?" the intruder said, amused. "You won't open it until you know?"

"No, I don't need to see anything." she said.

Kellan knew that with her protective shield in place, she would be safe from any darkness he projected. The images that followed were the most disturbing she'd seen yet: body parts, bruised faces of young girls, all blonde, all under twenty-five, and all drawn to meet a talent agent they thought had the power to make them famous. Their predator stood before her completely indifferent to his actions.

"Meet me at this address, and we'll shoot some rolls, see what we got. I'll have my make-up artist take real good care of you."

When he got them inside a hotel room, he would choke them unconscious, paint their faces like clowns, rape them, photograph them waking up, then stab them repeatedly. The blood would splatter sheets and walls like a Jackson Pollack painting. The maniac photographed his finished works. When the corpses were nothing more than masses of tissue and bone, he dismembered them with a circular saw, keeping select cuts for himself, and strewing the scraps around wooded areas and garbage dumps.

Closing her eyes never stopped the images, and plugging her ears did not stop the word Utah from repeating itself. Most of the killings took place there, she assumed, but he had been executed in Texas after serving twenty years in prison.

He blew a couple smoke rings and waited as Kellan went to the gate and glanced around the dark space inside the pitted bars. Nothing. Not that she expected to see anything in such blackness. She could open it quickly, he'd go, and she'd close it immediately. No problem.

Kellan did not look at him. When the gate was open, the man made no move to cross the threshold. Instead he smoked his cigarette and stared into her.

Urgency gripped her in the stomach. Kellan did not want to leave this gate open any longer than necessary.

"Go."

He took a long, patient last drag of his cigarette, dropped the butt to the floor, and ground it into a spot inside his astral world that looked to be her living room carpet. He stuffed his hands into his jeans, and stepped closer to her. She sucked in a breath not wishing to be in his energy field any further, even with her shield up. He leaned in as close as the shield would allow and sniffed her. Revulsion brought bile into in her throat, but she willed herself steadfast.

"I'll bet you'd have tasted real sweet."

Kellan worked hard not to make eye contact with the lingering wraith. "Move it."

The man smiled, took a step back, and laughed. "Until we meet again." And he stepped into the darkness. Quick as she could, she asked the gate to close. It had been open too long, but she didn't see or hear anything else. Prickling stroked the back of her neck and paranoia spun her around to survey her apartment. She saw nothing. Probably just the lingering hunger of the killer.

Cyrus had said she would not have to do this much longer. She prayed he was right. What was the point of evil people coming in her house, showing her their crimes before she opened the gate? Not like it would not open when they didn't. Why did she need to see the details, especially when they had no remorse?

Creepiness stuck to her like tree sap, and Kellan wished her last visitor's energy could be scraped off. For the first time since this adventure began, Kellan asked for help getting the feeling off of her.

"If there is someone available to help remove his energy from me, please do it. I'd be really grateful." She felt rather silly talking to no one, until a column of white sparkling threads shone down on her like a spotlight, with deep purple velvet drapes around its perimeter. Her eyes clamped shut from the brightness. Zaps sizzled as if there were flies landing on a bug light. Jade had mentioned this, during one of the times Kellan really wasn't interested, but now, she was glad Jade had been right. Kellan watched all her dark thoughts, globules of residual anger and pain, and negative dust burn away into the magical light. A sense of peace and safety followed. Kellan remained still for a few minutes, feeling reenergized, and grateful that her request had gotten such an immediate response. Hopefully, that would be the last of the truly horrible visitors.

Chapter 24

"Wake up, Kellan!"

Her head snapped up from the desk and she almost swallowed her tongue when she saw Trevor leaning over her. "It's loose."

"What?"

"Connor's Leech, It's loose. It slithered out when you were having a moment with your last guest."

Her mind was stuck in neutral. When it kicked into gear she recoiled. "The talent agent killer. I was not having a moment." Kellan stopped, remembering that she hadn't wanted to look at him. When he had leaned closer, she had taken her eyes from the gate. "Oh, God. Oh, my God, what do I do?"

"Be still. You can only find the creature if you have a still mind."

"Find It how?" She leapt from the chair and clamped both hands around her neck. She had not seen It leave the Gate. How was she supposed to find It? And when she did, how did she recapture It? Severing the cord attached to Connor had been little more than a reflex. What if she had no power over It?

Kellan collapsed onto the sofa. Trevor, in full battle regalia, pushed her down, straddled her waist, and held her by the shoulders. For a dead guy, he was awfully solid and powerfully strong.

"Stop thinking and be still. Focus on the Leech, Kellan."

"How am I supposed to do that with you on top of me?"

Trevor didn't seem to hear her. "You made contact when you cut the cord. Remember how it felt. Feel it now. Empty your mind of all other thoughts, and place only that feeling there."

"Anthony." Her breathing accelerated, and her head throbbed. She lay pinned on her couch, unconcerned about the man on top of her, petrified that Anthony was being hunted. Where was Anthony?

Her hazel eyes locked onto Trevor's black ones.

"What if I can't find It?"

His expression fell with his voice. "Then you will have broken your contract with Connor, and Anthony will be left alone to blindly defend himself."

"I thought he had protection," she squeaked.

"His shield is weak when his emotions are raw or he's exhausted. The Leech can disguise Itself to anyone. There is a gray area in what It considers to be an invitation. But you," he brightened, "you have the ability to *feel* It. Get to that thing before It gets to him, or he'll never see It coming."

Hard as Kellan tried to concentrate, panic swallowed her whole. Not to mention she had a dead guy sitting on her, watching her fail.

"Still your mind," Trevor ordered. "Focus."

Kellan clamped her eyes shut and saw only darkness. "I can't feel anything but you on top of me. Can't you do something?"

Trevor let go of her shoulders and his voice sounded matter-of-fact. "Are you asking for my help?"

"Yes!"

"Well, then, remember that you asked for it."

Kellan's eyes popped open just as a meaty fist connected with her forehead.

* * *

She likened the sensation to being shot from a cannon. Kellan moved so fast she feared the eruption of motion sickness. Colors flashed three hundred sixty degrees around. Bright arrows of sparkling light shot past, and starbursts exploded through the dark. The scent of metal and burning wood wafted past. The push had been such a shock she had forgotten to put up her protective shield. She hurried to do so, praying it would be strong regardless of her fear.

The prickling in her back alerted her to another presence. If smelling It wasn't bad enough, hearing Its voice brought back the cold loathing.

You think you're quick enough to catch me again? Its laugh darted around her like a bumble bee. *I know your fatal flaw. Soon you'll belong to me.*

* * *

Alarm grabbed her when Ramon DeSantos appeared in her line of sight. Kellan still had the sensation of moving swiftly through a dark tunnel with lights streaming overhead. Without being physically present, Kellan saw the entire scene play out as if on a large television screen. A shadow shifted behind Ramon as he walked a corridor of a hotel to stop at a guest room. He knocked on the door instead of entering with a card key. Kellan knew it was Anthony's room.

Don't open it. Please don't be there.

The blackness clung to the back of an unsuspecting Ramon, molding as perfectly to his back as his own shadow. The Leech had every intention of piggy-backing its way to Anthony, uninvited.

"It had to be invited somehow." Jade's words returned to her. If Anthony invited Ramon in, the Leech would view that as the gray area.

Why wasn't she there yet? Kellan flew jet fast, yet felt as if her body was hanging suspended.

Ramon must have sensed something because he tossed a paranoid glance behind him. His puzzled expression dropped when the door opened to reveal Anthony.

She heard the Leech delightedly mock, *Room service.*

Ramon stepped over the threshold, and the door clicked closed behind the three of them.

If she weren't in such a rush, Kellan would have paid more attention to the sensation that followed. The room door wrapped around her, a stiff but soft bread-like cushion pressed against her. The solidness yielded to membrane as it stretched thin, pulled apart, and deposited her astral body inside the room with them. Her protective shield had collapsed in the process, but Kellan wanted to include Anthony before restoring it.

The room now staged two men, the Leech, and the invisible woman. As Ramon and Anthony said goodnight at the door, the hitchhiker slid into the open portal of the bathroom. When the door closed, Kellan felt slightly relieved that Ramon was out of danger. Now she had to keep the Leech from attaching to Anthony before It spotted her. It had to know she was there, but Kellan wasn't sure if It had seen her.

Before Anthony could turn around, she had raised her energy to project a bubble of light large enough to house them both. The Leech launched Itself against the sphere a fraction of a second too late. Safely behind her layers of revolving razor wire, intermittent shrieks, and fitted octagonal panels of clear quartz crystal, Kellan worked to reinforce the astral orb with blue netting and a layer of pink mist for insulation. Pink was said to be the color of love, and the idea of repelling a creature so toxic with something so precious made her nauseated.

Oblivious, Anthony took off his watch, tidied up the night table, and turned off the reading lamp, leaving the television the only light source. The blue and white flickering was enough for her to see him climb into bed, snug as a bug.

You!

The Leech stretched itself over the shield as far as It could, as It searched for a crack, a hole, or any weakness to breach. Kellan could hear its cocky voice in her mind.

You can't hold that forever. You gave me plenty of time to gather my strength behind the gate, didn't you? And unlike you simple little nothings, I don't require sleep. I have nothing better to do but wait until you tire.

That frightened her. Kellan had to remain with Anthony long enough to keep him safe before she could return to her physical body. Having had brief outings with Connor and Cyrus in her astral body, she had no idea how long she could maintain the strength of the shield. There was one other option that would not only compromise the shield's integrity, but leave Anthony exposed. Kellan didn't like the idea, but it was all she could come up with. The only way for her to recapture the Leech would be to drop her shield of protection.

The Leech thinned Itself as It crawled and bulked up when the rest of the mass caught up to what appeared to be the front. Attack was hard to plot as the thing had no face or eyes, no appendages, or skeletal structure. Kellan could see no specific vulnerabilities. It appeared no more solid than a swatch of fabric. How did she conquer a shifty blanket that could move lightning fast?

Her eyes searched the protective sphere -- for what she did not know. Mentally, she focused on reinforcing the layers inside the shield that kept the Leech from her charge. Kellan risked a glance at Anthony, who had fallen asleep without turning off the television. For a guy who hadn't been sleeping, he certainly had no trouble this night. And now was the best possible time for exhaustion to catch up to him. She secured a position at the foot of his bed and turned her attention to the dark slithering predator.

You're not strong enough. You have no experience. No true knowledge of my power. You weaken, while I gain strength. I have all the time in the world to wait. Soon little one, soon you'll collapse, and I'll make quick work of you. It's a matter of time, you know. And then you'll pay for sticking your nose where it does not belong.

She didn't belong there, but until now, Kellan had never really belonged anywhere. Unless she figured out how to capture or kill It, Kellan knew the Leech would get exactly what It wanted. She could not give It the satisfaction. It did not appear to be able to read her thoughts. Another glance at Anthony safe in his slumber took her back to the first time she saw Connor.

The television offered far more light than had shone on Connor that night in the parking lot. She could smell Connor; feel his despair and resignation in her chest, his mental torment and anguish. She also felt the deep penetrating cold from the hellish space she found him in. Kellan could not allow It to take Anthony there.

The Leech sprawled above them looking like tar melting over a snow globe. In their last encounter Kellan had manifested a pair of gold scissors out of nowhere. What kind of weapon did she need? Did she need to know? If she did not consciously make that decision before, what had provoked the manifestation? And where was Trevor now that she was in desperate need of help?

Laugher filled the room without rousing Anthony.

You'll never get me. You'll have to destroy what protects you. Then you'll be forced to protect yourself, leaving our boy a sitting duck. I'm smarter, stronger, and faster than you could ever fathom. I'll have him with you or without you. Why waste time, when he's truly mine. Walk away and you'll be spared. Leave him to me and you'll be free.

Anger swelled inside her gut. Jade had said anger was what drew dark entities. Kellan turned to Anthony, worried that she did not have the wherewithal to fully protect him. What if the anger the Leech provoked made her weak? Anthony rested undisturbed as Kellan held her shield around them both while turning it over in her mind. When she had seen Connor tethered like a slave, she had been outraged at the injustice. The taking of a soul to serve selfish purposes had appalled her. The sheer hopelessness in Connor's voice when he told her not to cut the cord, that he wasn't worth it, brought the rage back. This was the feeling Trevor had told her to find.

Rage had provoked those scissors to appear; pure, raw, uninhibited emotion. The more she focused on that, the more powerful the rage grew. She imagined the Leech taking Anthony and gave herself over to the blind fury at Its entitlement. With every passing moment, she grew more furious with herself for having neglected the gate that allowed It to escape. If she had taken her gatekeeper role more seriously, Anthony would not be prey now.

Kellan focused on Anthony's face. His brow furrowed as he appeared to struggle with a dream. Her rage rose through her stomach, expanded into her chest, and shot into her shoulders and arms. The fury burned so hot, she cried out. Heat burned her arms and hands where she gripped something solid. No, two solid things. Kellan sucked in a stabilizing breath and lifted two silver swords to her eye level, amazed at their light weight. Yet she knew they were indestructible. If her astral body was doing the manifesting, then the swords must be in balance with it, and strong enough to do what they had been summoned to do.

Kellan did not dare drop her shield entirely, choosing instead to halt the movement of the rotating layers, silence the shrieks in the second layer, and dissolve one octagonal panel directly overhead. The crystalline pane vanished and what she hoped was the belly of the Leech lay exposed over the opening. In one swift move, she thrust the sword in her right hand straight up, unprepared for what followed.

The Leech had a protective shield of Its own that shot a bolt of unimaginable force through her body. Kellan was paralyzed.

She saw a hand first, then a face. Cyrus Clarke reached through a white mist, his face as relaxed as he had happened by on the way to lunch. His shirtsleeves rolled to his elbows and his gray slacks perfectly creased. She found his presence conflicting.

"Take my hand," he said, unhurried.

She did. Kellan saw only the mist around them. No Leech. No swords, no Anthony asleep at her feet. When her hand touched Cyrus', the mist evaporated, revealing a small room with two light gray reclining chairs and a white screen. Cyrus gently guided her to a chair and took the seat beside her without explanation.

The room dimmed, and the image of Connor brushing past her on the street appeared. Snow flurries fluttered down as she watched him enter the black door of his apartment building. The flurries grew so heavy the building vanished and the scene changed to be indoors.

A beautifully polished young woman with strawberry blonde hair was pleading with him. "Please don't do this, Connor."

"I'm not who you think I am," he shouted. "My own mother

wants to send me away so I don't embarrass her -- tell everyone I took a job overseas. And you're just the same."

"I never meant that," she sobbed. "I just wanted. . ."

Connor's face changed into something Kellan hadn't seen before. He threw something across the room. The girl ducked and screamed.

"You just wanted me gone. You don't know me. You don't know what I've become," he shouted. "You want me locked up, drugged into submission, watched like a psychotic. You're just worried what everyone will think."

"No," she cried. "I want you to be well."

"Well, now you can tell everyone Crazy Connor left you."

The girl's hands shook as she held them both out.

"Just stay away from me. Go join the rest of the lemmings." In his exit, Connor knocked some items off a table in the foyer, leaving the sobbing girl to curl into a ball after the door slammed.

The scene morphed to summer. Connor sat in his apartment shivering beneath every blanket he owned. Kellan heard the voice of a television meteorologist speak of record-breaking, triple-digit highs.

A flicker of the screen changed to the two young boys digging holes in the sand, running through the white foam of the surf. Giggles trailed their every step. Kellan couldn't help but think that had the boys been together at that time, Anthony might have sensed his urgency or seen the Leech again.

Abruptly the scene shifted indoors. Flashes of old memories bombarded Kellan. The housekeeper read in the corner while the boys camped in a tent pitched in the bedroom, built fortresses of couch cushions, and made terry cloth superhero capes far too big for their little bodies. Then they were in the dining room, giggling every time they slipped tidbits to their spaniel beneath a table. In the tub, the boys were naval submarine captains. In the car, heroes hurried to the front lines that awaited true leadership. Trips to the sea made them voyagers setting sail for new lands and discoveries, to design a new world.

Cyrus watched the images with such joy. Fond memories held no purpose to Kellan. She looked back at the screen. Now grown, Anthony and Connor bumped into each other on the street. Connor was nervous, talking rapidly, unable to meet his brother's eyes.

Inside a pub the pair sat before burgers and beer pretending they still knew each other. Audio was muted but Anthony turned angry and it took a split second for Connor to join him. Anthony sat back, arms folded, looking at his brother as if he had two heads. Bewilderment, sadness, rejection, pain, hurt, anger, frustration, loss; all this emotion passed between them as Connor pointed an accusing fork at his brother.

"He blamed me for a while," Cyrus said matter-of-factly. "He thought it was me that came for him. It mimicked my voice."

Connor looked exhausted at his mother's door. Naomi opened the door and threw herself into his arms. But Kellan could see the fear in her eyes.

"Just need to lie down in my room for a while," Connor told her.

"Take Anthony's."

Connor shot her a puzzled look.

"You always liked his room better and who knows when he'll be home again?" Naomi forced a smile. How hard she was trying.

Connor opened a white door to six-year-old Anthony standing on the bed wearing a white terry towel cape and paper crown. He held aloft a plastic sword borrowed from an old Halloween costume.

"I used to read them *The Tales of King Arthur*." Cyrus smiled. "Connor was always the dragon because he was bigger."

Adult Connor slumped when the scene dissolved and he stood alone in the empty room. He sat on Anthony's bed, pulled a pillow from beneath the covers, and buried his face in it. "This isn't me. You know me. You know me better than anyone. Why can't you be here?" Then he pulled the covers over his head and cried into the pillow.

Then he woke to the rasping whisper.

Only the timid escape in sleep. Little brother can't save you now. You're not worth it, you know. They worry over you. Weak little you! Look at you. You're nothing. You've made nothing of yourself. You don't belong with them. They are strong and beautiful. You are neither. Brought up with the same advantages and look at you, never finishing anything you start. You can't even hold down a decent job. You're not strong enough to sleep in your own bed. What good are you to them? You burden them. You shame them. You frighten them. How can they possibly care for you? You are nothing and deserve nothing from them. You belong to me.

Sun beat through the glass doors leading to the balcony. A hawk glided on a current, its wings stretched and motionless. He watched it glide past the window and disappear. Sitting up, he called, "Wait."

Kellan knew what came next. He had placed her on that hot balcony the night they'd met. She still remembered the burning in her fingers and did not want to go through it again, even as an observer. Panic welled into her throat as she looked to Cyrus.

"Did I fail him?"

Cyrus turned to her surprised. "If anyone failed him, it was me."

"By dying?"

"I didn't teach him how to be without me, or how to ask for the right kind of help." He looked back at the screen. "To have faith he wasn't alone."

"Mr. Clarke?"

"Cyrus."

"Aren't I supposed to be protecting Anthony?"

"That's up to Connor now."

Chapter 25

Anthony dreamed an odd and disjointed collage of imagery. He saw the woman who gave him the disk frozen like a statue, arm aloft, something large and dark canopied above her. He felt strangely on guard, his hackles up. A loud clank of metal meeting metal made him flinch. Water cascaded inside the room. The woman crumpled to the floor in a pile next to a pair of bare feet and jean covered legs.

Anthony heard a familiar voice. "Remember me?"

Light forced Anthony's eyes closed as if the sun rained powerful beams of energy down on him. The room seemed to move, and Anthony felt himself grab hold of something soft but solid. Connor! He was sure he had seen his brother's face. The tip of a sword rose to point at the black shadow that was scrunched into a lumpy ball in the corner of the room.

"I let you take me," Connor said to the mass, "but I will never let you take him." A shriek clawed through him, but Connor stood fast. The mass shifted, and bolted around the room trying to escape the water. Connor lowered the sword and, swinging his arm, released a glowing ball of fiery light. He crouched like a bowler holding his stance, waiting to see where the ball connected. It singed the great glob, causing it to shrink. Then It flattened Itself, and slithered beneath the half inch gap at the bottom of the hotel room door.

"Who is powerless now?" Connor said to himself. Then he noticed Anthony watching him. "Go back to sleep. You're safe."

Anthony reached out to him, felt his lips form his brother's name, and watched helplessly as Connor dissolved.

Anthony's eyes opened as light from the parking lot reached beneath the curtains that billowed from the air conditioner. He sat up to survey the room. A white piece of paper lay where the dark glob had been—the hotel bill.

His heart galloped like a frightened horse. The red numbers on the digital clock read 4:02 AM. Next to it was the pouch of herbs and twigs the voodoo priestess had given him. Sitting up, he fought to control his breath and lower his heart rate. When he was calm,

Anthony snapped on the light and dug out the laptop. Feeling around in the bag, he found no disk. Panic surged through him. Where had he put it?

Anthony had no idea what might be on it. Gibberish? Fantastical lies? A tale so ridiculous it might tear him apart? A part of him did not want to think about what had happened to his brother anymore. Connor, without a last word, had left him alone to get on with life without help from anyone. Still, another part of Anthony had to know if there was something, anything that could prove that his brother was not weak or mentally unstable.

The disk was not in the laptop case, so Anthony unzipped the camera bag, alarmed to find the camera's green light glowing. Perhaps movement had switched it on. He reached to turn it off, but yanked his hand out when he heard his name. Anthony held his breath to listen.

"Tony!" It had come as if from a distance, perhaps from the parking lot.

Anthony stepped to the curtains and yanked one open. He could see rows of cars in the well-lit lot. Nothing moved, and his room was on the third floor, which was a bit too far away to hear someone outside on the ground level.

"Tony!" The voice came again from the chair next to his leg where the bag sat.

Anthony heard someone suck in a gasp, and then felt stupid when he realized the sound had come from him. The camera was still on as he pulled it from the bag. The screen showed an empty chair. It took him a second to realize it was from the interview with Jerrik. He'd run the tape to the end, hadn't he? Anthony searched his memory. Jerrik had left after about four hours of taping. Had he forgotten to turn off the camera before he left?

Examining the frame, Anthony saw nothing, heard nothing. There was the chair next to a side table with an overflowing ashtray and a Diet Coke can. He made a note of the digital time read-out. Four hours, eight minutes. Anthony's thumb pressed reverse and he watched the frames until the picture moved, hit stop, then play. Eighteen minutes back and Jerrik rose from the chair. Anthony stepped into frame to remove the microphone from his shirt, and leaned over to stop the camera. The frame flashed and the picture was gone.

But in a beat, the picture returned. Someone had turned the

camera back on to film an empty chair. Anthony racked his brain. Had he come back into the room and bumped the tripod? Reviewed something, forgetting to turn it off? Turned it back on and gotten distracted with a phone call? From what he could remember, he'd used the bathroom, changed his shirt, grabbed his rental car key, thought about putting the camera away first, but decided to put the Do Not Disturb sign on the door handle instead.

Anthony watched the unmoving chair on screen while listening hard to the ambient room noise. Then he saw movement reflect in the glass of a watercolor hanging to the left of the chair. The corner of the picture went unnoticed in the upper right of the video frame as the studio light was angled away. Anthony's breath caught in his chest. Someone was standing just about where he had been sitting next to the camera during his interview. Fear flooded his brain. What the hell? The camera screen, mere inches wide, did not provide a clear enough view. A blurry figure that appeared to be wearing a white shirt moved toward the camera. Whoever it was had dark hair, but no clear facial features. Then the figure ducked out of the reflection of the glass. Anthony nearly panicked when it disappeared and he fumbled with the camera as though it were red hot.

He managed to press stop before diving into his bag for a connecting cable. Items from pockets littered the floor before he found it, and plugged his laptop into the camera. Anthony leaned over the fourteen inch screen. His breathing sounded as if he'd been running and, he swallowed a couple deep breaths.

After reversing and reaching the point where the figure appeared, he was disappointed to find that enlarging the picture only made it less distinct. Even cleaned up by a professional, he was sure the face would not be visible.

Anthony could hear his old mentor in his head. "Answers are like animals, kid. They sneak into the frame when they think they're alone."

He replayed the image at least twenty more times before letting the image run past the point where the figure bent out of frame. All that was left was the chair and the soda can.

"Tony!" a voice called, still sounding distant, but loud enough to startle Anthony, who reached for the chair behind him, missed it, and fell to the floor.

* * *

Kellan saw Connor's smile, peaceful and glorious, worry-free and happy. He touched her cheek with his hand. "You kept him safe until I got here. But you have to go back now."

"Back?"

Bright light blinded her. Everything was blurry, but she knew her own bedroom. Her throat was parched and, when she struggled to a sitting position, she noticed an IV needle taped to her hand. She automatically reached for her glasses on the nightstand while her eyes squinted at clear tubing that lead to a plastic bag clipped to the lamp. Kellan felt weak and heavy as if she'd been pulled from quicksand.

The bed bounced. Riley licked her face and wagged his tail while rocking the whole bed. She had to work to lift her shaky hand to rub his chest.

Stefan's voice came from the kitchen area. He was talking to someone on the phone. Sitting upright was an effort and she was shocked to find the rest of her body had the same tremor as her hand. Riley hopped off the bed and headed out of the room.

Stefan was headed for the bathroom when he caught sight of her. "Oh, my God! Wait, don't get up."

He rushed in to ease her back down into bed. Kellan tried to form words, but her mouth did not work.

"Don't try to talk. The doctor said you might be weak."

Kellan's brow wrinkled at the word doctor but her voice failed her.

"What do you need? Are you completely awake? Just blink or point or something." Stefan was practically vibrating.

Kellan searched her night table for a glass of water and found none. She offered a drinking gesture with the hand free of tubing.

"You want a drink of water?"

She closed her eyes.

"Ice?"

She shook her head. Stefan dashed from the room to get it. Why was Stefan here watching over her? He was back instantly, chattering as if he had one breath to get out all of his thoughts.

"Oh, my dear girl, thank God, you woke up. I mean, when the doctor said you weren't unconscious, just asleep, we didn't know what to think. After making phone calls all over the country, getting other doctors' opinions, they decided you were in Hiber-sleep, like a bear. Who knew that was possible with people? Well, our hero Duck convinced them that your HMO probably wouldn't cover a hospital stay, and with his EMT background, and his sister being a nurse, well, he got them to release you to his care. His sister Carol Ann was here this morning, acting like she had a stick up her ass. And of course, I took care of my mom back when she was in acute care, so here I am. But the doctors are fascinated. One calls all the time, wants to do a paper for some medical journal."

She drained the glass as if she'd been stranded in the desert for weeks. Gayle had been her savior and apparently he hadn't told Stefan they'd broken up.

"Not so fast. You don't want it coming back up." He took it from her. "More? Slower this time, K?"

She nodded, and he brought another glass. When he got back, she found a hint of voice. "How long?"

"Were you asleep?" He adjusted himself on the bed next to her. "Almost three days." He checked his watch. "Sixty three hours, give or take, since we found you."

Three days? Kellan grabbed his arm.

Stefan launched into explanation. "Missy Duress called the shop, said you were supposed to be picking up the flowers for Ellen Halverson's baby shower Saturday. When you didn't show, I called and called and nothing."

Kellan slumped at the idea of missing a work commitment. She had so little left.

"So I locked up and came right over. Riley was barking like the place was on fire. Well, I knew something was wrong. Mrs. Ramirez next door said he started barking at six in the morning, but she just figured you weren't home and turned her TV louder. The manager is in Miami Beach, so she didn't know who to call. I tried the firehouse and Duck made it here in three minutes flat. Swear to God."

Kellan winced.

"Well, then he gets here and doesn't have a key, which surprised me, but good girl." He patted the hand he was holding. "Not so helpful, but he drilled the deadbolt out with a cordless he had in his truck. Don't worry. He put a new lock on, too. Well, Riley had soiled the inside mat a couple times, so we knew it had been many hours since you were. . .well, out of it."

Kellan sipped at her water, barely able to keep up with the speed at which he was speaking.

"We tried everything to wake you. Smelling salts, ice water, yelling. He even slapped you once, which shocked the crap out of me, but. . ."

She had that coming, but hoped Gayle hadn't enjoyed it too much.

Stefan held both hands up. ". . . he scooped you up, and whisked you to the hospital. Of course, we had no idea what happened. No booze bottles around. No pills. You had a bruise on your forehead, but that's gone now."

Trevor. She'd be sure to give him her regards the next time he appeared. Then she felt a twinge of guilt. After all, if he hadn't helped, she might not have gotten to Anthony soon enough.

"Did you fall and hit your head on something?"

Kellan shrugged. What else could she do?

Stefan felt her forehead. "Well, your color is coming back. You were so white, you looked dead. I took Riley to my house and waited by the phone like an expectant father until Duck called to say that you were asleep. 'Asleep!' I said, 'What do you mean asleep? If she's asleep we should be able to wake her up.' The doctor said it was rare but there had been a few reported cases where a person in a trauma situation lapsed into Hiber-sleep and nothing could wake them."

Who would have thought a dead guy could knock you unconscious? With her fear that the Leech would get to Anthony, sleep might have sounded great. Anthony. Where was he now? Was he safe? That hotel could have been anywhere in the world. Where was Trevor? Wait, she had to assume Anthony was fine or Connor would not have appeared so peaceful. Kellan looked at the time on the clock. 4:02 PM. What day was it?

"Duck takes over watching you when he gets off at six."

Great. Kellan pointed at him. "Your shop?"

"Jade lent me Opal, who is really terrific," he said, "just not a nurse-maid. Jade has been worried sick. Canceled her appointments to stay in town and run her place. Now let's get to what scared you into hibernation. Do you remember anything? Wait, I should call everybody. Let them know you're awake."

Kellan couldn't ignore the pain in her bladder, and pointed to the bathroom.

"Can you stand?"

Only one way to find out. She threw the covers back and found she was wearing an oversized Carolina Panthers jersey and an adult diaper.

Stefan held up a hand. "All I could find, and Duck did the honors, so. . .We didn't think you should be in jeans indefinitely. And, not that it's any of my business, but your unmentionables could use some updating. You don't even own a night gown?"

Like now was the time for this conversation. She struggled to get out of bed while he wrapped himself around her. Kellan squeezed his arm. "Let me do it."

Stefan bit his lip instead of objecting, grabbed the glucose bag from the lampshade and followed, then realized she had meant alone. He tucked the bag under her arm, and held her elbow all the way inside the door before letting go.

It took Kellan longer than expected to do what she had to do, and she couldn't even feel bad about the diaper. At least they hadn't resorted to a catheter. The thought of Gayle doing all this to take care of her created nothing but guilt. Her movement was slow and shaky. Yet only one question burned in her mind: Was Anthony safe? Kellan had to risk calling Ramon whether he wanted to hear from her or not.

Stefan blocked her attempt to head down the hall to her desk. "What do you need? I'll bring it to you."

"Phone."

"I'll call whomever you like, but you need to be back in bed."

Kellan shook her head. "My cell."

"I put it in the charger, but shut it off because it was ringing a lot."

Her eyes widened, and she struggled to move past him.

He stopped her up against the wall and pulled his hands back. "All right, I will get your damned phone. But back in bed with you."

She obeyed, and lay back into the pillows, grateful for the support. Riley curled up against her, his body warm, solid, and safe. When Stefan returned, phone in hand, she reached for it with both hands like a baby for a bottle.

"I can call Duck for you and maybe he can lock up early," he said. "I should call him anyway just to--"

"No." Kellan shook her head, which made her woozy.

Stefan gave her a pensive look.

"Not yet," she said, "unless you need to leave?"

"No, I just thought. . ." He shook it off. "Never mind."

Kellan needed privacy for this, so she charged Stefan with a task.

"I'd kill for some cappuccino frozen yogurt," she said in a hoarse whisper.

"Zack's?" He started to head out of the room, but turned back. "Good for your throat and shouldn't be too hard on an empty stomach. But I'm not sure it's a good idea to leave you."

"I'm good. Really." She held up her phone, and pulled the covers back up to her chest. Riley rolled back to look at her upside down. She gave him a squeeze. "Where's Tallulah?"

"With Opal, little defector."

After Kellan raised her right hand and promised she'd stay put, Stefan re-hung her glucose bag, and headed down the hall. When she heard the door click, she dialed her voicemail box. There were seven calls from Missy Duress wondering where she was, but nothing from Anthony Clarke or Ramon DeSantos.

It rang four times before Ramon answered.

"Whatever it is, the answer is no." Emphasis on the no. He'd recognized her number, and she couldn't blame him for being angry.

"I just need to know he's okay," Kellan said, with all the voice she could muster.

"He's got a broken finger and eight stitches in his hand, if you call that okay." And he hung up.

* * *

Kellan could not tell if she was on another astral trip or swimming inside a dream. Anthony stood at a city crosswalk waiting for the light to change. He wore a white linen suit, white shirt, and white shoes. It struck her that people surrounding him wore darker colors making Anthony shine like an angel. Dear God, he wasn't. . .

Two yellow cabs rushed between them, followed by more traffic.

Kellan searched his face and could not read his blank expression. The scene flew forward and he stood before her while all the others milled around. His eyes waited, but his expression still offered nothing. As she started to speak, the noise of the city grew around her and Kellan feared not having enough voice.

"I'm so sorry," she said. "But he wouldn't go away. Connor wouldn't go away."

Anthony continued to stare, appearing almost lost. The noise overwhelmed her: car horns barked, diesel engines vibrated past, and truck doors banged and clacked. Kellan felt herself backing away, while Anthony's face searched for an explanation. He stood pristine and creaseless, and she would be the garbage truck that sprayed a mud puddle all over him.

What had she done? He was probably fine before Connor convinced her to meddle in his life. The man made films searching for truth and it mattered that she had none to offer that he might believe.

"I didn't ask for this," she said. "I never asked for this."

Her eyes opened to Gayle's. "Makes two of us."

Chapter 26

Gayle. What would she do about him? He did not deserve this. How could she expect him to understand? How could she explain the Leech and her being a Gatekeeper? Kellan would never be able to get him to understand the urgency of her actions or why she couldn't walk away.

She played with the conversation in her head knowing the obvious was forthcoming: What happened just before you were laid out on the couch?

My Roman guide punched me in the forehead because I couldn't stay calm enough to astral travel to Connor's brother on my own.

Uh, huh.

His mother's pastor would hose her down with holy water and rebuke the demons that had control of her. Well, not quite. This had to be how Connor felt when people demanded answers from him. Regular people didn't have any frame of reference for this parallel world. What they didn't see was not part of their reality, and therefore did not exist.

To Kellan, this was real, whether anyone else on this planet believed her or not. She knew with every fiber of her being what she had just experienced had happened. It was her truth. Even if Cyrus was right and she did not have to be a Gatekeeper much longer, her desire to know more about this parallel reality and her role in it had been fueled. Kellan was now as fascinated by it as she had been frightened in the beginning. Returning to cleaning houses would feel far too sedate and confining. Stagnation would settle into her bones and she would become someone she didn't recognize. Her definition of normal had been rewritten.

Kellan knew now she had done right by letting Gayle go. She would never have found contentment as the wife of a small town good guy, baking cookies for church bake sales, hosting Labor Day barbeques, and setting up parties for the wealthy at Christmas.

Gayle deserved a woman who could support his life instead of having it scared out of him. She could never ask such a rooted man to join her on this road riddled with potholes and crevices that sheltered hidden secrets. Kellan had no idea what was coming or if it would ever end, and no way to explain things in logical terms Gayle would understand.

"I know I've put you through a lot." Her gravelly voice wavered.

"I'm still alive." They shared a grin.

"Gayle, you're wonderful, and you didn't deserve any of this. I'm really sorry I hurt you. I know I can't fix what has been broken between us."

"Not asking you to," he said. "You're. . ." He looked around the bed. "This is a little more than I'm equipped to handle."

"I just want the best for you. . .for both of us." Kellan couldn't read his blank expression, but his eyes said that he did too.

***

An explosion of sound and color greeted Anthony and his crew when they pulled up to the cemetery in Santiago. Climbing out of the beat up rental van, they paused to take it in. Dia de Todos Los Santos looked more like a Fourth of July celebration than All Saints Day. They moved into the throng while Ramon's camera collected the vibrant abundance.

They shrugged past entire families gathered around elders telling stories at grave sites. Children squealed by, waving sparklers with reckless abandon. The pop of firecrackers sounded every couple minutes. People picnicked, sang, danced, laughed in a celebration of joy instead of sorrow.

Anthony leaned over to A.J., who was scouting the perimeter. "Do you know where we are going?"

"Look for," she searched around and pointed. "There, the one with the giant hawk."

Anthony saw several giant circular kites propped upright to the northwest of the cemetery. On the way, they stepped over people setting up altars of food, candles and candy. Some painted the tombstones bright festive colors while others planted orange marigolds around the graves.

Anthony slid past a group of men passing around a bottle of tequila and singing. One man wept openly. A flash of white caught Anthony's attention. An image sparked a memory of his brother in high school: polo shirt, blue jeans, brown hair long enough to cover his ears. His eyes focused on the figure shoving through the crowd, though he could only see his back. A good eight inches taller than any local, light skin tone. He had to be foreign. The closer he got to the man the more the crowd tried to push them apart. Anthony grew light-headed as faces came at him while the doppelganger blended into the wave of life.

The idea itself was illogical, merely his subconscious latching onto the image on the video or something he'd read on that disk the woman had given him. But what if what the Guatemalans believed was true and, on this day more than any other, Connor was able to make himself visible?

Colors swirled as Anthony maneuvered past children running off sugar highs and people laden with offerings. He searched frantically but could no longer see the white shirt. Inside he kicked himself for being gullible. He rolled his eyes to the sky feeling ridiculous. He'd almost bought it. He'd tasted the Kool-Aid, but couldn't bring himself to swallow it. Perhaps his mind was playing tricks on him, wanting what he'd wondered to be true.

Did he really wish Connor was still around watching? Or did he want Connor present so he could kill him again?

A.J. touched his arm from behind. He spun around, remembering he was not alone there.

"You okay?" A.J. stepped up to him.

"Always."

She hedged. "You're white. Well, whiter than normal."

Anthony did not comment as he turned to head for the giant kites.

Minutes later, Ramon had him inside the camera frame, hands on his hips, while A.J. counted the last three seconds on her fingers and pointed at him to speak.

"It's Dia de Todos los Santos here in Santiago, when people celebrate All Saints day with great respect for ancient traditions. Entire families come to the cemetery with offerings of food, stories, song, and dance to honor those who have departed this life for another. The Guatemalan people believe that the veil between the living and the dead is thinner on this day that any other. They attempt to pierce that veil by sending up enormous kites with the hope of communicating with their lost loved ones.

"This is the tenth anniversary of the Art Institute sponsoring this event here. As many as two hundred artists have converged to create spectacular pieces of artwork with a very specific purpose. You can see behind me several elaborate and colorful kites made of heavy paper and light-weight cane and bamboo. The larger ones are twenty to thirty feet in diameter, displaying images relevant to the spirit of the dead they honor.

"There is an enormous amount of work put into these kites. Most are only for exhibit, but a few of the family-made kites will actually take flight today, each representing a single family or extended family. You can see all around us there are many much smaller kites—the size you might have flown as a kid. But these big ones have their roots in Mayan culture, built round to represent the center of the earth."

A.J. watched the time and motioned for him to continue, pointing to the group next to him that was actively working on the final touches to their wheel of color.

"We've been talking with a group of visitors putting together sort of a collaborative kite, as they are not all from the same country, much less the same family."

Anthony pulled a middle-aged man aside from his work. "Can you tell me what you are doing here?" He glanced at Eddie who lowered the long arm holding a microphone over their heads, out of the frame.

"Tying a message on the tail," the man answered in accented English.

"A message to someone departed?"

The man smiled and nodded.

Anthony pointed to at least thirty pieces of rolled paper tied to the rope of the tail. "So when this is in the air, you think your message will reach the spirit of the person you intend it to?"

The man shrugged. "Is nice idea."

"Tail mail." Anthony felt silly the moment it passed his lips, but the group laughed.

A short, dark-skinned man next to his interviewee spoke broken English. "Only for fun now. You put one?"

In automatic response, Anthony held up a hand and shook his head, but someone was already passing him a piece of paper and a felt-tipped marker. Anthony couldn't be rude, and he knew it would play well for the piece if he just surrendered and wrote something, anything. He sucked in a breath, worried about what the camera was seeing play across his face. Ramon taped and A.J. made no move to cut it.

Time stopped, as did the noise around him. What message could he chose from the millions he had chewed over? *Was it you on the tape? Was it you in the crowd?* Anthony was painfully aware of the eyes on him, the camera that would pull in thousands more, as his hand scribbled the only two words that came to mind: Still here.

Everything in his body told him it was wrong. Too short, too impersonal. Nothing but an angry statement of fact. In those two words, he summed up all he could say to Connor without being able to see his eyes. The simple facts were that they had both lost their father. They had done what was necessary to grow up and keep going, and then Connor chose to leave. Anthony was still here shouldering responsibility for what remained of their shattered family.

Anthony rolled up the paper before the camera could capture what he'd written. The last thing he needed was his mother to see that. *You couldn't write something like I love you, or I miss you?* No. More like, how could you? Why would you?

Ambient noise returned as paper and pen were taken from him. Anthony stood speechless watching his message being tied to the tail. Hard as he tried, he couldn't grab onto a single coherent thought to say to the camera.

"Now we fly," the man announced with a big smile.

Anthony looked back to the camera, forcing brightness into his voice. "Now we fly."

He watched the group hold the giant kite off the ground as high as they could. The crowd parted so two men could run with the rope and help the kite catch a wind current. Anthony saw one of them morph into Connor, age eight, as he raced up the beach with a small red diamond kite bouncing behind him.

***

Nearly three months had passed since Kellan had knocked Anthony Clarke flat. And Connor visited once in a while giving her little details he hoped might help her story. Perhaps it was all he had in him. A list of details left out.

Time had a way of laying signposts and the distance between hers had stretched into miles. The drought of a long hot summer made for a very brown fall. Kellan had watched the fallen leaves blow into crevices and manage to disappear just as the many notions she had about her life. No child was raised to believe they should grow up to deal with the dead. Death meant lifelessness, the black hole, or the great void to some. Ashes to ashes, dust to dust. There were for others pearly gates, angelic music, and eternal happiness in the great retirement village in the sky. Some cultures communed with the dead as if they held all the answers denied to the living. And Kellan had to figure out where her loyalties lay. What did she really believe about death? And what role did she really have to play between it and life? What would her life consist of now?

Earthly pursuits seemed so trivial. Sure, she needed work to eat, pay rent, and put gas in the truck. But what was with people who lived to shop for material things? Why was a Mercedes so much better than a Chevy? What would anyone need with six thousand square feet of priceless antiques and twenty-four carat gold flatware? Kellan had never been a trend-setter or follower. So what was she?

The dead didn't seem to care where she lived, what she drove, or how much she didn't have to show for her small life. They found her anyway. Would she ever know how? Some people romanticized the ability she possessed as a gift, when really all it was to her was an aptitude. Some people found math easy, others language. Maybe that was all she would ever find easy. Being a translator for the dead. The word medium knotted her stomach.

But Kellan had no desire to hang out a shingle and take money for messages. Somehow that changed the value of them. And delivering them face to face, well, John Edward was a much stronger man than she. Had Connor not been so adamant that his purpose was so urgent, she would never have sought Anthony. And she never would again, since he had responded with thundering silence. She could live with playing receptionist, writing the messages down, and turning the truth into fiction to protect the innocent. In a recent television interview, actor Michael Caine had said he was advised not to write his memoirs, as they would surely bring lawsuits. Instead, he said, he would write his stories as fiction, in order to tell the truth. She could do that. Readers would get the message or not.

Writing was what had started this whole mess: her wish to write a story that mattered to someone. Note to self: be far more specific when making wishes. Taking Trevor's advice, she reworked the journal into a full novel, changing enough to disguise the family's identity, and having Anthony's character take care so he would move on to greatness.

But if Kellan was going to do any more stories for unheard voices, she would have to fine tune her hearing and clear her vision. Jade had given her the website address for The Rhine Institute of Parapsychology. After attending a couple lectures with her and Stefan, Kellan met other people with different abilities who had the same doubts as she. A practicing medium agreed to mentor Kellan and help uncover her strengths so she could develop whatever skills she found useful. Preventing Stefan from losing himself to his new obsession with ghost hunting was priority number two. The dangerous dead still found her on occasion. But with guidance, Kellan had opened the door to the regular souls who had more to say. They were much more reasonable to deal with than the living.

Life was smoothing out its rough edges, but her business had taken a serious blow. To compensate for her lost clients, Kellan took a part-time job at Starbucks where Gayle stopped by regularly to check on her. Much as she missed their relationship, she had no regrets. Gayle was free to find someone more suitable, or at least someone his mother would embrace.

Two days before Thanksgiving, Kellan stopped at the market on the way home from the coffee house. When she emerged, snowflakes were dancing their first waltz of the season. The temperature did not seem cold enough and November was too early for snow in the Carolinas. Kellan's mind catapulted to Connor brushing by in a long black wool coat, folded newspaper in hand. An anxious flutter in her abdomen had her searching for him. Nothing. Strange to miss someone she'd never known in life, yet she felt his absence deeper than Gayle's.

On the drive home, a lone hawk glided high above the road. Kellan smiled. She was still focused on the bird when she climbed out of the truck with her grocery bag, barely noticing the maroon Ford with rental tags parked in the guest space.

Then she caught sight of a man outside her door. Her heart crashed against her chest, the grocery bag slipped from her hand to the ground, and the air around her fell so silent she could hear the snowflakes land in her hair.

Anthony Clarke stood at the top of the stairs with his hands stuffed into the pockets of his jeans. The gears in Kellan's brain slammed into park and she could find no appropriate way to respond.

Anthony started to speak, but stopped.

Kellan waited, her body overtaken by shaking. Her mind was as frozen as her feet, and her labored breath so audible she could hear the fear inside it. Get a grip. You're a grown-up for god sake. What's the worst he can do? Shoot you?

"You armed?" she croaked, searching for signs of a concealed weapon beneath his clothing.

He shook his head with a puzzled look.

"Pissed off?"

He shook his head again and pulled his hands from his pockets in surrender. Both of them appeared back to normal.

Kellan held her head high in spite of her fear. "You lying?"

Anthony bit his lower lip, and kept his eyes on her as he descended the stairs.

Why wasn't he saying anything? She could not will herself to move without fear of collapse. Every molecule of her body told her to take flight on Anthony's approach. God, how he looked like his father, and the little boy Connor had shown her so many times. Why hadn't she noticed that at the hospital? When he offered his hand she actually flinched. Did he notice? The atmosphere felt void of time, sound, and oxygen. Awareness returned when she placed her shaky hand in his, drawing gentle strength and comfort from his steady grasp.

"Let's start over," he said. "I'm Anthony."

"Kellan." Her voice sounded small and hollow. "I only wished for a story. I didn't ask for--"

"Hell of a story." Anthony looked into her eyes as if they held the answer to all his questions.

"If you don't believe it...what did you come here to shoot the messenger?"

"I have some questions."

Of course he did. He was still searching for proof. "Doubt I'll have all the answers, and I don't have proof of anything."

Anthony let go of her hand and pulled the disk from his jacket pocket. "There are some details you couldn't have gotten from old news articles. Maybe you could help me understand."

Kellan relaxed a little, seeing his curiosity. "If this really is your brother, he wasn't ill, and he thought letting It take him was the best way to keep It from you."

Kellan let that settle in for a second. Anthony didn't move.

"Connor had the misfortune of being the easier target. Whatever weaknesses you thought he had, he doesn't have anymore."

Anthony said nothing and Kellan wished she could hear his thoughts like Trevor heard hers. His eyes seemed to reach for every crumb of information as if his next breath depended on it.

She kept going. "He only wanted to be heard. He was very private and would have preferred to write his own story. But he wanted you to remember."

He cocked his head. "What?"

"When you were almost eleven, you saw the thing in his room."

Anthony wrinkled his brow. "I don't remember any such thing."

"Fear can block disturbing memories. You told your mother about it, even tried to show her, but she thought you were lying and punished you. At least, that's what I was shown."

Anthony leaned back as if he wanted to retreat, but to his credit, stood fast. "I'd have to ask her."

"Doubt she'd cop to it at this point."

Kellan saw a trace of Connor in his expression, but she couldn't say all that his brother wanted him to know in one quick breath. Connor wished for Anthony to trust in the right people, to have faith that he had not been forsaken, and to let himself feel the love that he'd kept at arm's length. He wanted him to believe in things unseen so he could protect himself against them. But also to have faith that he'd never be alone. That was a little heavy to dump on the guy all at once. His cell phone rang and he gave her an apologetic glance before pulling it from his pocket. Anthony grimaced after checking the display and tucked the phone away.

A hopeful looking Connor appeared to his left.

Kellan could feel Connor's eagerness and remembered his fascination with the remote control at Ramon's apartment. "Your phone."

Anthony shrugged. "It's messed up. Scrambles text."

"Still here," she said.

"What?" He looked up.

"The message on your phone: still here."

Anthony gave her an odd look before pulling his Blackberry back out of his pocket. Kellan moved to his side to see the letters: STLHR.

Anthony had stopped breathing. Kellan thought if she sneezed, he might crumble into a pile of ash.

Connor studied his brother intently.

Kellan spoke for him. "He's still here, but wishes you would do the grieving you wouldn't let yourself do for him, for your father, then let them go so you can all be free."

Anthony was dazed. "I've probably gotten half a dozen of these in the last couple days."

She hoped he could hear her past his fixation with his phone. "Grief and anger weaken us; make us prey for the darker things. Disbelief doesn't erase their existence." Kellan gave him a long moment to process this. "You're not alone, but your brother seems to think you could use someone to take care of you the way you take care of other people. He also thinks you became a workaholic to avoid dealing with your feelings and being lonely."

He glanced at her then looked back at the phone. She could see he was struggling to maintain his composure. After a few seconds of silence, he cleared his throat and found his professional voice. "I don't know if I can believe in that dark thing or not. But since you do, you think it's still here, too?"

This man was a truth-seeker and, if there was any possibility the Leech could regain strength and wage a strike, Anthony had the right to know, whether he believed it to be true or not. "I haven't seen it. Connor did a pretty good job on It, but I suspect It could be holed up somewhere plotting the next attack. And you don't want to be exhausted if that happens."

Anthony looked around as if he might spy It in the trees.

"For now, you're well protected," she added. "But you have to deal with your emotions at some point. And this is him saying this, not me. 'Stop working yourself to death.'"

"And you?" His eyes were guarded but reached back to her through the now steady snow. "Are you well protected?"

Kellan forced a smile and hoped he wouldn't notice it hadn't come naturally. "So far. You know," she treaded carefully, "you couldn't have done anything to stop what happened to Connor. You can only build up a defense so It doesn't get to you."

He shook his head.

"You know, that thing is counting on you not believing me."

That got his eyes back to hers.

"Makes it easier for It."

They watched each other to see who might add something to bridge the gaping hole of discomfort. Anthony had a lot to process and nothing yet to say about it. Kellan didn't have the patience to wait him out. She started to feel the cold and tilted her head back feeling flakes melt on her face. "It was snowing in the first memory Connor showed me."

Anthony's face filled her with the hope that he might gain enough belief to muscle his skepticism aside. Kellan could hear the snow touching down on everything now.

Anthony fidgeted. "I'm sorry. You're just getting home. Maybe tomorrow we could--"

"Like either one of us will sleep tonight."

Anthony looked relieved.

Kellan grabbed the grocery bag by her feet and pulled the bottle of wine into view, amazed it had not broken. "I was going to make shrimp linguine; one of three things I can actually cook."

And that was the first time she saw Anthony smile.

"I'll cook and you can read what he told me since we collided."

"There's more?"

Kellan grinned as he took the grocery bag from her and let her lead the way up the stairs.

"Wait."

Kellan looked back at him as several emotions played across his face.

"Is it weird that I brought video?"

~

Sheila Englehart considers herself a believer with healthy skepticism, and has been on a continuous quest for knowledge of the afterlife for as long as she can remember. She's had more "real" jobs than she'd care to admit, while indulging in frequent journeys through uncharted territory in her writing. She lives in Winston-Salem with her husband and dog.

www.sheilaenglehart.com

Visit Indigo Sea Press

http://indigoseapress.com